KU-377-776

RIOT

A SCARRED SOULS NOVEL

TILLIE COLE

piatkus

PIATKUS

First published in the US in 2017 by St Martin's Press, New York
First published in Great Britain in 2017 by Piatkus

1 3 5 7 9 10 8 6 4 2

Copyright © Tillie Cole 2017

The moral right of the author has been asserted.

*All characters and events in this publication, other than those
clearly in the public domain, are fictitious and any resemblance
to real persons, living or dead, is purely coincidental.*

All rights reserved.
No part of this publication may be reproduced, stored in a
retrieval system, or transmitted in any form or by any means, without
the prior permission in writing of the publisher, nor be otherwise circulated
in any form of binding or cover other than that in which it is published
and without a similar condition including this condition being
imposed on the subsequent purchaser.

A CIP catalogue record for this book
is available from the British Library.

ISBN 978-0-349-41109-5

Printed and bound in Great Britain by
Clays Ltd, St Ives plc

Papers used by Piatkus are from well-managed forests
and other responsible sources.

MIX
Paper from
responsible sources
FSC® C104740

Piatkus
An imprint of
Little, Brown Book Group
Carmelite House
50 Victoria Embankment
London EC4Y 0DZ

An Hachette UK Company
www.hachette.co.uk

www.littlebrown.co.uk

For the Scarred Souls fans that have taken this epic journey with me.
May we see the dark romance revolution rise!

ACKNOWLEDGMENTS

Mam and Dad, thank you for all the support. Thank you to my husband, Stephen, for keeping me sane. Samantha, Marc, Taylor, Isaac, Archie, and Elias, love you all. Thessa, thank you for being the best assistant in the world. Liz, thank you for being my super agent and friend. Eileen and Dom, the best editors a girl could ask for, thank you from the bottom of my heart. Thank you to all the bloggers who have supported my career from the start. And lastly, thank you to the readers. Without you none of this would be possible.

RIOT

RIOT

Prologue

901

The Blood Pit
Georgia
Unknown Location

The coarse sand crunched under my feet as I pounded down the tunnel. The loud stomping of thousands of spectators—bloodthirsty, *rich* spectators—all slamming their feet against the ground above filled every inch of air around me. My muscles twitched as I held one of my Kindjals, my treasured Russian Cossack daggers, in each hand. I spun them as my blood rushed through my veins, igniting my bloodlust.

The thunderous, rhythmic stomping of the waiting crowd grew faster, as my legs pushed my body into a steady run. My lips rolled back over my teeth. A low growl tore from my mouth. The echoes of my heavy, excited breathing beat in tandem with my fast-moving feet.

The pitch-darkness of the tunnel gave way to light as I approached the ramp that led to the pit. The pit where hearts were pierced and monsters were slain. The pit where blood ran as freely as water, where flesh slipped from the bone as easily as the most tender of meats.

Where champions reigned supreme.

The pit where *I* held court. The king, the demon *shade,* the famed "Pit Bull." I was unbeaten. No one that Master dragged in from aboveground could take me down. They barely even made a scratch when they attacked. For years I'd reigned as champion.

I owned this sand.

I owned every soul freed in this ring.

In the Blood Pit, I was a god.

As the mouth of the pit came into sight, I picked up speed as the crowd roared above. Then I was free as I burst into the arena, rushing forward to slay anyone put in my path.

I swung. My treasured Kindjals, in seconds, sliced through not one but two males who ran at me without skill or a hint of competitive spirit. Their lifeless bodies slumped to the ground behind me, but I didn't look back. My eyes tracked the remaining three fighters, circling, craving my blood.

I smiled. I kept my head lowered and my eyes off theirs. They didn't stand a chance. These males were already dead to me. More fresh meat, soon to be disposed of.

The first ran at me, quickly followed by a second. I cut them down without breaking a sweat. Then the final opponent edged forward, swinging a bladed chain around his head. I ducked left, then immediately to the right, until we passed each other. I pushed by his side and sent my trusty blades into his torso. I kept my attention focused as the dying male fell to the ground. I heard the telltale thud of his body disturbing the sand . . . then the spectators roared their approval.

I stood upright, unmoving, as the crowd jumped to their feet, chanting my number over and over again.

"901! 901! 901!"

My eyes scanned the crowd, hatred dripping off me in waves, until my eyes found Master. Master was sitting on *his* seat, the gilded seat, which was central to the pit. And he glared. It was a glare filled with a mixture of pride and censure.

I waited, waited for *him* to give me permission to leave. When he did, with a dismissive flick of his wrist, I turned on my heel and stormed back down the tunnel. I trudged through the darkened hallway back to my cell, when Master suddenly appeared before me.

I stopped, remaining stock-still.

Immediately, I dropped my head in submission.

My eyes focused on Master's perfectly polished black shoes, his legs draped in the finest of suits. And I waited. I waited for him to speak.

"I told you to make it slower this time. I told you to create a show. You kill too quickly. You're costing me money. No one will bring their best fighters to face you unless you show an element of weakness. You don't ever appear beatable."

My jaw clenched at this harsh reprimand. My hands tightened on my Kindjals as they hung at my sides. "I don't lose," I grunted in reply.

Master's feet closed in until he was looking up at me. He was tall, dark, and broad. I was taller, I was broader, I was his prize killer. I was made of stacked, ripped muscles—he'd ensured it. I was brutal strength made real—he'd designed me to be that way. And best of all: I held no fear—Master had made sure I endured enough punishment that fear held no place in my black heart. He had been so thorough that I now didn't even fear the male who owned me.

"901," he chided, showing me that fear bubbled just under a veneer of calmness, "you are my best fighter. My champion. My Pit Bull." He stepped closer still. "Don't force me to hurt you." His hand lifted. In a move that always disgusted me beyond measure, he slowly stroked a finger down the side of my face. I froze as his fingertip ran over my lips and down over my chest. His finger traced the inked tattoo on my chest. My identity number: 901.

I risked a glance into his eyes as he stared, transfixed, at the ink. My veins filled with blazing fire. Flames replaced blood. Because Master was insane. Master lived for this, to dominate us: his slaves. In the Blood Pit he was a king. Worst of all, he believed it.

Clearing his throat, Master stepped back and withdrew his hand. My gaze dropped to the sand beneath my feet again. "901, you have no choice in this." In an instant, his personality switched. He lost his anger and sighed. "*Don't* make me punish you. It would pain me greatly to punish you, my champion of champions."

My skin pricked at his words. Because he *meant* it. Master would punish me. I had no doubt. He was feared by all, a predator, a born killer. He got off on inflicting pain on his slaves. But more than that, he got off on the mindfuck. The not knowing what he was thinking, not knowing if today would be the day he chose to have you killed.

His entire empire was built on a foundation of fear.

But I didn't have this fear. I was too important to him. I knew it. He knew it. Everyone knew it. I had no weakness for him to exploit.

That pissed him off more than anything else.

He waited for my answer. Taking in a deep breath, I replied, "I won't slow down. I won't be beat."

He shook his head and smiled. But there was no humor in his smile. There was only challenge. "That's where you are wrong, 901. Everyone has a weakness." His eyes flared and he added, "It's just a question of finding it."

Speaking against command, I replied, "I don't have a weakness. I don't allow myself weakness. Ever."

Master didn't respond. He remained still, directly in front of me, for several minutes. Silent. Pensive. Until he moved aside, which I took to be my cue to leave.

As I hurried down the hallway to my cell, Master shouted, "You'll yield, 901. I'll spare you for your insubordination this time. But don't think you are immune from punishment. Everyone is replaceable in the pit. Even you. Someone stronger and faster always comes along. Weaknesses will be found. And I assure you, they'll be exploited."

I stilled. His cold, lifeless voice washed slowly over my skin. Master's footsteps approached, the light padding of his shoes on the sand slicing through the cloying silence to where I stood. He hovered a moment, asserting his authority over me. Then, finally, he walked away.

When his footsteps died in the distance, I marched back to my cell. His words ran through my brain with every step, my lips curling in pure hatred.

Long ago I had resolved that no matter what he said or did, I would not let him break me. I wouldn't kill my opponents slower and I certainly wouldn't "put on a show"—feign failure and hide the power my body held. More important, I wouldn't show weakness. In my twenty-one years in this hellhole, I had never shown him weakness. Because this was the motherfucking Blood Pit. Weak males died. Champions fell. Only the most brutal killers survived.

And I too would die on this sand, but not until Master brought me someone who was worthy and ruthless enough to stop my heart. Only then would I breathe my last breath.

My strength, my refusal to bend to his will, was the only choice I had left in this life. He'd stripped me of everything else—freedom, happiness, free will. But my pride as a warrior was just for me, the only thing I called my own. I wouldn't let him take that, too.

I sucked in a deep breath and increased my speed. Safe in the knowledge that there was no one out there that could defeat me anytime soon.

Because I was the Russian Pit Bull.

The collector of souls.

This was my domain.

The Blood Pit was my arena.

And I'd fight until the end.

1

152

The Blood Pit
Georgia
Unknown Location

A warm breeze rippled over my skin, rousing me from sleep. My eyes were leaden as I tried to blink them open. When I finally succeeded, my vision was blurred. I tried to lift my head, but it ached, and pain pulsed down my spine.

A small cry left my lips as I tried to lift my arms and legs. They were racked by aches and featured the sensation of being pricked with a thousand needles. My mouth was dry. My eyes finally cleared enough to stare at the stone ceiling above me. The stone was a dull gray. Yet, in contrast to my surroundings, I lay on something soft and comfortable, my head sinking into what felt like the softest of down covered in silk.

My eyebrows pulled together in confusion. Managing to move my stiff fingers, I ran them along the soft fabric beneath me. Taking a deep breath, I held it in and forced myself to turn onto my side. I stifled a pained moan that was about to slip through my lips. I panted with exertion.

I squeezed my eyes shut. When the pain had subsided, I opened my eyes and stared at what was before me. I was in a . . . bed? A real bed. A large, soft bed. My head was thick with confusion. My heart raced in panic at being here. I had never earned the privilege of a bed.

This time I ignored the pain and shuffled my head higher on the luxurious pillow until the room loomed into view. It was large and decorated beautifully. White drapery hung from the ceiling, tenting the room. There were several carpets of the richest reds and what appeared to be old brown furniture, perfectly situated around the outskirts.

I tried to think of where I could be, but my mind was a thick fog. I shut my eyes, the harsh light forcing me to shy away. Then it dawned: I wasn't used to the light; I was used to darkness. But why? I didn't know! I racked my brain trying to remember. All that emerged were fragmented images: cages, needles, pain, red-hot fire in my veins, the unbearable need for it to be extinguished. Then darker visions followed: visions of males dressed in heavy suits of black, a house filled with children, those children being taken away. Ripped from their beds.

My hands began to shake, fingers curling into weak fists. *Wraiths. Night Wraiths,* my mind whispered as the words moved on.

Then a featureless face came forth. A brutally scarred, featureless face. The face of a monster, yet as scary as this huge muscled, scarred monster was, I felt no fear. In fact, it was the opposite—I felt safe. On seeing this face, warmth cocooned me. My hands stopped trembling. But the face remained. It gave way to a deep, raw voice assuring me that he would save me. At any cost. That he would come for me, wherever I was. That we'd once again be free.

I felt the soft, wet touch of a teardrop on my hand. Only then did I realize I was crying. My eyebrows furrowed, wondering why I was crying. Once again I racked my brain, trying in earnest to remember why this man was so important to me. I teetered on the very edge of this discovery, until the door to my right opened. I froze, as a young woman slowly entered the room. My eyes were wide and my breathing labored as I inspected her. She was small, dressed in a long, ill-fitted gray dress. She walked with a slight limp. When her head finally turned in my direction, I gasped audibly. The right side of her face was disfigured. No hair grew on that side of her head. The young female's dark features were marred by thick, ugly scars.

On her back, I noticed the unique identity tattoo that betrayed her status: a *chiri*. One of the "plagues." The lowest type of slave in the Blood Pit. Their tattoos read 000, denoting that they had no names. They were the shades of our world, the bit players who were so lowly they were not even worthy of a personal ID. I frowned at how I knew all of this information.

The Blood Pit . . . My mind raced with the realization of where I was. The place I feared most. I was *in* the Blood Pit. But how . . . where . . . why . . . ?

As if feeling my shocked stare, the *chiri*'s dark eyes met my own. She stilled, then quickly dropped her head. A lump clogged my throat. She looked no older than a teenager. Maybe fifteen or sixteen?

The *chiri* turned to scurry to the other side of the large room, but I managed to call out, "No, please don't." I swallowed hard, feeling as if a million shards of glass were massaging my throat.

I coughed to rid myself of the unpleasant sensation. As I did, the *chiri* rocked on her feet with indecision. Finally, her shoulders slumped and she dropped the linens she was holding in her hands and rushed to my bedside. I watched her as she poured water from the jug beside me into a glass. Without lifting her downcast eyes, she handed me the glass. I tried to lift my hand to take the drink, but the pain of moving even a muscle was too great. Tears welled in my eyes. The frustration of my confusing predicament too much to take.

As a teardrop fell to the pillow beneath me, the edge of the glass was suddenly placed at my lips. When I blinked back the tears blurring my vision, the *chiri* was gesturing for me to drink. As soon as the cool liquid hit my tongue, I closed my eyes. I drank and I drank until I had emptied the glass. The *chiri* refilled the glass and I drank that, too.

When she went to fill a third, I whispered, "No, that's enough. Thank you."

The young female kept her head down and went to walk away. Before she could, I begged, "No, please stay. I . . ." I shook my head, wincing at the ache it brought. Pushing the pain aside, I asked, "Where am I? Why am I in such a room? I'm so confused."

The *chiri* did as commanded, and without meeting my eyes, she replied, "You are in the High Mona suite, miss. Master commanded it."

In a split second of clarity, I remembered what I was. I was a *mona*. A slave used for her body, to give males pleasure whenever they wished.

Ice replaced the warm blood running through my veins. Shivers broke out along my skin and traveled down my spine.

High Mona?

Master?

Suite?

Master Arziani. That name sent a rapid shock to my heart, its beat increasing in speed. I wasn't sure why this Master scared me so, but again, I trusted my instincts, which told me to fear him greatly.

Dragging in a much needed breath, I asked, "I'm in the Blood Pit?" The question left my mouth, words laced with the confusion that still smogged my mind.

"Yes, miss. You were brought back six weeks ago. You have been gone awhile."

Shock rippled through my body. "Six weeks? Brought back?" I questioned. The *chiri* nodded once in response. I racked my brain trying to remember anything about where I had been, any morsel of memory from the past six weeks, but there was nothing. Panic flooded my senses.

"I don't remember," I said hoarsely. "I don't remember anything." The blurred scarred face of the male flickered through my mind yet again. I tried to hold on to the image of his face. I remembered that he had blue eyes. Somehow familiar blue eyes. But before I could understand why, he had disappeared, sucked back into whichever black hole was stealing all conscious thought.

My chest constricted and the ability to breathe was taken from me. My dry lips parted as I fought for air. Despite the pain, my hand moved to my chest and gripped over my heart. Panic surged through me and my feet began to kick. But my traitorous body wouldn't move. The aches and pains held it down. A whimper escaped from my lips. Suddenly, two hands gripped my arms and held me in place.

Frantically, I looked up. The *chiri* had leaned over the bed and was trying to keep me calm. "I . . . can't . . . breathe . . ." I forced out. The *chiri* finally met my gaze. Her eyes were dark and large. *She would have been pretty,* I thought, *if it had not been for the ravaged side of her face.*

"You're panicking," she said softly. "It's the drugs. You have been weaned off one and placed on another, a lower, less intense dosage. It's why you're in pain. It's why you're struggling to remember anything. Your brain needs time to adjust."

Reaching out, I gripped the *chiri*'s arms and followed the rhythm of her breathing. She inhaled slowly, as I attempted to fall into step with her calm rhythmical breathing. My heart had been beating so fast I was sure it would burst from my chest. But after minutes of controlled breathing, it regained its normal beat. I could once again breathe, my pulse slowed to a steady beat.

Yet I didn't let go of the *chiri*'s arms. Seeing I was calm, the *chiri* lowered her head. As she did, I studied her up close. My heart dropped. The disfigurement, what appeared to be a burn mark, was severe. Her hair was patchy, and her skin was red over her right cheek, neck, and ear. A wave of sorrow washed over me.

What had she been subjected to? How was this done? But worse, why was this considered normal? Why did seeing someone so brutally scarred not shock me?

Then I thought back to her words, as anxiety once again tried to hold me in its clutches. Drugs? The drugs? Opening my mouth, I whispered, "Drugs? You said . . . drugs?"

After a brief pause, the *chiri* replied, "Yes, miss."

"Please," I asked. "Explain. I . . . I find myself confused. My mind is a jumble of thoughts. I can't pin anything down."

The *chiri* paled. She shook her head. "I am not authorized to speak of such things. I've been sent to care for you, nothing more."

"Please," I begged. "Why am I here? *How* am I here? I need something to make sense." My head pounded as I grew silent.

It was several seconds before the *chiri* replied. "You were with Mistress Arziani for a long time. You were not in the Blood Pit. But Master called you back. So you returned. That's as much as I know."

I closed my eyes, trying to remember something, anything, but nothing was there. "I don't remember," I whispered.

"The drugs," the *chiri* repeated. Opening my eyes, I waited for her to explain. After rolling her lips together nervously, she said, "You were on the *monebi* drug. You have been subjected to it for years. When Master called you home, he ordered you be taken off it and instead put onto the High Mona formula."

"Why?"

"I do not know why, miss. I was simply brought in as your *chiri*. I have been assigned to your care while you are High Mona. Every High Mona is assisted. It's part of your privileges."

A million questions clogged my fuzzy mind, but I picked out one to ask. "High Mona?" I shook my head slightly. "Can you explain? I don't understand? What is a *High* Mona?"

The *chiri* looked up and with a deep breath stated, "Miss, you are Master's new personal consort. You have been elevated to be his. And *only his*. You are no longer the property of other males, as you were before."

All of the blood drained from my face as her words reached my ears. Releasing her arms, I stared down at my hands and saw them shaking. I searched my mind for why the news that I was Master's High Mona was a bad thing, but I couldn't remember. It was as though a high wall shielded my past from my mind's eye. Obscuring the answers to the many questions I had.

"Why am I shaking?" I asked nervously. "Why does this cause me to feel fear?" I clenched my hands together into fists, gritting my teeth through the aching pain. My eyes then scanned the room, at the luxury and the opulence. Nothing looked familiar. Instinctively, I just knew that I did not belong.

As that thought passed through my mind, another took its place. I felt the soft bed beneath me, breathed in the clean fragrant air, and asked, "If I am the new High Mona, what happened to the last?"

The air seemed to fill with tension. As I glanced up to the *chiri*, I pushed, "Tell me."

"She was killed, miss."

My heart dropped. "How?"

"I do not know, miss. She was disobedient. I don't know how or why, but Master put her to death. Publicly. In the pit."

"The pit?"

"The pit is where Master's fighters have their matches, miss."

Lifting my hand to my head, I gripped my hair. "I don't remember anything. Yet everything seems so familiar, if that makes any sense at all. It's like I hold the answers to all of my questions, but they are lost somewhere in my mind and I can't access them."

"You will remember them again, someday," the *chiri* informed. "The new High Mona drug you have been put on brings with it a clarity you were missing on the Type B drug. It takes awhile, but hopefully sooner rather than later you will remember things that seem out of reach now. The weaker drug is a better drug to be on, miss. Believe me. It shields you from pregnancy, yet it still gives you the need to be taken for Master's benefit. Though it will not hurt you and drive you insane like before. Master likes his High Monas to be aware of his touch. He likes you to be aware of him at all times. He wants you to feel every single second of being with him. He wants you to remember exactly who you are servicing."

"How do you know this?" I asked.

The *chiri* paused nervously, then said, "It is common knowledge among the slaves, miss. Master does not hide much."

Freeing my hair from my hands, I let them drop as fear began climbing back up my spine. Fear of being the solo consort to Master. A male I had no conscious memory of, but a male that my mind told me I already knew. Well.

Silence filled the room, then I asked, "Why me? Why have I been chosen? Has Master . . . taken me before? I feel like he may have. I feel like he has touched me before now."

The *chiri*'s shoulders stiffened, but she eventually whispered, "Yes, miss. He was the only male servicing you here in the first few weeks when the *monebi* drug still held you in its grasp. Since your initial need for his release calmed, he has been eagerly waiting for you to wake fully, with a clear mind." Her eyes flitted to mine, then quickly looked away.

"What?" I asked with dread. The *chiri* didn't add anything, so I shook her arm and pushed harder, "What? Tell me."

"You have caught his eye, miss. More than I've seen before. He has been visiting you every day, waiting for you to open your eyes. That is . . . that is not normal for him. He is Master, he can have anyone he desires, but he is solely focused on you."

"He is?" I asked, swallowing down my apprehension.

"Yes, miss. He will be very happy you're awake. He's been getting agitated. He hasn't even taken another *mona*. He wants only you."

Feeling my body aching, I slumped back against the pillows. The *chiri* hovered by, building up the courage to continue. "Miss, I've worked for the *monebi* all my life. Though you don't remember what you have been through yet, you should eventually. If you remember, you will be thankful that you have been elevated to this new status." She glanced down, then sighed. "The *monebi* life is one of violence and servitude. We are all owned and controlled by Master, but even though I am the lowest of the low, I would willingly take my *chiri* status over being a *mona* . . . the things they make you do." She swallowed, cheeks flushing with red, and quickly added, "If you submit and obey every command asked of you by Master, you will find yourself much better off."

The *chiri* then seized the opportunity to rush from the bed and commence her duties. I watched as she efficiently gathered fresh bed linens and put them in a dresser. Then she moved to a large bathtub and began filling it with water. She added some kind of liquid to the water, and the room quickly filled with the most beautiful perfumed scent.

I closed my eyes as the aroma washed over me. When I opened my eyes, the *chiri* was walking to the side of the room with a red dress in her hands. She laid it out on a table, then moved back toward the tub. She turned off the faucet and walked my way.

When she stood at the side of my bed, she said, "Miss, I have orders to bathe you. I was instructed by Master that the moment you wake I am to cleanse you, dress you and prepare you, then inform him."

Panic blossomed inside me again, but I held it back. I knew there was no way out of this. Something, some unknown voice inside my head, told me that I could not fight this fate, whatever it was. Pushing myself to sit up, I accepted the *chiri*'s offer of help to walk. I leaned heavily on her until I reached the tub. The *chiri* undressed me and helped me slip into the hot water.

As my body was enveloped in warmth, I sighed as my muscles relaxed, my pain evaporating with the rising steam. I closed my eyes, my eyelids pulled down by tiredness. As I did, the image of a dark-haired female towering over me came to mind. The vision was blurred, but I could see her ordering a male to take me as I writhed in pain on the floor. In the vision, I also saw the scarred male from my previous memory being restrained in the corner of a small room, a metal collar tightly fastened around his thick neck. And he was fighting to be free while I was on the hard floor, a deep, unbearable pain tearing me apart from inside. He was being forced to watch me being ravaged. And at the sight, his huge, built body radiated rage.

The scarred male roared as the one taking me released himself within me. But in that stranger's release, there was a dampening of the pain I was in. The release brought a brief moment of peace. I remembered closing my eyes, and as I did, the female ordered the scarred male to kill someone. She promised him that if he killed, I would be freed. Even in my drugged state I knew that her words held no truth; by the look on the scarred male's face I could see he knew it, too. Yet he did as instructed. In his expression, I could see that he would always do as she said . . . because next time could be the time I was set free.

The room I'd been kept in was cold and dark, but the male agreed to anything asked of him without question. Just as the vision began to disperse, a flood of guilt, shame, and sheer sadness blistered my heart.

I snapped my eyes open as I felt something from my left prick my skin, ripping me from my memory, ripping me from unanswered sorrow. The *chiri* was at my side, injecting something into my arm: a clear liquid. But I didn't fight against it. I somehow knew not to fight. Knew that this happened to me daily.

This was my life.

2

152

I felt the liquid from the needle begin to rush through my veins, and with it came lightness to my limbs. The pain and the ache in my muscles dissolved until all that was left was a heady feeling, a feeling of warmth. Then my eyelids fluttered as that warmth began to travel south between my legs. A whimper left my throat at the tension building at the apex of my thighs.

"Miss?" the *chiri* called gently. I slowly opened my eyes, feeling a blush on my cheeks. She stood beside me, holding out a soft, plush towel. Rising from the tub, I let her wrap me in the towel, not questioning why. I knew I *never* asked why. There was no explanation of anything in my life.

The *chiri* guided me to a chair. A large full-length mirror sat before me, and I stared at the female looking back. Blue eyes, dark hair, cheeks flushed with pink. She was slim and fairly tall. Her skin was a light olive color.

I stared and stared, numbed by the effects of the needle as the *chiri* fixed my waist-length hair and made up my face with powders and creams. I stood when she guided me to stand, then let her drape me in a long silken red dress, the floor-length material held together by two straps fastened with silver clasps at the shoulders. A large slit sat on either leg, showing the now glistening, fragrantly oiled skin beneath. I rocked on my feet as the ache between my legs increased. I clenched my thighs together, searching for release, but none came.

Just as I was sure I couldn't bear this searing ache anymore, a sound came from the door behind, and the *chiri* guided me to stand in the center of the room. The *chiri* immediately backed away and slunk into the shadows, keeping out of sight. Even in the light fog clouding my mind, I registered confusion at her behavior. She appeared terrified. Desperately afraid of whoever was about to show himself.

Then a male entered the room. A domineering, mysterious male. His dark eyes immediately collided with mine, and he stopped dead. He was dressed in a clean dark suit and green tie. His black hair was pushed off his head, his strong chiseled jaw dusted in dark stubble. I noticed that he was fairly handsome. Older than me by quite a lot of years, but handsome nonetheless.

Then he smiled.

And I stilled.

Before I could do anything else, a devastating wave of need took me in its hold, and a small cry left my mouth. The male's dark eyes flared with excitement and he walked forward, slowly and controlled.

Predatory.

The strong musky scent of his skin washed over me as he approached. I rocked on my feet as another wave of heat filled me inside, scorching my muscles. In reaction to my whimper, the male lifted his hand to my face. He towered over me in height and breadth. His large hands were smooth and soft.

"You're even more beautiful than a Greek goddess," he murmured, then ran his hand down over my neck. Pressure built between my legs at his touch, my body yearning for him to slip his hand lower to relieve the pressure. I gasped, unable to keep my eyes open, when another rush of heat filled me. I grew wet between my thighs. Suddenly, the male's hand dropped and cupped my core. I snapped my eyes open, my pulse racing with need.

The male's nostrils flared at my reaction, and he leaned in, running his nose over the tip of mine. His fingers at my core began to move toward my entrance, and I sighed at the feel, needing him to push them inside my channel. "Beautiful," he murmured as his mouth drifted to my ear, his fingers dancing along my hot flesh. "You need me, don't you, 152? You need Master to take away the pressure? To make you feel better? To make that pussy calm?"

I moaned in response, but I heard him. I heard his every word. This male was Master Arziani. This was the male I was meant to serve. I moaned again as his free hand twisted something on the shoulder of my dress and the fabric fell away to the floor, pooling at my feet. The cool air kissed at my naked skin.

A low, hungry groan left his throat, and in seconds, his eager mouth was on my breast. As his tongue flicked over my tight nipple, I cried out. His hands at my core worked faster, bringing me to the edge of relief. Just as the ache was about to be soothed, Master backed away and ordered, "Bed. Get on the bed. On your back." His voice had lowered to a stern rasp. I did as instructed as Master quickly shed himself of his clothes. The muscles rippled on his stomach as he approached, his strong thick legs covered in a dusting of dark hair.

Lying back, I spread my legs, inviting him inside me. Needing him above me. But when Master reached the end of the bed, instead of covering me with his body, he dropped to his knees and took me with his mouth. An ecstatic scream left my throat as I felt him flick over my bud with the tip of his tongue. I fisted the bed linen in my hands as a wave of pleasure crashed over me. But the pressure at the bottom of my spine didn't leave; instead, it heightened.

It built and built until my body was alive with the urge to be taken: rough, raw, and filled with Master's seed.

A light sheen of sweat covered my skin, and Master broke his mouth away from my core, crawling slowly and steadily until he was above me. My back arched, searching for more: his touch, his warmth, his hands. Our gazes collided, and he licked his lips as his hand palmed my breast.

I rolled my hips as Master placed himself between my legs, the feel of his hard length moving to wait at my entrance. I tried to push forward, but Master's hands reached to grip my wrists over my head. His grip was too tight to fight, and I thrashed, desperately needing some relief.

Master's face dropped to hover over mine, and he pressed kisses along my cheek. When he withdrew slightly, he said, "I knew it would be like this with you. You were born to be a High Mona. Your unrivaled looks, this body . . . this insatiable need for me to fuck you. Your Master." His pupils dilated and I bit my lip as I felt the tip of his length pushing inside me.

As he thrust forward, his grip on my wrists increased until a flash of pain crashed through me, eradicating the pleasure. But as I cried out from pain, he slammed inside me in one swift move, and I screamed at the feel. Too many conflicting sensations were running through me as he began slamming into me, each thrust bringing me closer and closer to the brink.

Master groaned above me, with me moaning in reply as his hard chest brushed against my breasts. Master's warm breath ghosted over my face. Moving his mouth closer to my ear, he growled, "I own you, *mona*. I own every part of you. You're mine."

I cried out as his grip on my wrists tightened, causing a brutal pain to override the pleasure. "Do you hear me?" he asked, suddenly pausing in his taking of me. His handsome face was stern and un-yielding, staring me down.

I moaned in protest, trying to roll my hips to feel him move within me once again. But he held still, his eyes hard and crazed with the need for my response.

"Yes," I replied breathlessly. I screamed as his grip became so hard on my wrists that I feared the bones would break. "Master," he hissed, "Show your fucking respect, *mona*."

"Yes, Master," I corrected quickly, holding my breath immediately afterward. Master's face softened, his anger dissipated, and his grip on my wrists slackened. "That's better," he praised, and released one of my wrists to place his hand on my cheek.

Ensuring I looked him in the eyes with a firm grip on my jaw, he scolded, "I won't tolerate any disobedience from you, *mona*. You belong to me, as such I'll treat you like a queen." His mouth moved to my ear and he whispered, "But disobey me in any way, and I'll make you regret the day you were born."

He raised his hands and kissed my lips softly, sweetly—in stark contrast to the threatening words issuing from his mouth. Fisting my hair and abruptly ripping my head back, he demanded, "Do you understand, *mona*? Tell me you understand my every word."

White-hot pain spread along my scalp under his grip, the unbearable feeling stood in contrast to the need between my legs. "Yes, Master," I gulped, as tears left the corner of my eyes.

Master released my hair and a devastatingly handsome smile spread on his full lips. "Good," he announced proudly, his fingers now massaging the scalp he'd just bruised. His smile dropped as his hard length twitched and pulsed within me. I waited for what would happen next, unsure if it would be pleasure or pain. Then, still inside me, he abruptly spun me around until I straddled his hips.

His hands ran over my thighs, finally gripping my hips as my palms landed flat on his broad muscled chest. "Fuck me," he ordered, his dark eyes blazing in excitement. His hands tightened on my hips until I was sure they would leave a bruise. "Take me until I fill you."

And I did. Needing his release, I let his harsh grip guide me until my eyes closed and my head snapped back, embracing the rapture. Body stiffening, I cried out a long loud moan, digging my nails into the flesh on Master's chest as he stilled beneath me, roaring out his own pleasure. As his seed filled me, it soothed the heat within my channel. My skin tingled as I remained poised over his hips, slowly rocking back and forth as Master's length jerked inside me.

I didn't know how much time had passed, but as my breathing slowed to calm, I lowered my head and fluttered open my eyes. I was met with a dark, satisfied gaze. A gaze that watched my every move, a predator, a true Master of the pit.

A cold sensation began creeping up my spine and continued spreading all over my body, as I remained transfixed by his stare. As the insatiable need to be taken ebbed, the reality of this moment hit me hard. This was Master. The male who controlled all fates in the pit. The person who decided whether we lived or died.

And I had been selected to please him.

Real, true fear settled in my heart.

"My delicate pretty petal," Master purred, voice low. His fingertips drifted off my hips and brushed along my stomach until they dropped to my core. He ran his fingers through my wetness, and as they did, his hips raised, tearing another moan from my mouth.

"You like that, petal?" he asked. I drew in a deep breath, but before I could speak, he bit out, "Answer me!"

My eyes opened as I flinched at the aggression in his voice. "Yes, Master," I replied quickly. "I like that, Master."

My words were a balm to Master, and he relaxed back on the bed. Glancing down at my hands on his chest, I paled when I saw nail marks on his skin, blood gathering underneath. I snatched my hands back and watched, in trepidation, as Master glanced down at the blood. My heart pounded in terror at what he might do next. But to my surprise, a wide, happy smile spread on his lips, and his eyes grew leaden with desire.

I swallowed down my trepidation when Master's hand rubbed over the small speckles of blood. Then to my surprise, he raised his finger to his lips and sucked the blood off the tip. When he lowered his finger, he looked at me and said, "I knew you were born to be mine." His hands landed on my waist and dragged along my skin until they cupped my breasts, palming the soft flesh. My nostrils flared as his touch reignited my desire, and my hips began to rock back and forth. "I knew when I watched you on those cameras, when you were with my bitch of a sister, that you were who I'd been waiting for. That the other High Monas couldn't hold a candle to you."

Master's length began to harden within me again, and he softly thrust his hips, increasing my pleasure. I moaned, and Master groaned in reply.

I worked my hips faster still, until I started to search for release. Master's hands tightened on my breasts, and I cried out as his grip bordered on pain. "That's it, petal," he murmured, "take me hard as you feel this pain." Pleasure overriding the pain he gave, pressure built at my core and tingles spread over my skin as I chased the pleasure coming over the horizon.

Master groaned and began to slam into me with vigor. As he did so, it wasn't long before I fell over the precipice and burst apart with light. I fell forward, slumping onto Master's chest as he thrust into me three more times and spilled his seed within me, extinguishing the embers of desire that the shot of the new drug had ignited. Master's arms wrapped around me, but I could tell it wasn't in affection but possession. His grip was unyielding, his arms a cage of flesh and bone. He held me close, my eyes squeezing shut at the hum of fear that still buzzed under the surface of my skin. Now that the effects of the drug had faded, with its false desire muted and still, I had no idea what to do next.

My memories were silent, but I was sure I'd never been with a male drug-free before. I simply had no idea how to act.

Master's fingertips traced lazy circles on my back. I breathed slowly, trying to stifle a cry. "Do you know why I call you petal, 152?" he asked softly, a gentler, more affectionate side appearing at the forefront of his personality.

"No, Master," I replied timidly.

Master's hand ran up to my hair and combed through the dark tresses. His hand stilled. He turned his head toward my face to answer, "Because just like a petal, you can be easily destroyed. But while intact you are so very beautiful to admire."

Although spoken tenderly, the weight of his words hung like a dagger over my head. Master continued stroking my hair like he hadn't issued a threat, a threat I knew was just as every bit a promise.

"Yes, Master," I answered weakly. Master sighed happily in response.

He turned his face to mine and began peppering kisses up and down my cheek. "You smell and taste so good, petal," he murmured.

I closed my eyes and let him do as he pleased. But I realized, as I lay in his arms, that I did not like his touch. Although this male was handsome, there lurked a cruel monster beneath. If I was the petal of a flower, then he was most certainly the thorn.

"Come," said Master finally, after minutes of running his hands over my body. As his now flaccid length was withdrawn from my body, I rolled to the side and allowed him to rise. As he stood up from the bed, he pointed to something in the dark side of the room. A door then opened and the *chiri* from before entered the room. A guard had let her in. A guard who, I quickly realized, had watched Master take me.

The *Night Wraiths,* a faint echo in my head stated. The thought fled as someone took hold of my elbow and guided me to a sectioned-off room. When I looked down, I saw the person's nape; the identity tattoo read 000. The *chiri.*

"Come, miss," she urged, and pulled me into what appeared to be a bathroom, a gold gilded opulent bathroom. A toilet, basin, and extra tub filled the vast space on one side. On the other was a plush seating area.

The *chiri* pulled me toward the tub. Wetting a cloth, she began to wipe away Master's seed from my thighs and core. I stared at the stone wall before me, dazed, fighting the fuzziness that still occupied my mind.

After the *chiri* dried my thighs with a soft towel, she led me to the seating area and guided me down to a seat. She made quick work of opening a large set of double doors. I looked up to see rows and rows of dresses, beautiful vibrantly colored dresses.

The *chiri* pulled another out and I stood as she clothed me. As I looked down at this dress, I saw it was a deep green. I idly thought how beautiful this color was. I frowned, wondering if I had ever noticed the color of anything before. Currently, the images in my head were revealed only in gray scale. As I scanned this room, I realized that life here was lived in color, yet it did not hold within it any form of beauty the vibrant colors should bring.

The *chiri* backed away two steps and nodded her head. "You look beautiful, miss. Master will be pleased."

On hearing the *chiri*'s words, I stared at her. Her head was downcast. I could see a blush on her neck, creeping to her face. Stepping forward, I placed my hand on her shoulder. She tensed. "You don't need to bow your head to me, *chiri.*"

But the *chiri* didn't raise her head. Instead she replied, "I'm a *chiri,* miss. We are below everyone. Master commands it to be so." She paused, then added, "And you are High Mona, miss. You are elevated in status. From whatever that was. This is who you are now. There's no going back once Master commands it."

My hand fell from her shoulder, and once it did, the *chiri* scuttled out of the room, waiting in the doorway for me to follow. Knowing that I had no other choice, I followed. We entered the room where Master was waiting. As soon as he saw me, his eyes flared and his lips tightened as though he was fighting for breath.

Once again he was dressed impeccably in his suit, not a hair out of place. Master held out his hand. Forcing my feet to move, I walked to where he stood, placing my palm against his. Lifting my hand to his mouth, he placed a kiss on the back of my hand and pulled me beside him, linking his arm through mine.

Turning us to the only door in the room, he paused, looked at me, and declared, "You look beautiful, 152. Like a vision."

Bowing my head, I replied, "Thank you, Master."

Leaning in close, he brushed a strand of hair from my neck, placed a single kiss over my pulse, and added, "And a quick study. Let's hope you stay this obedient. My High Monebi have a habit of breaking my trust and consequently losing their lives." He nuzzled his rough cheek against my cheek and said, "I would really dislike it if you forced my hand. I'd hate to see such beauty fall."

"Yes, Master," I whispered, my hands shaking.

Master straightened and smiled wide. "That's what I like to hear." Securing my arm through his, he led us out the door, past a guard dressed in a jet-black uniform. I glanced back at the guard, just to see his hard eyes staring at us as we left.

A trickle of ice-cold shivers ghosted over the nape of my neck as an image sprang to mind of two children—an older boy and a younger girl hiding under a bed. A deep sense of sorrow followed.

I racked my brain, fighting to keep tight hold of the memory, as Master guided us through a dank, dark hallway and down a set of stone stairs.

Guards lined the hallways every so often, and as we passed, they stood attention and saluted Master. He paid no heed to their obvious show of allegiance and respect. He just kept his head high and his attention straightforward.

As the faint sound of clattering metal and shouts increased in volume the farther we walked, I began to wonder where we were going. I didn't have to wonder long, for as we turned a corner, the mouth of the hallway revealed the answer to my question.

I stared, gaping at the vast expanse before me. A space so wide that I struggled to interpret exactly what I was seeing.

Master stepped forward and held out his free hand. "The Blood Pit," he announced, his voice laced with pride and conceit.

The Blood Pit . . . My eyes struggled to absorb the many males, segregated into hundreds of small sand pits. And they were fighting. Weapons of all descriptions were being used. The males were of all shapes and sizes, but most were huge; muscle packed upon muscle as they circled one another, sparring and drawing blood. They were all dressed the same: bare torsos, bare feet, and black pants.

Guards lined the sides of the pits. Most held metal prods, sparking at their tips with what appeared to be arcs of blue fire. If a male stepped out-of-bounds or stopped fighting, he was struck with the prod. Most fell to the ground in obvious pain, like boiling-hot lead was scalding them from within.

Suddenly, the image of the scarred male that had plagued my thoughts since I'd awoken filled my mind. I could see him, as clear as day, standing before me as a boy, a large tattoo on his chest, as he was forced to fight . . . forced to fight as I was forced to watch . . . just like this.

And he did. He fought everyone, as commanded, reaching for me when all of his opponents had been defeated. But as had happened every day since, I was taken away. And then . . . then . . .

I didn't know.

As my vision cleared, I whispered, "I have seen this before. I've been here before."

Master stiffened beside me, then asked, "What?"

My heart raced with the fear. I shouldn't have spoken of my own accord. Swallowing back my nerves, I repeated, "I said, I think I have been here before." I frowned, struggling to remember. Master's dark eyes narrowed. Straightening my shoulders, I continued, "But I do not remember how, why, or when. Surely I must be mistaken?"

Master did not move for several seconds, nor did his expression change. Eventually, he moved to stand before me, blocking out the view of hundreds of males fighting. His hands reached up to cup my cheeks, and he smiled. "You were raised here, 152. You have spent many days here as a child and as a teen, one of our most standout *monebi*." Suddenly, his face frosted over as he unleashed his anger. "If I had known you before, you would have been with me from a young age. But my sister found you first. And now, you are home . . ."

He stepped back and linked my arm through his again. ". . . To my empire," he added. My attention was immediately drawn to his face. I studied his expression and saw the happiness radiating through. "I am the only male on the planet who has this as his kingdom." He gestured with a sweep of his arm, then continued, "A Caesar for the modern age. An empire built on strength and skill. A gladiatorial Rome right here in Georgia. An arena where we root out the gods from the men. The arena where my word is law, where lives are saved or taken by the simple flick of my wrist."

In a split second, Master dropped his exuberant, insane excitement and assumed a neutral air of composure. My head ached with his constant change of moods. But more than anything, my fear of him grew minute by minute. In the short time I had spent with him, he had shown many versions of himself—none of which I liked. All of which were terrifying.

Master patted my hand and pulled me forward along a path that ran around the edge of the sunken pits. From our vantage point we could see every strain of bare muscle, every drop of sweat glistening over scarred skin, and we could hear every grunt of exertion. Such energies generated a highly charged static, which hovered in the musty air. This place stank of violence and death. The male beside me, the male who had just taken me, was truly the master of all he surveyed and king of these slaves.

Master pointed out certain pits as we passed. "New fighters, they'll be first-round fighters only," he explained without feeling, casually talking about the group of males in training as though their days were numbered. He pointed to a pit farther across the room. It was a larger ring filled with larger men. "New transfers from our gulags in Western Europe. We're still determining their capabilities." As my eyes focused on the males in training, one looked up and blatantly stared my way. Master tensed beside me. Then I cried out when his opponent swung his ax and buried its blade straight into the chest of the staring male. The male dropped to his knees. I stopped. Yet I didn't react. My nerves were altogether too calm, my demeanor too collected. I instinctively knew that I had seen death before. Death just like this: quick, brutal, violent, senseless.

Many deaths.

Master continued my tour as though a male had not just lost his life. Glancing back, I stared at the number on his chest, 129. I repeated the number in my head. I silently mouthed the number on my lips. I did it because I knew, without thought, that no one else would ever remember the male who had just died here in the pits.

Merely one of many nameless to needlessly perish.

I frowned at this flicker of knowledge. Then Master pointed out other groups to me as we slowly circled his enterprise—paired fighters, group fighters, veterans, those brought in from gulags from all areas of the world. I listened enough to show I was attentive and nodded in all of the right places, and I offered a "Yes, Master" or "No, Master" response when it was expected.

Then we stopped. We stopped at a secluded pit in the far rear of the training space. As I glanced into the sunken pit below, I saw the biggest male I had ever seen, dressed only in black pants, menacingly circling another male.

"And here is the most important pit of all," Master explained. I looked to his face and watched as a smile, a maniacal smile, spread on his lips. But he didn't look to me; instead his attention was fixed on the male in the pit. I followed his gaze. Just then, the male turned, his large chest facing us. His identity number was showcased for all to see: 901.

As if feeling my stare, 901 glanced up. Blue eyes met mine. But these were not kind blue eyes. They were cold and devoid of life. No warmth lived in that stare. No, all that glared up at me from this pit were the eyes of a killer. A brutal, and what appeared to be the most successful, killer under Master's command.

Master squeezed my hand and announced, "901 is my prized champion. The undefeated 'Pit Bull' of the Arziani pits. No one can touch him. He's infallible." Master stopped abruptly, his jaw tensed. "Or so he tells me," he added. I noted a hint of venom in his voice. Master dropped his head to the side as he stared at his champion, and he said, almost to himself, "But he has a weakness. I just need to find it."

Then Master appeared to freeze. When I looked down into the pit, trying to fathom what held him so captivated, I once again found the cold, hard stare of 901. He was still looking at me.

My heart pounded under 901's scrutiny. I ducked my head to the side, edging closer to Master. He did not make me feel much safer, but 901's rawness and harsh attention seemed the greater threat to me right now.

Then Master glanced to me. His eyes watched me and his lips curled in anger. Before I could understand what had triggered his rage, he called, "901, come here."

Master's loud command caused me to flinch, and I almost whimpered aloud as his grip on my arm became unyielding, to the point of pain. I kept my eyes down but heard the heavy thud of footsteps crunching on sand, approaching our vantage point.

A fresh scent washed over me, then I saw two large bare feet stop in my line of sight. Master eventually slackened his grip on me to guide my head up with a finger under my chin. I obeyed this silent order and lifted my head. But Master wasn't watching me. His attention was on the male standing a mere foot in front of us.

"901, this is my new High Mona, 152," Master announced. My attention remained with Master, but then Master's thumb and forefinger gripped my chin and forced my head to turn. Turn and meet the blue eyes of the champion of the pits.

If I had thought 901 huge before, it was nothing to how he appeared now, standing before me. His chest was double my width, and his height towered above me, my head in line with his chest. Every inch of him was ripped with muscles, wide veins cording in his arms and neck. Despite myself, I noticed his face, mostly how handsome he could be if his stare wasn't so cruel. Master was beautiful, his dark features staggering and elite. But 901 was the epitome of rough and raw; every inch of skin was marred with the scars of cruel tattoos: blood drops, decapitated heads, and what looked like images of shreds of torn flesh.

My pulse raced as he held his stare. I felt a blush creep up my cheeks and sprout, clearly, on my skin. As Master's grip tightened, I winced at the pain. "Petal, meet 901, the Pit Bull of my arena." Master leaned closer to 901 without letting me go, then added with obvious disdain, "My most successful *pet*."

My eyes, of their own accord, examined 901's face for a reaction. None was forthcoming, save for the slightest creases that formed at the corners of his severe eyes. And then I knew. I knew that being called Master's *pet* had struck a nerve.

Master stepped closer to me, released my face, and leaned down to press a wet kiss on the side of my neck. 901 remained stoic, unmoving and completely unshaken. "What do you think, 901?" Master asked, as he pressed against me, his lips still grazing my skin. "Don't you think my *mona* is simply the most beautiful creature ever created?"

Master then kissed up along my cheek. I breathed through the discomfort his touch brought.

Realizing 901 wouldn't react, Master withdrew his hand and flicked his chin. "Get back to training. You have a match this weekend." He leaned in closer to his fighter and added, "Remember what I said. We have high rollers attending that night. I want them to return."

901 said nothing. Eventually Master flicked his wrist and 901 marched away. He reentered the pit, picked up two short-bladed weapons, one in each hand, and commenced sparring. Master guided me to leave by his hand upon my elbow. As he did so, I glanced back to the pit, where a now familiar face was looking my way, his hard blue stare penetrating mine.

As Master guided us around the pits, it took all that I could muster not to look back to the champion's training area. To the large beast that dominated its domain.

The male with the cruel eyes.
The infallible killer.
The Pit Bull of the Arziani empire.
Master's living god among men.

3

LUKA

Brooklyn, New York

"So are we talking thousands or hundreds?" I asked Valentin.

He, Zaal, and I were stationed around the table in my house.

Valentin's eyes narrowed in thought. I watched the newest member of our Bratva as he straightened in his seat.

Cracking his wide neck from side to side, he replied, "Hundreds, one or two depending if there is a match. Master Arziani brings in more of his males if his associates come in. They fly to the pit from all over the world, many traveling days to get there." Valentin's fists clenched on the tabletop, large muscles bunching under his black shirt.

The veins in his forearms corded with the anger ripping through him. I glanced to Zaal, who studied his new brother-in-law. Zaal briefly met my eyes before leaning forward and saying to Valentin, "Be calm. Breathe through it."

Valentin's nostrils flared. I could see that Zaal's words were having no effect on him whatsoever. Instead, Valentin rose from the table and began to pace back and forth in front of the fireplace. He was panting with rage. Given his sheer size and scarred face, and the permanent raised red scar collaring his neck, Valentin appeared every inch the monster he was renowned to be.

"Why are we wasting time with all this shit?" he snarled, pointing at the maps we'd had constructed of the Blood Pit based on his memory. I never took my eyes off him. The map lay in the center of the table, our notes scattered around the edges of the wooden top. Our intel regarding Arziani's pit was gradually building day by day.

"We sit here, like fucking fearful morons, as that prick sits on his throne, doing fuck knows what to my sister," he roared, then stopped dead in his tracks. His fists shook so much that his entire body seemed to convulse.

As calmly as possible, I leaned back in my chair at the head of the table and said, "Arziani is the biggest threat we've ever faced." I pointed to Zaal, then to myself, and finally to Valentin. "I'm not just talking about within the Bratva or the Georgian brotherhood. I'm talking about us three, too: in the gulag, under Jakhua, and with that bitch, Mistress Arziani. The Blood Pit is like nothing we've ever experienced."

Valentin's hot glare locked on me. He slapped his fist on his broad chest. "I know this more than any of you. I was raised in that hell. I spent day after day in those pits, until I was chosen as an *Ubiytsa*. Do not lecture me on what *I* had to endure."

I chased back the annoyance of his disrespect. "Then I don't need to explain why detailed planning is essential, why we need to know exactly what we'll be facing. Above all, we need to find a way in. The Blood Pit is underground, heavily fortified, and manned by many, many guards. It's impossible, unless we can identify a secure way in—*unseen*." Valentin remained motionless while I talked. Leaning forward, I rested my elbows on the table and asserted, "We are heavily outnumbered. Besides us three, the males under our command are soldiers of the street. They fight with guns. They have no idea how to overcome an organization such as this, how to fight male prisoners like us. Even if we made it into the pit, the guards are too many. Even if we overcame the guards, the conditioned male fighters would surely tear them apart. And we would all die. Each of us is unbeatable in a death match, but even we cannot defeat hundreds of enslaved fighters and *Ubiytsy*."

For a second I thought that I had gotten through to Valentin. But suddenly a pained roar burst from his throat, and he struck out at the mirror hanging on the wall. The sound of shattering glass echoed around the room. But Valentin didn't stop there. Lost in his rage, he swept his arm along the mantelpiece, destroying Kisa's ornaments.

Zaal looked to me in concern, but I slowly shook my head. Valentin was fresh from his long imprisonment. Worse, his sister was under the control of that sadistic bastard Arziani. The deep fear of this was steadily eroding any peace he could find, day by day, hour by hour, minute by minute.

When Valentin's gaze snapped to us, I could see that he had been overwhelmed by the monster that lived within. I nodded my head. Zaal shifted on his seat, ready to fight. But there was only one person that could quell his rage. She brought with her the same calm each of us had found latterly in this dark hell of a life. She brought water to the fire, the balm to our conditioned rage.

"Zoya!" Zaal bellowed, never taking his eyes off Valentin, who was bracing to fight.

Light footsteps padded on the wooden floorboards of the hallway. In seconds there was a light knock on the door. "Enter!" I called. The doorknob turned.

Zoya Kostava entered, long black hair hanging to her back. She was dressed in black jeans and a sweater. Without any need for explanation, Zoya's dark gaze zeroed in on an increasingly agitated Valentin. Zaal pushed back his chair, readying to protect his sister.

But she gestured for him to stop. As she looked to her brother, she shook her head. Zaal stilled, though he remained primed to strike if needed. As was I.

Zoya stepped forward. As she did so, Valentin's lost eyes slammed to greet her. She walked forward, no fear in her stride. Valentin's muscled shoulders relaxed in response. His scarred face melted to one of deep sorrow.

"Valentin," Zoya murmured softly, as she approached her male. Valentin reached out and drew her in to press against his chest. I watched as his eyes squeezed shut and he breathed in her scent.

Zoya's hands lifted to run over his head. "You're okay," she murmured in Russian, speaking Valentin's native language to help calm the savage beast within.

I could see the tension leave Valentin the second Zoya was in his arms. I glanced to Zaal, who was watching the scarred Russian like a hawk. Zaal had slowly, but steadily, grown to accept Valentin over these past few weeks. Worryingly, Valentin's mood was unstable. A whole lot more unstable than either Zaal or I had been when freed from captivity. We knew that most of this stemmed from a desperate need to save his sister, Inessa. The rest was due to his many years as a slave killer for the Arzianis. Valentin wasn't adjusting to the outside world as well as we had hoped. His conditioning to kill, only to kill, ran far too deep to undo quickly. But it was his anger that troubled us most. We all had anger. We all had to tamp down its burning heat. To be "normal" in this world was a challenge every unforgiving second, round the clock. But for Valentin, it was much worse. Only Zoya could tame his anger.

"You're okay," Zoya murmured gently. Rearing back, Valentin looked down at his female and sighed deeply. His hand cupped her face and he slowly nodded, an unspoken message of love traveling between them.

They stayed that way for several seconds, communicating silently. Then Zoya turned her head to me and asked, "Can we go home?" I could see the desperation in her torn expression. She needed to be alone with Valentin. She needed privacy to truly calm him.

I nodded. Zoya took Valentin's hand in her own. Without another word, Zoya guided him from my office and out of the house.

As the front door closed, Zaal slumped back in his seat and pushed his long hair from his face. I sat back too, glaring at the blueprints of the Blood Pit, trying to figure out how the hell we could break in safely.

"We need to get into that fucking pit," Zaal said eventually.

Sighing, I ran my hands down my face and nodded. "I know. But with their numbers and their home-field advantage, I can't visualize how to take these fuckers down."

Zaal glanced out the window to the street beyond and admitted, "Valentin isn't coping. He needs his sister back to fully heal and move on." He turned back to me. His face darkened. "I've only just gotten Zoya back. I will not see her destroyed because she alone can calm him down. It's affecting her. I can see it in her face every time she enters the room and sees his rage."

He was right. We could all see it.

"I am the *Lideri* of the Georgians. You are the *knayz* of the Bratva. We run this city. I know this. The New York underworld is ours and ours alone. But if we don't find Inessa soon, before long Valentin will snap and he will kill." Zaal shook his head. "Even we cannot prevent him from killing in public twenty-four/seven." Zaal's hands flattened on the tabletop, and he added, "Then people would realize he wasn't like them. That he was different. Changed. Too many questions would fall back on us.

"The real world isn't ready to handle our reality. How could they accept that the gulags, the drugs, and the Blood Pit are real? It is the stuff of nightmares. How could they believe that males are being raised as killers, for sport and greed?

"Worse, it would surely implicate the Bratva and my people in too many ways. We can fight the police and the system *here* in our city, but we can't take on the whole world." Zaal shrugged and tapped the map of the Blood Pit. "We need a way in. We need a solid plan, and we need it fast. I won't have our freedom jeopardized. I won't have what I've found with my Talia taken away from me, after being without her all of these years." He raised his brow. "And we know you won't give up Kisa. We need to act, Luka, and we need to do it soon."

Lifting the glass of water sitting beside me, I brought it to my lips and drained it in one motion. Zaal stood up. As he passed by, he pressed his hand on my shoulder. I didn't move until I heard him leaving my house with Talia, who had been sitting with Kisa.

Pushing back from the table, I got to my feet and walked down the hallway. In the living room, Kisa was waiting for me on the couch, hand lying on her swollen stomach.

She took one look at me, her face sympathetic. Silently, she held out her hand. I took it in an instant and dropped to the couch beside her. Kisa fell against my chest and her hand landed on my stomach.

She didn't say anything. Once I'd fought through my pride, I admitted, "I can't see a way to defeat Arziani." The minute I had confessed what was torturing my mind, a heavy weight lifted from my chest.

Kisa froze, then tilted up her chin to meet my eyes. I stared down at my beautiful wife and sighed. "They run a damn fortress, *solnyshko*. Arziani seems insane from what Valentin has said. He's deluded, thinks he's some kind of king, some Roman Caesar. The king of his prisoners. Males, just like me, he drugs them and forces

them to fight on until they die. Kids plucked from families and orphanages, made into his monsters."

I ran my hand over my tired eyes and asked, "How the hell do
we stop him? How do we even breach his Blood Pit?"

Kisa sat up and brought her face to hover above mine. "You'll
find a way, baby. I trust you, we all do."

I shook my head. "And that's the problem," I said harshly.
"Everyone expects me to work this out. Everyone expects me to
find a way in and execute a plan to bring Arziani down." I pressed
my hand to Kisa's pregnant stomach, to our baby she was carrying.
"But more than that, I need this Arziani to be fucking killed. I need
to cut off the head of the snake. Everything, *everything* we have all
been through starts with Arziani. The gulags, his contact with the
Durovs. Levan Jakhua worked with Arziani, using Anri and Zaal
as his prototypes. Then we found out how he keeps so hidden—by
using drugged killers as assassins. They take out anyone who is a
threat."

Kisa blinked, then blinked again when what I was saying hit
home. "You believe he's coming for us. You believe that now we
know about him, he'll send another Valentin." Her words were not
a question. Because she knew what she said was exactly what I'd
been thinking.

An ache caved in my chest, and I leaned in to run my lips over
hers. "If he came for you. If someone took you away from me . . ."
I couldn't finish the sentence.

"Stop," Kisa said, moving back to press her finger over my lips.

I took her hand in mine. My mind took me back to the gulag.
I could still smell the dankness of the cells. I could still smell the
richness of the blood spilled hourly in the ring. I could still feel the
heavy veil of death that draped us all, waiting to strike, waiting to
deliver another soul to hell.

"Luka, *lyubov moya*, come back to me."

I gasped as I heard Kisa's soft voice cut through the memory. I tightened my grip on her hand. Once again I looked down to her stomach. My teeth clenched together, then I said, "I have to find a way to take him down. I can't, *I won't,* have our baby brought into this world knowing that the male who condemned me, us all, to that life is still breathing, still stealing children from homes, forcing them to be killers."

A tear escaped Kisa's eye to fall to our clasped hands. "Luka," she whispered, "this man scares me more than anything else in the world."

Dropping my forehead to rest against hers, I replied, "That's another reason why he needs to be put out of our misery. I want *our* version of a normal life. I want this Bratva life with you, with my new brothers and our families. But as long as that prick lives, it can never happen." I paused. My hand, still on Kisa's stomach, felt a tiny kick.

My eyes darted to my wife's stomach. Kisa laughed a single watery laugh. She covered my hand with her own, just as our baby kicked again.

Leaning forward, Kisa pressed her lips to mine. When she pulled back and I saw the love she had for me written on her stunning face, I knew I had to remedy the Arziani problem quickly.

I had two months until our child came into this world.

What that world would look like depended on me.

A world free from any threat to our lives.

That meant Arziani dead.

His guards slaughtered.

And the Blood Pit burned to ash.

4

901

Stoically, I sat in my cell as I waited for my turn. I could hear the faint roar of the crowd and the stomping of feet coming from the pit. The first round had come and gone, as had the second and the third. The better matches were happening now, then my match would follow.

The main event.

I rolled my neck from side to side as I spun my beloved Kindjals in my hands. The handles were warm. My eyes stared straight ahead as I envisioned how this fight would go. I had no idea whom I was fighting. Master no longer informed me. He wanted me unprepared, going in blind to my opponent's weapon of choice and level of skill.

He wanted a fucking show.

A show he would never get from me.

The sound of cell doors clattering against the walls came from down the hallway, and I knew it would be a Wraith for me. My cell was at the end of the champions' quarter. It offered a bed, basin, and flush toilet. Master gave his champion the best accommodations. With this cell came more privacy. It was the only thing I really appreciated about this prison. I liked to be alone. I didn't want a connection with anyone else. Liking, or even tolerating, another fighter made you weak. I never even took a *mona* when they were sent to me. I wouldn't fuck a female, even though I wanted to. They were forced into fucking as much as I was forced into killing. I didn't have any sympathy for them, but neither would I use them. I'd seen too many fighters brought down by becoming attached to a gifted female. They'd grown so attached that it had messed with their fighting skills.

Females were a distraction from the most important thing in this place: staying alive.

Suddenly, my cell door opened and a guard walked in, gun in hand. He was dressed in a black uniform, the match night uniform. Master was nothing if not a showman for his investors.

"Up," the guard ordered.

I obeyed and walked to where he stood. The guard looked up at me and said, "Master has ordered you to draw out the kill. To let your opponent get in a few strikes against you. He said you are to allow the Chinese investors' fighter to believe he is winning, to ensure a rise in the stakes for your next match."

Disgust at participating in such a pathetic show flooded through me. I wouldn't do it. Master knew it, but he ordered it just the same. He lived for the day when he mastered me completely. It wouldn't ever happen.

"You understand?" the guard checked. Instead of snapping his neck to shut his whining mouth, I pushed past him and pounded down the hallway. As with every match, the sound of the spectators increased in volume. And, as always, I broke into a slow, steady run, my feet kicking up sand with every stride.

When I neared the end of the tunnel, I concentrated on the pit. I could see a huge man circling the sand, a spear in each fist. My lips curled up in excitement. This male actually looked like he could contend.

We would see.

Picking up speed, I burst through the mouth of the tunnel and charged at the male now standing at the center of the pit. Obviously expecting me to act quickly, the male stuck out his spear. My right Kindjal immediately struck the wooden handle, splintering the weapon in two. The blurred calls from the crowd rose in volume as I plunged my blade straight through the heart of my opponent. As I forced my blade farther into his flesh, I watched his eyes widen and blood spill from his mouth.

Leaning back, I lifted my foot and pushed against his chest, forcing his lifeless corpse off my blade. As he dropped to the floor, the crowd cheered. I towered over the dead male, breathing faster but barely having even broken a sweat.

Then the crowd grew silent. I turned to face Master's seat. The moment I looked up at him in the stands, I could see the rage simmering in his eyes. Of course, his always perfect public persona remained firmly in place. But I knew better. Inside, Master was erupting at my blatant disrespect of his orders.

Then, as Master stood to address me, my eyes moved to the female sitting on the floor at his feet. I swallowed hard. It was the High Mona.

The most beautiful female I had ever seen.

"901," Master's firm voice suddenly called out, snapping me from staring at the *mona* dressed in blue, whose eyes were focused on the floor. "Another victory," Master complimented. But I caught the venom in his words. I fought back a satisfied smirk.

As Master was about to speak again, a male sitting a few seats to his left stated coldly, "You told me this match would be a good fight. Your animal just slaughtered mine in ten seconds flat." The male stared Master right in the eye. He continued, "You had seen my fighter; therefore, you knew his skill level." The male then looked to me and curled his lips. "This fighter far exceeded him in skill, which leads me to question your honor, Arziani."

At that, the crowd began talking in hushed whispers. Arziani's cheek twitched, betraying his rage at being questioned in his own house. No one questioned Arziani in this arena. So whoever this male was, he must have been important enough for Master not to order his immediate execution.

Master's anger didn't show; instead a wide smile spread on his lips and he assured, "I promise you this was an even match. But I take your point, 901 is a highly exceptional fighter." He paused, then his livid gaze fell on me. "Perhaps even the best fighter my empire boasts." His head tipped to the side. The anger that lay in his eyes gradually faded.

His hand dropped to his side. As my eyes followed the action, he ran his hands through the High Mona's dark hair. The *mona* stiffened as he did so, and I had to work hard to restrain a sudden urge to rip his arm off.

I felt my teeth grind together of their own accord. Before I showed my anger toward Master, I masked my expression. But as I refocused on him, I caught him watching me closely, very closely. My stomach sank as his lips hooked into a brief smirk. Then, as if nothing had transpired between us, he held out his hands to the crowd and announced, "To show that my pit isn't rigged, I shall stage a death-match tournament, the likes of which you have never seen before. It will be the greatest of challenges, pitting together my empire's skilled and most ruthless killers. No rules, no restrictions— any weapon of choice, but no guns, of course." The crowd cheered Master's turn of phrase. "Any man can fight." Master nodded in excitement and looked directly at me. He continued, "Then we shall truly see who is the best death-match warrior of all. We shall call on the champions from each of the gulags"—he turned to the male who had complained and added—"and my associates, that would be you, are free to enter whomever they wish."

The male whose fighter I had just slain didn't react, save to curtly nod his head. "Deal," he replied, then flicked his wrist for his entourage to follow him out of the stands surrounding the pit.

Master reached down and took hold of the *mona*'s arm. He pulled her to her feet, and without dismissing me as protocol demanded, he moved in for a kiss. The *mona* submitted, as did they all. But as I watched Master's eyes open and stare at me without breaking from her mouth, scalding fire traveled through my already twitching muscles.

When he pulled back, he dragged the *mona* away from the stands, flicking his wrist my way, my signal to leave the pit. Turning on my heel, I jogged to the tunnel and ran all the way to my cell. Just as I was about to reach the door, Master walked through a side door to meet me. Alone. He stopped directly in front of me.

He glared. I could see his intense hatred of me in every tense muscle under his suit. I stood fully upright, glaring right back at him, very obviously standing my ground. His jaw clenched. "You disobeyed a direct order," he hissed coldly.

I didn't flinch. I didn't react. I didn't do shit.

He stepped closer. "You have fucked me over for the very last time, 901. I have needed you these past few years, and you've known it. You wouldn't dare act this way if you didn't know. You are unrivaled here in the Blood Pit, that's beyond question. And now you have forced my hand with this fucking Ultimate Death Match." Then he smiled, his head tipping to the side. "But now that I've calmed down, the more I think about it, the more it feels . . . *right*." He paused, then shrugged. "Think of all the gulag champions, brought to Georgia, fighting in my Blood Pit. Think of the money that will be made from them ripping one another apart."

His eyes flared and he inched closer. His warm breath washed over me, then he added, "Among the gulag champions, or my business associate's own fighters, there may be one that can defeat you." His cheek twitched. "Imagine that? Imagine finding a diamond in the rough, one that is stronger than you, quicker than you, more skilled." He stepped even closer. "One that is obedient, bends to my will. Not one that is ungrateful and rebellious." My anger boiled. *Ungrateful.*

As if reading my mind, he held out his arms and said, "I've made you into what you are: a fighter no one can match. I've given you this life, a warrior for the modern age. In this place, to the spectators I bring in, you are a champion." He paused, then added, "You are a god." He dropped his arms, his face switching back to a livid expression. "*I* gave you it. And this is how you repay *me*?"

I bit my tongue, forcing myself not to snarl that I bore no gratitude whatsoever to *my master* for condemning me to this hellish life. That I bore no gratitude for being drugged and forced to fight as a kid. That I bore no fucking gratitude to the male who had bestowed on me a life of solitude, where having feelings toward someone else made you weak.

No gratitude, only red-hot hatred.

So I welcomed this tournament. Maybe Master would bring me a fighter to finally end this life for me, save me from being Master's pet. But I wouldn't go easily, and that was his problem. My honor was all I had left, the only thing he could take away. I had fought and killed hundreds upon hundreds of opponents—so many I had lost count. But not once had any of them come close to ending me.

Master stepped back at my silence and laughed. "You think you can beat them all, 901? Is that why you disobey my every order, because you don't fear death? You really believe you're unbeatable."

My hands tightened on the handles of my Kindjals. Master noticed and another laugh burst from his lips. "You do. You really believe you can't be beaten, do you?"

I lowered my eyes to focus on the ground. When Master didn't speak, I raised them. I detected something in his gaze. Inhaling, he folded his arms and declared, "Then you've just raised the stakes."

I fought a frown at what he meant. But Master didn't say anything else. Instead he clicked his fingers at a nearby guard. My cell door was opened and I was locked inside.

I watched Master turn on his heel and leave the champions' quarter with a sadistic smile on his face. As much as I tried, I couldn't help but wonder what that smile had in store for me.

My skin dripped with sweat as I returned from sparring in the training pit. As I reached my cell door, a loud roar came from the cell opposite my own. I glanced that way as a louder, more pained roar ricocheted off the dank stone walls.

The roars were relentless. Scream after scream, then hollow thuds. I took a step in that direction, then another, stopping outside the cell next door to where the screams were coming from.

Suddenly, 667, a fellow champion, came to his barred door. I didn't turn his way. I never spoke to him, though he always tried to speak to me. As per Blood Pit rules, the top champions never fought one another. Although we were all Master's "champions," I had gained more kills, was broader and taller than 667. The other one, 140, was no match for me, either. They were all skilled and vicious in combat, but we all knew that if Master was ever to pit us against one another, I would slaughter them all.

Master needed champions to pull in bigger numbers for championship matches. He had never had only one "champion." At least he hadn't before. I heard rumors from the trainers as I sparred that Master's upcoming tournament wanted to find only one. The truest warrior of all.

The champion of all champions.

Suddenly, 140 charged his cell door, his sheer bulk almost taking down the heavy iron bars. 667 shook his head. "Fuck," he hissed.

This time, wanting to know why the warrior was acting strangely, I asked, "What happened?"

667's eyebrows rose in surprise as I spoke. As 140 charged his cell once again, I growled, "Answer me!"

667 wrapped his hands around the bars and said, "The Wraiths took his *mona*."

140 roared out in pain and began tearing up his cell, lifting the mattress from the floor to throw it across the room.

"Took her?" I questioned.

667's face dropped. Sighing, he replied, "Took her from his cell, shut his door, and slit her throat in front of him."

My eyes dipped to inspect the dark stone ground before 140's cell. My eyes narrowed in concentration, struggling to focus in the half-light of the dim wall lamp. But then I saw it—freshly spilled blood.

As 140's huge body slumped to the ground, I leaned against the cell door, a fire ignited within me. "Master," I hissed. 667 nodded. "Why?" I questioned, never taking my eyes off 140, his blank and torn face now staring lifelessly at the blood splashed before him, just out of reach.

"He disobeyed," 667 informed. "He killed a guard. The guard had tried to fuck his *mona* while he trained. 140 broke the guard's neck when he returned before he could take her." 667's hands tightened on the bars. "When another Wraith informed Master, Master ordered his *mona* to die." 667 paused, then said, "The guard that killed her made it slow and painful. He was seeking revenge for the slain guard."

I watched 140. His skin was pale and his hands were shaking.

Worst of all was the look in his eyes. 140 was gone. He was broken. He wouldn't survive his next match. This male was already dead.

"She made him weak," I said, and turned my back to walk to my cell.

"She was his *mona*!" 667 bit at me.

I stopped and looked back over my shoulder. "She was his weakness. Master thrives off weakness. The fool offered his demise on a plate."

"She was his heart," 667 said with even more bite. "Just as my *mona* is *mine*."

Cracking my neck, my bones clicking, I slowly faced him. Holding out my Kindjal toward where he stood, I said, "And, like him"—I pointed my blade to 140's broken, slumped form—"she too will be your downfall."

I urged my feet to walk, when 667 shouted, "I would rather die knowing my *mona*'s touch and comfort than to live a long life like you will. Cold and alone in your cell. Never knowing anything but blood and death and pain."

This time I didn't stop. I kept walking until I was in my cell and a guard slammed the door shut. But even when the guard had walked away, I remained rooted to the spot, my Kindjals still in my iron-tight grip.

I would rather die knowing my mona's *touch and comfort than to live a long life like you will. Cold and alone in your cell. Never knowing anything but blood and death and pain.*

667's words circled my mind. They jabbed at my brain like the sharpest of knives. The coldness of my cell lashed at my cooling skin. Dropping the blades, I slumped to the mattress on the floor. As I stared forward at the dark stone walls, against my will, the face of Master's High Mona swam into view.

I tried to chase this vision away, but 667's words prevented me.

Her dark hair and blue eyes, her perfect body, and how she looked in her dresses.

Then, as if it were real life, I saw her standing before me, holding out her hand. But just as I went to reach for that hand, a Wraith stepped behind her, knife in his hand. Before I could react, he struck at her throat. The *mona*'s pretty eyes widened with shock. She dropped to the ground in front of me, life fading quickly with the outflow of her blood.

Shaking my head, I forced myself to lie back on my bed, still trying to push the image from my head.

Because wanting her would make me weak.

I wouldn't ever give my heart to another. Doing that only brought pain.

I wouldn't be weak. I refused.

I fell asleep still picturing pooled blood at my feet. Pooled blood and 140's lifeless, vacant eyes.

5

152

I woke with a groan. As my eyes opened, I tried to move my numb arms and legs, but I couldn't. As I tried again, I panicked. A cry left my lips, as I glanced up to my arms and saw them secured to the bedpost with rope.

Focusing my attention on my feet, I saw that the same ropes were fastened around my ankles. Tears blurred my vision as I looked to the spot beside me in bed. It was empty. I stared at the bloodied linen, then at my stomach and thighs. I fought back sickness. My skin was peppered with bruises.

Closing my eyes, I thought back to last night. Master had arrived and injected my arm. I pushed through the light fog the drug brought with it to remember what he had done. Master had been rough.

Master had many sides to his personality. And last night saw him at his most wicked. From the moment he had arrived, I remembered seeing his hard eyes. He walked to me, shedding his clothes. He'd grabbed my arm and bruised my lips as he crashed his mouth to mine. But this kiss wasn't gentle, nor was it softly petting as he sometimes gave me. No, this kiss was vicious and cruel. As was the rest of our night together.

The tears from my eyes ran over my cheeks as I thought back to him tying me to the posts until I couldn't move. I remembered him placing himself between my thighs and slamming inside me, over and over, with brutal thrusts. His hands had nipped and dug into my skin, but the drug made me crave him more. And Master gave it to me. Gave me his seed over and over, hard and harder until he made me bleed. Until I couldn't take any more.

He was punishing me.

Punishing me for what? I didn't know.

Then he left. Different from all our other nights together, he hadn't forced me into his arms so he could fall asleep with his cheek upon my breast. Instead he had left me tied up to the bed, in pain, unclean.

He'd left without so much as a backward glance.

Fear held me captive as I thought of the previous High Mona. I wondered what she had done to deserve her death. I was terrified that I had done something similar. Though what? I had no idea.

I shifted on the mattress, trying to find some relief from the pain, when the door to my room opened. My eyes darted to whoever was there. I prayed it wasn't Master or, worse, a guard to take me away.

My heart beat fast, then strong relief surged through me when I saw my *chiri* enter. When she shut the door, her eyes searched the room for me. When she saw me on the bed, restrained, her dark eyes flared. Then I could see shock and sympathy in her stare.

The *chiri* rushed to where I lay, and her hands hovered over the ropes. "Miss," she whispered when she saw the blood and welts.

Her head moved as she scanned the room. She ran into the washroom, then returned with a short sharp blade. In silence, the *chiri* began to cut my ties.

I tried to hold back the cries of pain, but even the slightest movement of the rope at my wrists and ankles caused a searing blast of pain to rip through my body.

"Sorry, miss," the *chiri* said, as she tried to quickly and efficiently remove my restraints.

One by one, the ropes fell away. As they did, my numb limbs fell lifelessly to the mattress. When all were removed, the *chiri* began massaging my arms and legs, bringing the blood back to my muscles. I stifled a cry as they filled with what felt like an onslaught of needles.

"It will help eventually, miss," the *chiri* soothed. I nodded, telling her I understood. For several minutes, I let her massage my limbs until, though weakened, they returned to something near normal.

When the *chiri* withdrew her hands, she slid from the bed and crossed the room to fill the large sunken tub on the other side of the chamber. Unmoving, I watched her go about her work. I watched her long, ill-fitting gray dress hang loosely on her starved frame. I stared at her scar.

"I'll get you out of here." I started as the echo of a voice spoke into my ear. Wanting to hear more, I shut my eyes and tried to recall the voice. The scar, I thought. The scar had made the voice speak? Thinking of the *chiri*'s scar, I prayed the voice would return.

"I promise. I won't stop until I find a way from this hell." My heart raced as the voice returned, this time with greater clarity and strength.

I stared at the male hovering over me. I lay in a corner of a dark cell, and I smiled. "I know you will. I trust you. I believe in you."

My weak, shaking hand lifted to stroke the male's face, and he sucked in a deep breath. His bright blue eyes closed at my touch. My stomach rolled when a single tear fell from the corner of his eye.

"Don't cry," I murmured, chasing the tear away with the pad of my thumb. "I will wait. However long it takes, I will wait."

The scarred man opened his eyes. Gathering me in his arms, he held me close. My body was tired and I could barely move. But I felt safe in his arms. "How long until they inject me again?" *I asked.*

"Soon," *he replied, and his huge body tensed.*

"It's okay," *I soothed.* "One day, I'll wake and I'll be free. You will have freed me."

"I promise," *he rasped.* "You have my word. You're my blood. I'll never stop trying."

"Miss?" a distant voice whispered. Something touched my arm. "Miss?" the voice spoke again. I fluttered my eyes open, the memory spiraling into a black void.

I turned my head to the voice, but my vision was blurred. Gentle fingers wiped away the tears. "Miss? Are you okay?"

I swallowed back the lump in my throat. The vision had been so real. The care of the scarred man, a male who should have scared me, brought me the first sense of peace since I'd awoken in my gilded cage.

"Yes," I replied. The *chiri* sat silently, awaiting my response. I lifted my hand to my head, breathing through the ache in my arm. "My mind keeps showing me things." I frowned. "I'm never sure if they are real memories or illusions."

The *chiri* nodded, then took hold of my hand. "Miss, you must bathe." Her eyes dropped to my body, specifically my thighs, which were covered in a mixture of my blood and Master's release.

Forcing my legs to move, I slid them over the side of the mattress and held on to the *chiri* to help me stand. As I swayed on my feet, I leaned against her and used her to walk to the tub. I groaned as I stepped into the hot water; the marks from the ropes burned.

Gritting my teeth, I sat down and closed my eyes as the steam billowed around me, stinging my sores and soothing my aching muscles.

The water's scent was delicious. "What is in the water?" I asked, and opened my eyes to see the *chiri* dipping a cloth into the water before running it down my arms. I watched as the cloth wiped away the blood. The bruises remained. Nothing could wash those marks away.

"It's called lavender, miss. Master requires his High Monas to be bathed in it. It's his favorite scent."

I nodded, then rested my head back against the tub. The *chiri* washed my body, careful not to touch the bigger, darker bruises. I stared up at her as she worked and asked, "How did you become a *chiri*?"

She stilled, then dropping her eyes, she said, "My father sold me to the Wraiths. I was ten."

My eyes widened. "Your father sold you?"

The *chiri* nodded. The cloth stopped on my arm as she felt the heavy weight of my shocked stare. She sighed. "Starvation forces desperate people do the most despicable things, miss. My mother had died, there were six of us, no food." She shrugged. "I understood why he did it." Her gaze lost focus as she continued, "Though I'm sure he had no idea where I would be sent."

"I'm sorry," I whispered, hearing the edge of sadness in her plain words. The *chiri* flickered a watery smile my way. Only the left side of her mouth lifted, the right too deeply scarred to move. As I studied her tied-back dark hair and her dress, my heart clenched. I asked, "And they raised you to be a *chiri*?"

This time, she withdrew her hand, and then, after a pause of several seconds, she shook her head. Eventually she met my eyes and replied, "I was brought in to be a *mona* . . . just like you."

I stared at her. Then, without intention, my gaze fell upon her scar. Clearly seeing my confusion, she added, "I made the mistake of resisting the training." She pointed at her disfigured cheek. "This was my punishment."

"Why? How?" I asked, feeling a flood of sadness wash through my soul.

The *chiri*'s bottom lip trembled, but she pulled herself together enough to answer, "Acid. They threw acid over my face." She inhaled a shuddering breath. "I was punished for rejecting a guard's advances. So he ensured I would never look beautiful again." She paused, then added reluctantly, "It was at Master's instruction. He came to see how the new wave of *monebi* were progressing. He saw my defiance and decided to make an example of me. He ordered me to stand forward, then instructed the guard I'd refused to ruin my face."

Ice crept up my spine. My eyes drifted to my rope-marked wrists, to my heavy bruising and thighs. *Yes,* I thought. *Master is more than capable of ordering such a cruel act.*

"I'm so sorry," I said in a hushed voice. When I looked up, I saw something new in the *chiri*'s eyes—a kinship. A common understanding of what it felt like to be on the receiving end of Master's cruelty.

"What did you do?" the *chiri* asked, and commenced cleaning my body.

I dropped my hand into the water, watching as it rippled around me. "I don't know," I confessed, repeating the action just for something to do. "He was so angry, his eyes so possessive of me. It was as if he was furious that he wanted me so much. It was as though I was being punished for how much he wanted to take me." I shook my head. "Which I do not understand. Master has made no secret of how much he wants me since I was elevated to this High Mona status." I looked to the *chiri* and asked, "So why, now, does he seem to resent it?"

"I don't know," she admitted. I could see the confusion I was feeling showcased on her face. Moving to the head of the tub, the *chiri* made quick work of washing my hair.

Just as she was rinsing out the soap, I asked, "Do you have a name?" My eyebrows pulled down and I asked, "Do I have a name . . . I can't . . . I can't remember?"

The *chiri* dropped down to crouch by my side. She studied me, seeming to search my face for something. Eventually, her shoulders slumped and she said, "Yes, miss. I once had a name, though I haven't been called it for many years." She took in a breath and continued, "You will, too. We all have names, all who are enslaved in this place. We were all someone once, though Master makes quick work of making us forget."

"A name," I whispered, and tried to rack my brain for what I was called. But it was to no avail. The only name I had, the only identity my brain could find was 152. I was 152, I had only ever been 152. "I don't remember," I said sadly.

The *chiri* went to move, but I reached out and took hold of her arm despite the protests of my aching muscles. "Wait," I begged. The *chiri* froze. "Do you remember your name? Do you have a name?"

The *chiri*'s face paled, and then I knew. She did. She remembered her name. I sat up as quickly as I could manage and pushed. "What is it? Please, tell me."

The *chiri* shook her head, biting her bottom lip as her eyes glossed over. Her head dipped forward and she said, "I could be killed for telling you, miss. It is forbidden by Master for any of us who remember to speak of it." Her arm began trembling beneath my touch, and she said, "I know what he is capable of, and although I hate this life, here in this prison, I still want to live. I live for the day we will be free. I remember the outside world. Not all of it, but enough." She closed her eyes and inhaled. "I remember the sun and the fresh air. I won't lose hope we'll get that again."

Deflated, I sank back into the water. "I understand," I said soothingly, and meant it. I would never put her in danger.

I stayed in the bath for a few more minutes, then the *chiri* helped me out. As she did every day, she dried my hair and then led me to the seat in the side room, fixing my hair and beautifying my face. I watched her as she picked out a bright red dress. Only this dress was different from the others. It was made of a fabric so sheer that you could see clearly what was underneath.

As the *chiri* took my hand for me to stand and then began to wrap me in the dress, securing it at my shoulders, I frowned. Reading my confusion, she said, "Master ordered me to dress you for seduction. I'm to take you to him now."

I swallowed in trepidation and replied, "Okay."

As the *chiri* walked toward the door, she suddenly turned and stopped dead. I wondered what was wrong. Dropping her chin to touch her chest, she whispered, "Maya." I opened my mouth to speak, to ask what she had said, when she met my eyes with her own and repeated, "My name . . . my name is . . . Maya."

I felt warmth swell in my heart. With the revelation of her name, the *chiri* before me transformed into a young girl. A young girl with a *name*. She was no longer a "plague," she was a *person*.

Unable to keep from smiling, I let the happiness of her confidence in me show. Maya's cheeks blushed at this gesture. "It's beautiful," I said. Maya's cheeks reddened even more.

Stepping closer to her, I reached for her hand and said, "Thank you for telling me. I swear, I will never tell another soul."

"Thank you," she replied, then, checking over her shoulder, turned to me and said, "I don't know your name, miss. But I heard Master talking about you. He said you were twenty-one years old. I know that isn't much information, but it's something. You have an age. That's more than most in this place have."

My pulse sprinted, rushing the blood through my ears. "Twenty-one," I said quietly. I briefly closed my eyes and repeated with increasing confidence, "Twenty-one. I'm twenty-one."

"Yes, miss," Maya said in support. I had to hold back from taking her in my arms. If I were caught embracing a *chiri,* it would be punishment for us both.

"Thank you," I hushed out.

Maya bowed her head, then pointed to the door. "We must go, miss. Master will not be happy if we are late." I glanced down at my sheer dress and felt my cheeks heat with embarrassment. The dress was entirely see-through. You could see every part of my naked body underneath. My breasts, but shockingly, my most private area was clearly visible.

"All *monebi* here in the pit wear this garment, miss. It is only the High Mona that is covered. To show she is Master's and Master's alone." I nodded in relief, only for fear to spike in its wake.

"Does this mean I am no longer High Mona? Have I been relegated to being a *mona* once again?" Pure terror then shot to my heart when I confessed, "I don't want to be drugged again. I don't want to forget who I am again."

Sympathy flooded Maya's gaze. "I do not know, miss. I know nothing more than instructed."

Before I could respond, there was a loud bang on the door. "Master will be waiting!" We both jumped as a guard shouted. Maya's eyes grew large and she said, "We must hurry."

Steeling my nerves, I followed her out the door, ducking my head when the guard by the door stared lustfully at my state of undress. Maya led me swiftly through a maze of hallways, all dark stone lit only by dim lights, until we arrived at a forked section. Three hallways led to different areas of the pit. Maya headed down the hallway farthest to our left and I dutifully followed. We had walked only a few steps when the hallway changed from stone to sterile white walls, with many lights that almost blinded me.

I tried to understand what I was seeing, but I couldn't. When we arrived at a silver door, Maya opened it and I stepped through.

A large room lay before me. Several cages were lined along the walls. Then my heart sank when I saw what was inside. Four young boys, appearing to be between six and eighteen years of age, sat in the cages. Three were rocking back and forth, sweating and restless. One was staring straight forward, like he was alive but no longer aware of the world around him.

I tried to look for Maya for explanation, but she had already crossed the room to another door. I rushed to catch up. As I arrived at the door, Maya had opened it to reveal another room. This one was smaller. A narrow bed lay in the center. Along one of the walls were collars of all shapes and sizes. Thick metal collars. I closed my eyes when an image of the scarred male came to my mind. In my vision, he was wearing a collar. It was wrapped tightly around his neck. Then the vision deepened and in my mind's eye I heard a hiss spring from the collar, and it tightened around the scarred male's neck. His muscled neck corded and his blue eyes flared until the blue was eradicated by black.

Then the scarred male was no longer friendly. He was no longer safe. He was dangerous, becoming the most brutal of killers.

"Miss?" Maya's soft voice brought me from my thoughts, and she pointed to the bed. "You must sit on here and wait for Master."

I stared at the narrow bed, at its restraints hanging to the sides, and I feared the worst, but I did as instructed. I had just climbed onto the bed when the door opened again and a male in a white coat walked through. He saw me but didn't even flinch at my state of undress. Instead he walked to the wall housing the collars and took the smallest one from its rack.

I never moved my eyes from him as he silently worked. My hands were linked on my lap so the male couldn't see me shake.

I was so focused on the mental image of the male with the collar that I neither saw nor heard Master enter the room. I knew he had materialized only when I felt a finger drift over my arm and brush over the rope burn on my wrist. I sucked in a sharp breath at the raw tenderness, then my eyes collided with Master's.

I quickly bowed my head and saw his feet step as close as they could to the bed. His hand lifted, and I braced for a strike. Unexpectedly, it ran softly down my face. I scrunched up my face in confusion. I had expected the wicked Master from last night. But before me was the gentle and loving male from days ago.

"Such a beautiful petal," he whispered tenderly and placed his finger under my chin to raise my head. I did as instructed and lifted my face to look at his.

Master's gaze roved down to study my body, his eyes twitching in annoyance when he took in the bruises on my arm. He shook his head and leaning forward, ran his lips over my forehead. "I had no choice. I had to take you that way." He reared back and said, "You're so beautiful, too beautiful. I can hardly bear what I'm about to do, what I have to do to make sure my empire stays strong."

Pure terror took hold of my senses at his words, and the regretful, sad tone of his voice. Lifting his hand, he cupped my cheeks and stared into my eyes. As always, I could see the crazed possession staring back. He shook his head and licked his lips. "My very own Helen of Troy." He paused after those words, but I didn't understand what he meant, or who he was referring to.

"Your beauty is too coveted, but also extremely useful." I inhaled a ragged breath, and he added, "And now I must whore you out to an animal."

This time my heart kicked into a heady sprint. *Whore me out to an animal?* My mind raced, trying to piece together what was to happen. Suddenly, Master pushed me back onto the bed and shackled my wrists and feet. I didn't fight back.

Every part of me trembled as Master stayed beside me, stroking his hand along my cheek, his blazing, crazed eyes almost undressing me.

The male in the white coat moved beside me and took hold of my hand in a shackle. He moved up the cuff until my wrist was bare. It took me a moment to see what was in his hand.

The collar.

I flinched, imagining it going around my neck. But when I looked closer, I saw that it was too small. It was a bracelet. Then my short-lived sense of relief faded fast when I spotted the inside of the bracelet. It contained small needles, clear pellets of liquid behind each one.

The male lifted my wrist. Suddenly, he attached the bracelet to my skin and clasped it shut. A scream escaped my throat when the needles pierced my skin, sending a searing pain up my arm.

"Shh, petal," Master soothed, as I tried to breathe though the torment. His palm pressed against my forehead and he moved in to nibble my lips with his teeth, then cover them with his own. I whimpered at the unwanted affection, but Master didn't seem to care.

When he reared back, he said, "I have to do this. This task you must undertake is bigger than us both." He gestured around the room. "All of this. Our empire rests on the shoulders of one man." I tried to understand what he was saying, but the pain was too much.

"He has no weaknesses. And as much as it incenses me, I need him. He will win my tournament for me. But first, I need to break him. I must have him fully under my instruction. I need him to fully bend to my will." He talked to me like I knew what he meant. "My investors expect a show. They expect it to be a close match, not a cull. For that, I need him to *obey*." Master's finger drifted down my chest and stopped at my breast. His fingertip circled my nipple, and his nostrils flared.

"In all of the years under my command, he has given me no way to fully overpower him." He let that sentence hang in the air, until he looked to me again and said, "Until *you*. Until I saw him stare at you. My champion, my cold, unfeeling killer, affected by this face."

He nuzzled his cheek against mine and said, "*He* wants you." He stilled. In a flash, the cruel soul from last night possessed his being. Snapping his head up, lips curling, he hissed, "*My* High Mona. *My* pretty delicate petal. I don't want to let you go, but it will serve a higher purpose." His cheeks flushed with excitement. "Then I can own you completely. When my empire is secure, I can have you all day and all night. I will possess you in every possible way."

My blood turned cold at his words. Feeling a wetness on my wrist, I glanced over and saw blood trickling downward. Master saw it too and clicked his fingers at Maya, who was hovering like a shadow in the corner. "Clean it, *chiri*," he snarled. Maya rushed to the water and wet a cloth, immediately cleaning my wrist. I tried to meet her eyes, but she kept her head down.

When my wrist was clean, I stared at the silver bracelet and immediately knew it was the drugs. Instead of a single injection, this would give me regular, automatic doses. The male in the white coat quickly moved around the table, unshackling me from the bed. Master helped me stand. When he did, he stepped back and ranged his gaze all over me.

"Perfection," he whispered. I could see genuine pride in his expression. Reaching down to his crotch, Master palmed his hardening length. "So fucking perfect," he murmured. No sooner had his words left his mouth and he withdrew his hand than the ruthless Master of the Blood Pit suddenly reappeared.

With a surreal blankness now on his face, he walked out the door and called for a guard. When a Wraith arrived, Master instructed, "Take her to him. Lock her in his cell." He smiled that sadistic smile and added, "Don't let him out until he fucks her."

I heard Maya's almost inaudible gasp beside me. But I raised my head and prayed that my fear wasn't showing. Master pointed to the guard. "Follow him."

I walked forward. Just before I reached the guard, Master gripped my arm and slammed my back against the wall. Before I could catch my breath, he smashed his lips to mine, ravishing my mouth with his.

Master abruptly pulled back, then stormed toward Maya. I didn't understand what he was about to do, until he gripped her by the back of her neck and slammed her small body against the wall. I stood, motionless, as Master lifted his hand and sliced it across her face. He was taking everything out on her. She was too young to take such a cruel hand!

Desperate, my eyes drifted to Maya's, and my heart cracked when I saw in her eyes that she was no longer in the room. Mercifully, she had taken herself elsewhere.

By her reaction, I realized this wasn't something new. Master had done this to the young girl before. Beat her. Hurt her, as though she was nothing . . . not even a human at all.

I felt sick to my stomach.

"Move!" The guard beside me ordered, as I stared helplessly at Maya hurting on the floor.

The male who had attached the bracelet worked on something at the back of the room, offering Maya no help. A surge of anger burned within me.

"I said move!" the guard snapped. I forced myself to follow him out of the room, ignoring the young boys in the cages, and into the hallway. When we reached the forked section, this time we went down the right hallway and descended. Unlike the left hallway, where it grew lighter the farther we walked, this hallway grew darker and danker.

My fear grew with every step we took. Then we reached a narrow hallway. There was a wider hallway to the left. I started when, from that direction, I heard the loud sound of males shouting. I swallowed back my nerves when the guard walked straight ahead. The noise faded the farther we traveled, until we arrived at a small section housing only a few cells. It was much quieter here.

I tried to understand where we were. The guard walked past the cells. I tried to peer in, but unlike others I had seen, these had some semblance of privacy. I heard soft moans coming from one. Instinctively, I knew that a female was being pleasured.

The guard stopped and reached for the door before us. When the door opened, the guard looked at me and snapped, "Get in." I hesitated when I looked inside. I couldn't see anyone in there, the room was so dark.

When I didn't move, the guard gripped my arm and hauled me forward. He pushed me inside. I stumbled, landing on the hard ground of the cell. My heart beat hard as I lifted my head. When I did, pure terror seized me.

Sitting on a mattress before me was *him*. The Blood Pit Champion. The Arziani Pit Bull. Master's greatest warrior.

Warrior 901.

And he was glaring at me.

Unmoving. Hatred spewed from his hard gaze.

I drew in a short breath, but it was cut off when 901 rolled to his feet. He stepped forward, his huge body towering above me. I choked back a scream.

He was the most intimidating male I had ever encountered.

And I was trapped in his cell.

Completely alone. In the unwelcome company of a killer.

And there was absolutely nothing I could do.

6

901

I stared at the High Mona on the ground. She was shaking and looked up at me with her huge blue eyes. I swallowed as I met her gaze. I could see, could almost *smell* the fear pulsing off her perfect body.

Lifting my head, I got up and marched to the door. Spotting the guard through the bars, I snapped, "What is this? Why is she in here?"

The guard slowly turned and smiled. "Master has gifted you his female." The guard leaned in farther, his smile doing nothing more than pissing me the hell off. "A reward for all of your victories in the ring."

The guard moved back before I could pull him close and snap his neck. I growled, "Take her back. I don't want her."

The guard shook his head. "My orders are to leave her here with you. Regardless of what you said." He turned his back to me, adding, "Master thinks you could do with a good fuck." He shrugged. "Personally, I do, too. It might calm you down." Glancing over his shoulder, he said, "I've worked in these quarters for years and you've refused every chance at a *mona* you've been given." His gaze dropped to my crotch, and he said, "Your balls must be so damn blue."

Unable to stop the rage bursting free, I released a loud roar and slammed my hands against the iron bars. "GET HER THE FUCK OUT!"

The guard looked back at me, then walked away, leaving me alone with the *mona*. I stood at the bars, the metal still vibrating from my hit. I worked on breathing, sucking in long, deep breaths. But no matter how hard I tried to calm, I couldn't. I could feel the female's eyes on my back, watching me. Her perfumed scent was hitting my nose. My cell always smelled of the wet rot of earth in the walls. The *mona*'s scent was better.

Better, but unwelcome.

Making myself turn, I ignored where she sat and made my way to my bed. With my back still turned, I paused, then made myself sit on the mattress. The muscles in my shoulders and neck ached with tension, at how much having a female in my quarters disturbed me.

On a heavy sigh, I kept my eyes to the ground. Out of the corner of my eye, I could see the *mona* on the floor, trembling. My teeth gritted together in annoyance.

She was a weakling.

I wondered why the hell Master had given her to me. He was obsessed with her. All of us could see it, the way he watched her every move, walked her through our training pits daily. He kept her close and smiled at her like he wasn't a sadistic prick intent on ruining all our lives.

But more than that, and what I suspected she didn't know about, were the many males that had been punished or slain for even looking her way.

All except me.

Then the anger returned. Clenching my hand into a fist, I

threw my head back and slammed it into the wall behind me. I heard the *mona* whimper and scurry to the far corner. When I looked up, she'd tucked herself into a small ball, her head buried in her hands.

This time I studied her. And what I saw shot straight to my dick. Sitting like this, I could see how the *mona* was dressed. The red fabric was see-through. And I could see her naked body beneath—her perfect tits, every bare inch revealed for me.

It only pissed me off more.

Her dark hair was pulled to one side, falling over her shoulder. Then my eyes found the metal collar around her wrist. All of the blood fell from my face.

I'd seen that collar on the *Ubiytsa*. The collar discharged the Type A pellets intermittently, to keep them under Master's control. Though I suspected that her collar wasn't filled with Type A.

It would be Type B. Which meant she would need . . .

My hands shook with rage. Then, through that rage I felt my stomach fall. In all my years I had never been with a female. From a young age, I had seen what females did to the males. I saw the males becoming attached to their *monebi*. I saw them slowly be used against them. And worse still, I saw them killed or passed on to make the men submit to the guards. But Master's favorite was when he gifted the same *mona* to two males, then watched them tear each other apart in the pit, fighting for dominance.

But Master never rewarded the winner with the female. Instead he would use her as bait to do his bidding. Until his sick game grew tired and he disposed of them both.

Pawns. All of us were pawns in his empire. He was the true king.

Then I stilled, eyes closing when I realized he had seen me looking. No female had ever pulled my attention. But with Master's High Mona, from the second I saw her in the training pit, it had been different. She appeared different from the rest of his females. She walked differently. She was shy and timid.

She was beautiful.

So fucking beautiful that she rocked me back on my heels.

I thought back to the match against the Chinese fighter, and then I knew. I remembered the moment Master had caught my attention, and for one split second, I had lost control of myself and paid the female heed. I had looked at her as she sat on the floor at his feet in fear. I had been pissed.

I had fucked up.

He knew. He knew I had noticed her. He'd told me he'd find a weakness. And after all these years, he'd finally found one. I'd sleepwalked right into his trap.

As I glanced to the *mona,* still hunched in the corner, shaking in fear, I felt a part of my self-imposed coldness warm. I felt a fissure fracture through my dead heart. She was tiny compared to me. She was frightened.

And she was beautiful. It was obvious why she'd caught Master's eye.

When I caught myself, I pushed those feelings away and lay back on my bed. I stared at the dark ceiling, listening to the *mona*'s breathing catch.

I closed my eyes and made myself ignore her presence. If I ignored her, if I didn't touch her, Master would take her back and I'd be safe. I simply had to resist, and then this would all go away.

I wouldn't be weak.

Not even for a female as beautiful as her.

A hissing sound was the first thing I heard. The strange sound, followed by a sharp cry. I blinked into the dark room, confused by sleep. Then my dick twitched when I heard a breathless female whimper cut across the silent cell.

My body froze, and then I remembered the female in the corner. Another cry filled the room, and my heart started beating when I thought back to last night. To the guard throwing the High Mona into my cell. The *mona* that wore a collar around her wrist.

A long, needy moan pierced the air, and I gritted my teeth as my erect cock began to throb. Rolling to my side, I focused on the corner and saw the *mona*'s slumped form on the ground beginning to move. I watched, holding my breath, as her legs began to twitch. Her eyes were still shut, clearly still asleep. But when my eyes narrowed and I saw the wrist collar, I could see small movements from underneath, something pressing into her skin.

Drugs injecting into her veins.

I fisted the linen on my mattress as a louder, more desperate moan tore from her lips. This time the *mona*'s back arched and, even in this dim light, I could see her nipples erect as they pushed against the fabric.

My jaw ached from the strain, my dick pushing against my black pants. But I stayed still. I wouldn't move. I wouldn't submit to Master's plan.

I couldn't. I couldn't give him the final part of my will.

Movement from the hallway caught my attention, and a guard called out, "You better fuck her, 901. The only way to make her stop is to spill inside her."

I growled, low and threatening, but the guard moved away, leaving me alone with her again. When I looked back her way, her eyes were open. Her pupils were blown, and she looked right at me. Her wide eyes, leaden with lust and need, seared mine as she cried out, her hands moving to cup her full tits.

I couldn't stop the groan from leaving my throat at the sight of her writhing on the floor. But I kept strong. It would pass. Her need would pass. I'd resist.

But the minutes ticked by and her need grew stronger. The

mona writhed on the floor more and more. Her cries increased. They grew so pained and loud that I rose from the bed and slammed my fists against the metal bars. "Get her the fuck out!" I roared to the guards I knew were close, when I couldn't take it anymore.

But no one came. Then I heard the hissing sound again, and every muscle in my body tensed when the *mona* paused in breathing, then screamed so loud that I flinched at the pain in her cries.

Moving back, I charged the metal bars with my shoulder, hearing them groan from the force. This time a guard turned with his gun held high. "Get back," he ordered. I bared my teeth.

"Take her away!" I repeated, and wrapped my hands around the bars. I held them so tightly that my fingers ached and the veins in my muscles corded at the strain. "Remove her from here," I threatened.

The guard flicked his gun at me, then lowered it to lean forward and order, "Screw her. I can't stand her wailing anymore. Master gave her to you, so take her and shut the bitch up!"

The guard walked away, and I screamed, "Get back here!" but I heard the sound of a door closing and I knew he'd left us alone.

The *mona* screamed out again, and I closed my eyes, lowering my forehead to the bar. The cold metal cooled my burning skin, but my cock was still hard and testing my restraint.

When she cried out again, I held back a roar.

"You need to help her," a deep voice called from across the hallway. Opening my eyes, I peered over to 667's cell and saw him at his cell door. When I met his eyes, he said, "She needs your release. This will only get worse if you don't."

"I won't," I snarled, anger lacing each word. "I won't bow to Master's games."

"She won't stop," he repeated. I glared at him. 667 was broad with shoulder-length dark-blond hair. His blue eyes stayed fixed on mine and he said, "She's in pain." He shook his head when I didn't move. "You remember all the drugs we were given as children? How they made us ache and scream in pain?" He pointed to my cell. "That's what she's feeling now."

I lowered my gaze, and he continued, "My *mona* feels it every night, so I care for her. I don't let the pain get to her."

"I won't do it," I bit as she cried out. I risked a glance behind and saw her pressing her hand against her pussy. The sight sent the ache in my dick soaring. But it wasn't right. I didn't want her, she didn't want me. I wouldn't take her because of some damn drug that she was forced to take.

Turning back to stare out into the hallway, 667 said, "Is she breaking out in a sweat?"

I frowned at his question. I didn't want to care if she was, but no matter how much I tried to block out her cries, I couldn't. When I couldn't see from my place by the cell door, I turned and edged closer. As I moved, her dilated eyes fixed on mine and I caught her flushed face—it was dripping with sweat. She had a fever, her skin was red from the heat.

"Is she?" 667 asked.

I roughly replied, "Yes." I gripped the cell bars again and closed my eyes. I tried to breathe in the dry clogged air from the hallway, but the *mona's* enticing smell filled my lungs and nose.

I cursed inside.

"Listen to me," 667 demanded. I glared at his strict command. My lips curled, but he didn't care. "You need to take her," he said calmly. "If she has broken out in sweat, it means that the drugs are too strong for her body to cope with." He paused. Then making sure he got his point across, he added, "Some *monas* have died if their host males refused them."

My stomach sliced in two at that, but disguising my reaction, I said, "Then she can die."

667's face dropped. He hit his hand against the bars and hissed,

"If I could get out of here, I'd do it myself." His faced flushed with anger, and he added, "Then I'd kill you." He jabbed his finger through the bars of the cell and bit out, "That female is as much a prisoner as us." He spat on the hallway floor and said, "You may be the champion, but you are not a brother to any of us. I hope Master slaughters you slowly and painfully."

With that, he moved from his cell door, and I closed my eyes in frustration as the *mona's* cries became so fast that she barely took a breath in between. Unable to stand here anymore, I turned and began to pace the floor before her. My hands were balled into fists at my sides.

I allowed myself to look to the female writhing on the floor and the sweat dripping from her forehead. Her skin was pale and her hands were shaking. Then my heart almost stopped when she began convulsing, a pained scream almost deafening me.

I caught frustrated shouting from the hallway and knew that my refusal to take her wasn't infuriating only 667. The other males nearby also were beginning to react to her cries.

I stopped dead, warring with what to do, when the female suddenly went silent. My gaze shot to hers. She was staring at me blankly, panting for breath. Then she held out her shaking arm and whispered, "Help me . . . please . . ."

Her soft voice was weak and hoarse. I squeezed my eyes shut at the desperation in her voice. My resolve weakened when I saw her beautiful face staring at me with such hope.

In a second, I knew Master's plan had worked. As cold a bastard as I knew I was, I couldn't stand seeing her so pained and weak.

I wouldn't be the cause of her death.

Slowly, and in measured steps, I approached where she lay. I bit my tongue in frustration, when a hissing sound broke through the calm and more of the drug was injected into her veins.

A new kind of cry slipped from her full lips, one so agonized it caused me to immediately drop by her side. My huge body towered over her. I had no idea what to do next. That wasn't a problem for long, as the *mona* reached for my hand and brought it straight between her legs.

She moaned again, but this time there was a hint of relief in her cry as my fingers met her wetness. I swallowed at the feel of her warmth under my fingers.

Letting her guide my hand, she pushed my fingers back and forth along her lips, her hips bucking as I passed over a certain spot. My teeth gritted at the sight of her eyes fluttering closed at my touch.

My blood ran hot as my dick throbbed in my pants. The female moaned and, going on instinct, I plunged my fingers into her channel, feeling the tightness wrap around them.

152 screamed out and gripped my wrist, guiding the movement of my fingers in faster and faster, until I was breathless. With my free hand I reached into my pants and pulled out my cock. My fist ran up and down its hard length.

I growled low at the simultaneous feel of the female's wet heat and my hand on my cock. I tried to keep tight hold of my control, but when the female arched her back high and spread her legs wide, all of my treasured control snapped apart.

Pulling my fingers from within her, I released my cock and shifted above where she lay. I groaned at how perfect she looked beneath me. When she arched again, I reached for the fabric of her dress and, with my hands on the neckline, used my strength to rip it in two. When the *mona*'s bare skin came into view, waiting for my dick, I moved forward until my chest met her tits, skin to skin, heat to heat.

My breathing was ragged. Then I groaned low as her legs wrapped around my waist and tried to guide me to her center. Reaching down, I pushed my pants down my legs, then placed my hands on either side of her head. The *mona*'s eyes met mine, and for a moment I froze at how stunning she was this close.

When a cry left her mouth, I moved back and braced my dick at her entrance. My arms shook as I pressed my tip to her channel. I closed my eyes and paused. I had never taken a female before, never felt what it was like to spill my seed inside.

I had no idea how to take her.

When the *mona*'s fingernails scraped along the skin of my back, something inside of me broke and I slammed forward, engulfing my cock in her heat, roaring out as the new sensation took its hold. My lips parted and I panted in short, sharp breaths. My eyes rolled as 152 clamped around my thickness. The muscles in my neck strained at the feel . . . and then she started to move. The *mona*, searching for my release, rolled her hips, ripping a snarl from my throat.

"Shit," I bit out as my hips began to move in response.

The *mona* whimpered below me. Her hands slid up my back to grip my neck. My eyes snapped open as she pulled me close, her eyes trapping me in their stare. My heart jumped as she watched me taking her. Her cries lost their pain and turned into cries of pleasure. My cock jerked inside her channel, the *mona*'s soft skin flushing at the feel.

My thrusts increased in speed as tingles spread along my thighs and a pressure built at the bottom of my spine. With each roll of her hips, I took her harder and harder, her warm, sweet breath flowing over my face.

Her hands tightened around my neck. Her eyes glazed, and I felt her pussy contracting around my dick. I growled, unable to tear my eyes away from her. As her mouth dropped open and her head threw back, she screamed out in release. Seeing her so beautiful, so unrestrained, and with the tightness of her core, the pressure in my spine broke apart and I spilled inside her, a deafening roar ripping from my throat.

My hips slammed fast, then slow, as I gave her what she needed most. My hands balled into fists on either side of her head, then the *mona*'s eyes opened as I watched her in the following calm.

When her gaze met mine, her pupils reduced in size and her breathing softened to a steady pace. Suddenly, my hips stilled, and the air between us thickened. Because looking back at me was the *mona* without the drugs.

It was the slave freed.

I waited with bated breath for her fear to arrive. Instead, a tear formed at the corner of her eye and she simply whispered, "Thank you."

My heart slammed against my chest at the tenderness of her voice. I didn't know what to do next, but that was remedied when she lifted a shaking hand to my cheek and hushed out, "This isn't over." Her eyes lowered in embarrassment, and her cheeks flushed. "It takes more . . ." She trailed off. "It lasts awhile."

My throat clogged at the sadness in her voice. But even more, something inside me cracked at the feel of her small hand against my cheek. It was strange, because being with her was like nothing I could have ever imagined, but her warm palm on my face was something else entirely.

For the briefest of moments, it pumped life back into my dead heart.

For a split second, it made me feel alive.

And in that short second, I was reborn.

I swallowed, still uneasy, unsure what to do next, when the *mona*'s legs twitched and her hands moved to grip my shoulders. I wondered what was happening. When I studied her face and watched her pupils blow, I knew the drug had taken her again.

My softening dick began to harden as her hips started to roll. I ducked my head at the too-good sensation and pushed forward, the *mona*'s pleasured cry making my pulse beat furiously.

I thought about the fact that I had refused to ever take a female, about how I had resisted it with everything that I was. As I sank into her hot depths, I called myself a fool.

Hours passed and the *mona*'s drugs kept strong. I wasn't immune; the cocktail I was injected with every morning kept me strong. Kept my cock reacting to her needy moans, made me able to release inside her every time she needed me . . .

Until finally her pupils reduced in size and stayed that way. Sweat dripped off our slick bodies in the aftermath. The *mona* fell asleep through exhaustion, saving me from the awkwardness of what came next.

My arms shook on either side of her head as I stared down at her pale cheeks. Every time I had taken her, I could see more blood draining from her flushed skin. I could feel her limbs becoming weaker with exhaustion, yet the drug overrode her need to stop. It led her on and on, it pushed me more and more, until no energy ran in our blood. Until we had no more left to give. Until she passed out.

She was young. Lying here, her once contorted face now relaxed in sleep, I could truly study her. Checking there was no guard behind me watching my moment of interest, I slowly lifted my hand and brought my fingers to her face. I frowned at the size of my hand compared to her face. My hand was scarred and rough from too many fights. Against her perfect skin and pretty features, it didn't look right. It didn't belong anywhere near her face.

But I lowered my fingertips anyway, brushing them across the cooling skin of her forehead. The *mona* stilled for a second, as did my hand. I froze, but then a breathy sigh left her mouth and she fell back to sleep. I waited, hovering above her for a full minute, before moving my fingers around her eyes, my lips twitching at her long black lashes kissing her cheeks. I extended a finger and brought it down her small nose, then down to her full lips.

For some reason, I had to stare at those lips. As a boy, Master had made us watch the pit fights that would become our future—but rather than watch the fights, I would focus on the people in the crowd. I would study each of them, both males and females. I would wonder where they had come from. I would wonder why they were there.

My eyebrows lowered as I remembered seeing a male seated beside Master lean down and place his lips against the female beside him. My tongue ran around my lips as I wondered what it would be like to press my lips to this *mona*'s.

Without thinking, I felt my head lowering toward hers, my lips hovering a fraction from hers. The *mona*'s warm breath spread across my face. I abruptly drew my head back, pulse thundering in my neck.

A wave of molten anger ripped through my veins. I wrenched out of the *mona*'s channel and staggered to my feet. My legs shook from too much exertion. My hands lifted to grip my hair, and I pulled, a growl spilling from between my taut lips.

What was I doing? I silently asked myself. *Why was I trying to touch her lips?*

Needing to calm down, I began to pace back and forth on the stone floor. My teeth ground in frustration, my neck muscles tightened to the point of pain, my hands clenched into tight fists.

Master was trying to mess with my mind. I knew it. That sick motherfucker knew it. He knew what putting her in this cell would do to me. He knew what having her in need, arching and moaning on the ground, would do. He knew that the aggression drugs I was given would ensure my dick responded.

I serviced her.

I calmed her fire with my release.

But I wanted none of the rest. I couldn't let myself care what she looked like when she came. I couldn't let myself care how sad she sounded when her pupils shrank back to normal size and she thanked me for temporarily setting her free from the pain.

And I couldn't let myself care about her lips. I couldn't let myself care about her at all. She had to be just a *mona, Master's* mona. *I must not let her destroy me.*

Without a second glance, I lay down on my mattress and turned my back to her sleeping body. I closed my eyes, pushing all thoughts from my mind. My rage simmered as I focused on not smelling the *mona's* scent on my skin. But it didn't last for long; exhausted, sleep took me in its hold and quickly pulled me under.

When my eyes opened, a guard was at my door. I immediately sat up, my eyes narrowing at the glare of victory in his gaze. "Up," he commanded when he saw me watching him.

I got to my feet, ignoring the aches in my arms and legs. When the guard opened the door, I resisted the urge to turn and look at the *mona* on the ground.

I had failed. Master had won this round. But I was a warrior through and through. He wouldn't win the ultimate battle. I could take her without feeling. I would *make* myself feel nothing.

I had succeeded for years. This challenge would be no different.

I walked down the hallway to the medical room, joining the line of waiting males. Someone moved behind me, and when I heard, "You did the right thing," I turned around.

667 met my eyes. 140 stood directly behind him, his eyes focused past me, staring at nothing.

"You saved her," 667 added. My lips rolled over my teeth in annoyance of his praise.

"I fucked her to shut her the hell up," I snapped back, and saw his censure toward my response flash across his livid expression.

"Good," 140 remarked, his voice low and raw. "Keep it that way. Fuck and forget. You'll be better off."

The entire time he spoke, 140 stared straight forward, never facing me. Maybe I'd been mistaken. Maybe Master killing his *mona* wouldn't kill him, maybe it made him more of a threat.

The line moved quickly until I was at the front. An old female *chiri* jabbed the injection into my arm. Then I made my way to the training pits. My trainer stood waiting for me, my Kindjals ready for my hands. I picked them up, feeling complete now that the metal was in my palms.

My energy spiked, having just received my drugs. My trainer struggled to take my relentless slices and strikes with his shield. But I didn't stop, hammering blow after blow, until a whistle was blown—the sign that Master wanted to speak.

As conditioned, we all walked to the center pit. A podium towered above us. I had to fight back a snarl when Master climbed up to speak.

He was dressed all in black, hair slicked back, and his hard eyes tracked over his prime males. I watched as he inhaled deeply, before he clapped his hands together and said, "I have an announcement to make. In four weeks' time, all our lives will change." The males around me began rocking on their feet, too pumped up with the drug to stand still and listen. We were fighters. That's all we knew.

"In four weeks' time," he repeated, "the Blood Pit will be hosting its very first death-match championship." Males moved to stand either side of me. In my peripheral vision, I noticed they were 667 and 140.

The champions of the pit were standing in line.

The movement caught Master's attention, and he looked at his current champions standing side by side. A slow grin spread on his lips and he said, "We have Blood Pit Champions"—he pointed our way, then dropped his arm—"but I own many gulags around the world, all boasting their own champions." He paused, then continued. "In four weeks' time, those champions will be brought here to my arena. Three champions from each, along with some of my associates' personal fighters." His eyes swept over the many males listening to his every word. "This tournament will weed out the weak and unskilled warriors. This tournament will test you all in ways you have never been tested before." His eyes fell upon me, and he emphasized, "Those who will be entered—and they will be only a select few of my best fighters—will represent this pit." He took a deep breath and announced, "And from all the champions of the death-match world, only one will remain. The ultimate champion. And that champion . . ." he paused for effect, "will win his *freedom*."

Murmurs broke out among the males standing around me, their eyes lit with the excitement and the prospect of freedom. But I stayed stoic, my eyes never leaving Master. I watched him absorb the reaction from the males. But he wouldn't get one from me. I knew his games. I couldn't let myself believe that this was true.

Master played with our minds, gave us false promises time and time again. It was what held his pleasure.

This couldn't be real.

As I heard the excitement from the other males, I knew I was the only one doubting this news.

Master raised his arms, and the guards moved around us with electric prods to calm us down. The males quieted and Master stepped forward. "In the coming four weeks, we will be holding rounds for who shall compete." He then focused on us three champions. "And my champions, who have already secured a place in the tournament, will engage in demonstration matches to ensure we have my associates firmly on board."

Master stayed silent, drinking in the euphoria from the males below him, then he swiftly turned and left the podium. A whistle sounded, and we all walked back to our pits to resume training. As I swung away, honing my skills, I could hear that the grunts of exertion were stronger from the other fighters. I could hear the louder clanging of metal on shields. I could hear the trainers ordering more effort. I could feel the sense of hunger from the males.

Hunger for freedom.

My trainer blocked and fought back against my blows, but he suddenly stopped when a figure appeared before my pit. I knew who it was before looking up. Only one male drew that much respect. Or obedience. In this Blood Pit, those lines were blurred.

"901," Master called. My shoulders tensed. Calming my inner flames, I turned and met his stare. Master jumped down into the pit and strode to where I stood. He stopped only when he was as close as he could get without touching. He looked up into my eyes and smiled. His head dropped to the side. "Tell me, 901. How was my High Mona last night?"

I glared but stayed silent. Master shrugged. "My guard tells me that you tried to resist." He paused, then leaned in to say, "But no man could resist her, could he?" He glanced away like he was picturing something in his mind. When he faced me again, he said, "Tell me, did you taste her, 901?"

When I didn't respond, he pushed, "Did she scream out when you made her come . . . did she rake your skin?" Master walked around to my back. I knew he would see her nail marks. I expected him to gloat, but when he walked back to stand before me, his face was no longer rapt with victory. Instead, I could see the fury in his tight expression. Could see the rage, the psychotic possession he had for 152 in his unhinged glare.

Turning his back, he went to walk away, and I let my anger free and bit, "I took her all night long. Until she passed out." He stilled, and I added, "Last night I made her mine."

I watched as Master's shoulders tensed, then he whipped round.

Taking my hand, he guided my Kindjal's tip to my throat. I didn't even flinch as his lips drew back to bare his teeth and his face flushed a deep red color.

He wouldn't do it.

Out of the corner of my eye I saw the guards lining up around my pit, their guns ready to take me out if I lashed out in reaction and tried to kill their king. Lowering my head, I pressed the tip harder to my throat, feeling my blood trickle down my neck. Master's jaw pulsed. I could see him fighting back his desperate need to kill me.

"Do it," I hissed. And only for him to hear: "Do. It."

Then, in a flash, Master drew back, a neutral expression commandeering his face. He righted his suit, then walked away as if he hadn't just nearly taken out his prized fighter. The prized fighter who had just taken his most prized possession.

As Master walked out of view and away from my training pit, I let the blood trickle down my chest and turned to charge at my trainer.

I wasn't going to win this championship for my freedom. I was sure that would never come.

No, I was going to win it to fuck with Master's mind. Just the way he loved to fuck with mine.

And I would. Because I never lost.

I was the motherfucking champion.

Not even the taste of 152 could take away my fire.

7

152

I stayed huddled in the corner, my body shivering at the cold drifting in through the large cell doors. I looked down at my torn dress and closed my eyes as I pictured 901 ripping it from my body with his bare hands.

My cheeks flushed as I replayed the events of last night in my head. I flinched when I remembered the pain. Embarrassment rushed through me when I remembered hearing 901 screaming for me to be taken away as he charged the bars of his—our—cell door.

Then I remembered him dropping to the floor beside me. I remembered his face melting from anger to something much more kind as he stared into my eyes. I remembered the soft touch of his hand as he pushed a fallen strand of hair from my face. In fact, thinking back to last night, this simple touch, this gentle gesture from a man so raw and hard, shined most brightly in my mind.

I lowered my head to my clasped hands as another chill slapped against my bare body. Looking to the mattress on the floor across the room, I checked that the door was clear of the guards and scurried over to take the thick linen covering the base. I wrapped it around my body and quickly sat back down.

When I had awoken this morning, the cell was empty. 901 had left, probably to train. And I was glad of that fact. I racked my brain to remember if, with the exception of Master, I had ever had to face a male the morning after he had had to take me. I couldn't remember, but I had the feeling that I hadn't. 901 intimidated me more than anyone. I knew I would have been terrified to face him this morning. My stomach rolled when I thought back to how much he hadn't wanted to pleasure me. But then I pictured him after he had reached his release the first time. There had been a look of wonder and awe in his blue eyes as he had stared into mine. His sharply featured face had relaxed to betray softness. That expression had created a home in my heart when my palm touched his rough cheek.

I blinked to break the trance I had fallen into, tucking my head into the bundled linen at my chest to stave off the cold. When I did, I was engulfed by the strong musk scent of 901. My thighs clenched together as the aroma infused my lungs. I closed my eyes, once again seeing him rocking above me, his bulging arms flexing and tensing beside my head.

The sudden sound of the cell door made me jump. When I looked up, a guard was in the doorway. He flicked his chin and ordered, "Move."

I immediately got to my feet. As he turned to lead me out of this cell, a momentary sense of regret sprouted within me. For a second, I didn't want to leave. 901 might not want me here, but he was a better alternative than Master. Trepidation ran over my skin as I walked down the familiar hallway toward my quarters. I didn't want to return to Master. I didn't want him to hurt me.

I didn't want him to cherish me, either. His crazed possession was almost as terrifying as his harsh hand.

When we reached my quarters, the guard opened the door and I walked through. My eyes immediately searched the room for Master, to try to foresee what would happen to me today. But I relaxed when from the side room came Maya.

The guard shut the door, and when he did, I smiled. Until I remembered yesterday. Until I remembered that Master had hurt her in the room where I had been given my bracelet.

A sudden sadness propelled my legs to move, and surprising Maya, I wrapped her in my arms. Maya gasped as I held her.

When I drew back, I searched her dark eyes. She appeared uncomfortable and lost.

"Are you okay?" I asked, and she blinked blankly.

"Yes, miss. Why?" she questioned in a timid voice.

Chasing away the lump in my throat, I replied, "Because of yesterday. Because of the way Master hurt you."

"Hurt me, miss?"

I held up my bracelet and said, "In the room where I received this. He hit you." I shook my head and knew I was showing my confusion now. I lifted my hand to my head. "It felt wrong to me that he did that."

Maya shook her head and reached for my hand. "No, miss. It isn't wrong. Master does whatever he wants, whenever he wants. He beats us frequently." Maya swallowed, then added, "I am a *chiri*, miss. I have no say in anything that happens in my life."

I nodded, understanding that I was mistaken, but something in my heart felt off. Like Maya's statement was false. Like we *shouldn't* be treated this way.

A pain ached in my brain when I tried to understand why I had this thought in my mind. I couldn't remember.

"Come, miss," Maya said, and led me from the center of the room to the table at the far side. I sat down and she poured me a glass of water. She next placed a plate of food in front of me. Maya went to remove the linen from around my body. I was in the middle of bringing a lump of bread to my mouth, when I dropped it to pull the linen back.

My cheeks flushed under Maya's raised brows. "I . . . I just want to stay like this a moment longer," I said quickly.

Maya nodded dutifully and moved to walk away. I reached for her wrist, and she stopped dead. Not wanting to be alone again, I asked, "Please, stay." I pointed to the food. "Eat with me."

Maya shook her head. "I can't, miss. It's forbidden."

A flick of anger burned in my chest, and I pulled out the chair beside me. "Sit down, Maya. Please."

She glanced over her shoulder to the door, but it was clear. There was no sign of Master or the guards. Maya slowly sat down, then waited for me to speak.

So I told her about last night. About 901.

"Why would he do it?" Maya questioned, confused, when I had finished speaking. "Why would Master give you to his best fighter?" She checked the door again and, when it was clear, said, "Master acts so differently toward you, miss." Maya's gaze dropped to stare at the floor like she was thinking things through, then her head snapped up. "Maybe it was why he hurt you so badly the night before last. Because he knew he was giving you away." She ran her hand over the linen I was still wrapped in and continued. "It was why he ordered you dressed in the transparent fabric. It was so you could seduce the champion."

"You're right," I rasped, her explanation making sense of the Master's recent actions.

"But why?"

"The guard told him I was a gift. For him being so efficient in the pit."

Maya leaned forward. "But there are many *monebi* in the left section of this place. Why would he give you to him? You are the High Mona."

I rubbed my hand over my forehead. "I don't know."

Maya lost her questioning gaze, then placed her hand on my bare arm. When I felt her watching me, I looked her way. "Was it okay, miss? Did . . . did he hurt you?"

Feeling my cheeks blushing, I shook my head. "No. No," I repeated, "he didn't hurt me."

Maya nodded, then said, "Some of the *monebi* I have cared for, they have been hurt by the fighters." She leaned even closer and whispered, "The males are given a drug that sometimes makes them uncontrollable and rough. They lose their minds and only know how to fight and hurt people—including the *monebi* who are sent in to help calm them down."

I thought back to 901. I knew he was nothing like that. In fact, he did not seem to be under a drug's influence at all. "I don't think this fighter was on anything like that."

Maya nodded. "Some are on lesser doses if they are compliant. They are given something to make them aggressive and short-tempered, but if they have been here for years, they are accustomed to how we live."

I soaked in every word, then asked, "How do you know so much, Maya? You are so young?"

Maya flinched, her face contorting at something I had said. "What?" I questioned, and reached for her hand. Her head bowed, avoiding my gaze. "Maya?" I pushed again. She flinched. When she lifted her head, I saw tears fill her eyes. "What is it?"

"You called me by my name," she hushed out in response.

My stomach plummeted. Squeezing her hand, I said, "Maya is your name."

Maya shook her head. "No, I'm *chiri*, I'm a 000. I lost my name when I lost my face. It melted away the same time the acid melted my flesh."

This time I leaned forward and ducked my eyes until I held her attention. "In this room, you are Maya." I inhaled slowly through my nose, and the words, "You are someone. You're more than a number," spilled from my lips. I suddenly sat up straight when I abruptly pictured a dark cell in my mind, a rough hand brushing over my face to move away sweat-ridden strands of hair. I couldn't see him, but I heard his voice tell me those exact words. *You are someone. You're more than a number . . .*

"Miss?" Maya questioned worriedly.

I forced a smile and said, "To me, you are Maya."

A teardrop trickled down her cheek and she whispered, "Thank you."

I waited until she had found some composure, and repeated my question. "Maya, how do you know so much about what happens in this place?" I rubbed my fingers over my forehead and said, "From what I know, I have spent most of my life here, yet I remember almost nothing. I can barely recall being trained to be a *mona*." I turned to face her and said, "Please, explain everything to me. How does this place function?"

Maya said nothing for several moments. I thought she could not tell me, but eventually she spoke. "Miss, when you are a *chiri,* you are nothing to Master and the Wraiths." She shrugged. "That is both a blessing and a curse. It takes awhile to be ignored like you don't even exist. But in this place, I have discovered that it may be the best thing of all. I can walk freely, without suspicion. I also see parts of this Blood Pit that no one else gets to, and hear conversations that others would never hear." A flicker of a smile pulled on her lips, and she said, "I know a lot about this place because I am a no one."

"Maya," I whispered in sympathy.

"The *monebi* are housed in a section of the pit." Her eyes dropped, then she confessed nervously, "I have asked some of the older *chiri* about you. They remember you, miss. They were here when you were trained. Some even assisted you when you were used as a guard's *mona*."

I blanched at that news. "I wasn't given to the fighters?"

Maya shook her head. "No, miss." She lowered her voice and said, "Master Arziani had a sister. He sent her away because she was a hindrance to him here in the pit. But the Mistress was part of the drug program. She and her lover helped develop the drugs everyone in this place is given." Maya swallowed and continued, "She was the one that brought you in as a child. You were part of her personal section. You were used solely for her guards." Maya shrugged. "I don't know much else, miss. But I am trying to find out for you. I promise."

"Thank you," I said, trying to remember anything about that time. Flashes of that dark room, me and someone else hiding under a bed came to mind. I remembered high walls and being led down some steps. And I remembered . . .

"I waved," I whispered, and tried to push my mind to remember more.

"Miss?"

Looking up, the hazy vision fading, I repeated, "I was young, I was taken from something I loved with my entire heart . . . and I waved. I remember waving."

A crack felt like it broke across my heart. I felt overcome with emotion. I placed my hand over my chest as if to stop the pain throbbing inside.

"Someone you loved?" she questioned. Feeling the ache build in pressure in my head, I said, "I don't know."

Maya handed me the glass of water and I drained the liquid, feeling better when I did. I sat back in my chair, completely exhausted.

Maya clearly saw this and took hold of my hand. She stood up. "Come, miss. You need to rest."

I let her lead me to the bed, where I climbed in. As soon as my head hit the soft pillow, I drifted off to sleep. The last thing I saw in my mind was a female towering over a boy as I looked back and waved. Beating him, causing him pain as the boy tried to reach me.

A female I knew I recognized.

A female that looked not too dissimilar to Master.

I glanced in the mirror and stared at the dress I was placed in tonight. It was dark green and made of the same transparent fabric as last night. Maya placed large earrings in my ears and curled my hair until it was pulled to one side and hung over one shoulder.

Master had left me alone all day. When I woke, it was to hear Maya running me a bath. And now as I stood in front of the mirror, I knew I was returning to 901. Or another fighter. According to Maya, Master would never receive me dressed in such a way.

This was purely for seduction.

As Maya ensured my dress was secured at my shoulders, I looked to the large wooden dresser in the corner of the side room. I had pushed the linen from 901's cell behind it. I didn't know why, but I wanted to keep it. Unwashed. Unchanged. Today I had slept the best I had since I woke here in the Blood Pit, fully conscious and aware of my surroundings. It was his scent that had kept me safe. I couldn't explain why, but it was certainly the case.

A guard, just as last night, pounded on the door. "Move!" he ordered, and I followed Maya out the door. She stepped to the side as I followed the guard. When I glanced back, Maya was walking in the opposite direction. I wondered where she stayed when she wasn't assisting me. I made a mental note to ask.

The same guard from last night led the way, down the same hallway. My heart raced when I saw we were heading for the fighters' quarters. To 901? I still wasn't sure. My jeweled sandals padded lightly on the stone floor beneath my feet, and we entered the section of the connected hallways where the fighters resided.

Loud, raucous noises came from my left. The guard suddenly paused. His attention was drawn to the cacophony. My face blanched when I thought we would be taking this route tonight. But the noise quietened when several gunshots sounded. I jumped as the sound of bullets echoed through to where we stood.

The guard, clearly sensing it was safe, pushed forward. Relief reentered my body with every step we took toward the champions' quarters. In just a few minutes we had reached the secluded cluster of cells. Of course the guard stopped before a familiar cell—the largest.

901's cell.

The guard opened the door. Needing no instruction, I hurried through, the heavy barred door slamming shut behind me. I could feel the guard hovering close. Lifting my head, I scanned the cell. At first I couldn't see him, but then, in the far-off corner, was 901. He was exercising on the floor. His arms were lifting his body up and down, his bare torso and back muscles bunching with the effort.

I wasn't sure if he had heard me enter. But then he stopped and jumped to his feet. And he glared right at me.

I staggered back when a flash of anger crossed his face. His teeth bared. Taken aback at his massive height, I stepped out of the way when he rushed past me to the door. He met the eyes of the guard and snarled, "Again?"

The guard stared at him blankly. "Master's gift. The way you fucked her last night, I'm surprised you've forgotten her pussy this quickly."

"Why has she returned?" he demanded. "I did what Master wanted. I *obeyed*."

The guard responded, "Then I guess he wants you to do it again," and with that he walked away, leaving us alone together in the cell. I stepped back until my back rested closely against the wall.

My stomach rolled at the tone of his voice. *I did what Master wanted. I obeyed* . . .

I squeezed my eyes shut at the hurt those harsh words brought. Then I felt him move past me. I opened my eyes and saw 901 walk back to the darkened section of the cell and commence his exercises. Though this time they were done with much more aggression.

I worked my way along the wall of the cell, then sank down into the corner I had slept in last night. A pit had caved in my stomach at his angry rejection.

901 was a cold, tough-minded warrior. I knew this. I could see this clearly, yet I was hurt also, because this wasn't my choice, either. I had been ordered here. Ordered to serve *him* by Master. Like him, *I* had no choice but to obey.

I clasped my hands together on my raised knees as they began trembling with fear. My gaze fell to the bracelet around my wrist. I fought back tears when I thought of how, sometime tonight, it would inject me with a drug and 901 would have to take me.

I risked a glance to him panting heavily across the room. He was now on his back. His knees were raised as he curled himself into his torso, his abdominal muscles flexing and bulging at the action. When I thought of the drugs that would soon flood my veins, I wished that he would just let me be. A hollow feeling caved in my chest, and this time I prayed that he'd leave me writhing on the floor. Last night I had heard the warrior across the hall tell 901 that if he left me, I could die.

I thought back to the past few weeks trapped under Master's ever-changing moods, his false affection and now being forced to serve 901 as some kind of punishment to his disobedience. More and more, I felt myself wanting to be left alone. Jailed with a male that I repulsed, I scanned the dank, dark cell. In doing so, I felt a peaceful sensation take root in my heart at the thought of never waking up again once the drugs had taken their evil hold.

A sound at the cell door made me look up. A guard was there, opening the door for an old *chiri* female who held a tray of food with trembling hands. My eyes widened at the mountain of different foods and the large pitcher of water.

The *chiri* entered silently and left the food on the floor. She turned without ever meeting my eyes. With a deep exhale, 901 jumped to his feet, cracking his thick neck from side to side as he kept his eyes straight forward.

He walked to the food and dropped to sit in the floor. Without pause, he dived into the pile of food. I watched as he raced through his meal. He had so much food that my mind boggled. I had only ever been fed the tiniest of meals. My stomach growled as I watched him wolf his food down.

901 paused when this sound filled the large room. I blushed in embarrassment when he flicked his harsh eyes my way, a strand of his blond hair falling over his forehead with the quick movement. I didn't know why, but that fallen piece of light hair made him look almost . . . approachable?

For a split second, he did not look like the hardened warrior I knew him to be.

901's cheek twitched in annoyance as my stomach growled again. Dropping his food, he cursed, *"Whore."*

Without thinking, I snapped my head up and responded, "Yes, I am a whore. One who wishes she wasn't handed off to you."

As the words left my mouth, my eyes widened. Lifting my fingers to my lips, I paled. Out of the corner of my eye I caught 901's head tip to the side. When I looked up, his angered expression had disappeared, replaced by one of shock.

I replayed his words in my head, then my response. I racked

my brain, searching for the answer. Because it wasn't the native language of Master or the guards. It wasn't the native language Maya spoke to me in. It was another. A language I knew, one that felt as natural as breathing but one that I had no idea of how or why I could.

I swallowed, shaking my head in confusion at what I had spoken, when 901 said gruffly, "You speak Russian?"

"I am Russian," I replied automatically. I shifted on the spot, my hand covering my mouth in shock. I dropped it, and whispered, "I am Russian?" My eyebrows pulled down in confusion. I looked up to find 901 watching me—very carefully. Only this time there was something else flickering in his unyielding gaze.

Acceptance.

"Russian," I hushed out. I inched forward and asked, "What is Russian?"

901 angled his body to face me. Lifting his hand, he tapped it over his chest, right over his heart. "This is Russian. *I* am Russian."

He stilled, then used his hand to point between us. "You and I, right now, are speaking Russian."

It took me a moment to realize that I was still speaking to him in this not-so-strange language. Then, as if plunged back into a dream, I pictured the scarred male from my visions—speaking to me in Russian. *You are more than a number . . .* He had spoken to me in Russian. *I will free you from this life, I promise. Just hold on . . .*

The male had held out his little finger, and I had linked mine within his. *I promise,* I had replied. Then everything went dark.

I blinked away the dream. Addressing 901, I said, "A male I dream of spoke to me in this language. He told me he would come for me. He told me he would free me." A surge of emotion welled within me. I held up my little finger and I choked out, "He held my finger and made me promise."

"Who was he?" 901 rasped.

"I don't know." I tapped my head. "I see him in my dreams, but I don't know who he is."

901 was silent for several minutes as he stared at the wall beside me, lost in his thoughts. I sat back, tucking myself in the corner of the cell, trying my hardest to remember something, anything. But nothing came.

"It's a country," 901 said, breaking through my silence.

I looked up at him. His eyes remained straight forward. "What?"

901 blinked, then faced me. "Russia. It's a country. We are in Georgia. He pounded his fist over his heart again. "Russia is my home. I am Russian." He spoke the words almost like he was trying to convince himself about what he was saying . . .

As if he was also trying to make himself remember.

My stomach flipped, a mixture of sympathy and excitement. 901 then held out his finger. Pointing to me, he said, "You are Russian, too. The way you speak the words . . . it is not learned. It comes from your heart."

Leaning forward, I asked, "What is it like?" I glanced around the cell. Thinking of the Blood Pit, I wondered out loud, "Is it like the Blood Pit?"

901 frowned and shook his head. He regarded me strangely. "No, it's a country. The Blood Pit, here, is a place. A place Master created." He gritted his teeth and hissed, "This is hell."

I flinched at the harsh tone of his voice. I lowered my eyes and admitted, "I don't know what you mean. I don't know about anything outside of these walls." I tapped my head. Catching 901's attention, I added, "In my head, I see some things not of this pit." I licked my bottom lip and continued. "I hid under a bed, the room was cold . . . but they found us." Tears filled my eyes. I could feel the sadness and fear I felt at that moment like it had just happened yesterday.

"Who found you?"

My stomach dropped and my face paled. "The Wraiths. They came and took us." Letting a teardrop fall, I added, "And I waved. I waved to a boy who tried to get me to stay with him." Taking a much-needed deep breath, I asked, "Was that Russia? The place where the Wraiths came? Was that in Russia?"

"Yes," 901 replied. I watched the thick muscles in his neck and shoulders tense, and he confessed, "I was taken by the Wraiths, too. From Russia."

My heart pounded so hard I heard its pulse in my ears. "You were like me," I confirmed, and shuffled closer still. "And I was like you."

901 stared at me. He didn't respond. He didn't utter a single word. He simply stared until he reached for a chunk of bread on his plate and handed it to me. I took it and sat back against the wall.

We ate in silence. I watched him as we did. 901 didn't look my way. When the growling in my stomach stopped, I leaned back against the wall and asked, "You don't want me with you, in here, do you?"

901 froze. I waited for several seconds before he shook his head and answered, "No."

I felt my heart deflate at his honest reply.

"Females make the warriors in this pit weak. I don't want to be weak, and I don't want to fuck you. I don't *want* anyone. I don't *need* anyone."

I wasn't a pleasant gift to him, like Maya had told me the *monebi* were to other warriors. I was nothing but a nuisance.

I didn't know why, but a slice of pain cut through me at this stark rejection. Sighing deeply, I shuffled back to my corner and meekly said, "I understand."

901 remained unmoving until the *chiri* came to take away his food. I closed my eyes, praying for sleep to hurry and take me . . .

when I heard the soft hiss of the bracelet, and then I felt the searing pain of the drugs injecting me.

I stifled a cry as the drugs shot through my blood like a flow of flames. It took only a minute for my thighs to clench together and my core to pulse in need.

"No!" I heard 901 bite out.

Opening my eyes, still able to speak through the drugs, I said, "Don't." 901 had jumped to his feet. At my words, he stilled. As a wave of blistering heat poured through me, crashing at the apex of my thighs, I met his furious gaze and commanded, "Don't." I gritted my teeth when my stomach cramped. "Just leave me."

901's head whipped back in shock. "You'll die." I saw his hands ball into fists at his sides. A moan escaped my mouth as I slid down the wall, placing my hand between my legs. 901's chest moved up and down, the sign of his ragged breathing. I could see his length hardening under the thin fabric of his black pants. My need was causing him to react.

He cursed, then took a reluctant step forward. "No! Stop!" I shouted. He did.

"You'll die!" he snarled, sounding angry this time.

Even as the pain, the unbearable need, built within me, I managed to demand, "Then let me die."

I saw the impact my words had on the warrior. He staggered back, my response seeming like a physical blow.

Recovering quickly, he moved to my side, his expression determined and stern. "I won't let you die."

A bead of sweat dropped off my head as he glared at me. My heart sank when I realized he meant every word. But I wanted to. I wanted to let go. Then, as 901 hovered close by, I also heard the scarred male from my dreams telling me to hold on. I felt my little finger twitch, as if I could still feel his finger wrapped in mine.

I squeezed my eyes shut as a bolt of pain forced my back to arch. Panting, breathless, I opened my eyes and pointed to the cell door. 901 followed my finger and asked, "What?"

"Guard . . ." I rasped. "Get the guard to take me."

This time, 901's gaze wasn't hard or stern, it was positively savage. "You want a guard over me?"

Unable to keep fighting, my body sagged on the floor and I said, "I don't want you to take me . . . because . . ." I hissed as my channel contracted, then forced myself to add, "you don't want me. You don't want this . . . I couldn't stand to be the one who took away your choice."

I stretched my body, trying to fight off the cramp seizing my limbs. My vision became blurry as the drugs built and built, making it almost impossible to endure. 901's expression became engulfed with pain. As quickly as it came, it disappeared. As I pressed my fingers to my core, 901 kneeled beside me, his blue eyes beaming down, directly at mine.

I watched as his breathing increased. I watched as his hands hooked onto the waistband of his pants and pulled the fabric down. I shifted as his hard length came into view and he stroked it with his hand. My legs opened as he began crawling over me. His huge chest covered mine, his arms bracing on either side of my head as he lay at my entrance.

I shook my head, feeling the cold floor beneath me. But 901 leaned down, and in a familiar tender move, brushed back the sweaty strand of hair from my forehead. I paused, the pain momentarily forgotten as he watched me. A small blush covered his stubbled cheeks as he studied my face. In this moment, an unfamiliar feeling sprouted in my heart. This feeling caused me to raise my hand and place it on his cheek. 901 gasped at my touch, his lips parting at the feel.

And we stayed that way, paused in time, locked in the moment, just his gaze trapped in mine.

As another wave hit me, 901 began pushing inside me, quickly extinguishing the brunt of the pain. I gripped his heavy arms as a loud needy cry spilled from my lips. Sliding his hand from my head to my chin, 901 made me look into his eyes as he said, "I do want you, *krasivaya*. I won't let you die. I'll take you, but I just can't let you have me . . . it'll make me weak."

Beautiful, my mind translated. 901 had called me beautiful.

I moaned as he slammed into me, his thrusts soothing my pain. As I lost my mind to the drugs, *krasivaya, krasivaya, krasivaya* . . . circled my head.

Beautiful, he had said. *Krasivaya.*

901 thought me beautiful.

And he had told me so in Russian.

In the language of our hearts.

The language of our home.

I smiled as his chest brushed against my breasts. I smiled as I looped my arms around his strong neck. Because I also thought this deadly warrior was beautiful.

He was simply . . . more.

8

LUKA

"Again!" Valentin demanded as I circled him in the ring. I stretched my fingers, then formed them back into fists. I watched as Valentin jumped to his feet, a trickle of blood running down his chin from his lip.

I charged, slamming my fist into his face. Valentin's head whipped back, but recovering quickly, he shook off the blow and delivered a hook shot to my ribs. My breath was taken away, but before he could gain advantage, I swept his ankle and dropped him to the ground.

I saw Zaal pacing the ring, desperate for his chance to spar. But when Valentin flipped me onto my back, I quickly focused on the task at hand. Valentin's hands wrapped around my neck, his scarred face hovering close as his eyes shone brightly with bloodlust.

Lifting my hands to wrap around his neck, I squeezed hard, each of us robbing the other of breath. I could feel my face reddening under Valentin's grip, but he was faring no better than I was. Our bodies were screaming for air.

"Enough!" Zaal called, his hand slapping on the floor, but I stared into the eyes of this killer trying to take my life. I could see in his blue eyes that he wouldn't give up. Lifting my leg, I kicked out, unbalancing the male sitting above me. Rolling over, I straddled his waist, knocking his hands off my neck. My grip slipped from his neck. Zaal then pulled me from Valentin as he roared and went to strike again.

I panted, muscles braced to react as Valentin paced the floor of the ring, his deadly gaze slicing over Zaal to mine. I pushed off Zaal and rushed to Valentin, standing toe-to-toe with the psychotic male.

"I want to kill you," he snarled, then pushed me back.

I moved back directly in his path and ordered, "Resist it."

Valentin's balled fist smacked at the side of his head. He growled low and said, "I need to kill you!" His fingers dragged down to circle the collar scar marring his neck.

"Resist it," I ordered again, and watched the newest member of our Bratva war with the monster living inside.

"No," he replied, abruptly standing still, every packed muscle in his huge body tensed and shaking as he tried to restrain his rage. "I want to kill!" he bellowed.

Zaal moved beside me, crossing his arms over his chest. His black hair hung down over his chest, dripping with sweat. "Fight it," he ordered, too. Valentin's stare almost eviscerated him on the spot.

"I'm a killer!" he hissed, his neck cording at the effort it was taking not to kill us where we stood. "I fucking kill!"

This time neither Zaal nor I spoke. If Valentin was to stand with us as a future Bratva king, if he was to stay and build our brotherhood to be unrivaled and feared, he had to learn how to conquer his conditioned instinct to strike.

Zaal stepped closer and Valentin bared his teeth. "For Zoya," he said. The words immediately had an impact on our brother. Valentin stilled. He held Zaal's gaze and Zaal held his.

As the minutes passed, the rage within Valentin reduced to a simmer. That was as low as it got for the scarred Russian. He was always angry, always filled with pain.

The three of us stood there silently, until I said, "To be a fighter, you have to know when to contain your rage. You must use it to fuel your need to kill but hold it back enough to not let it blind you."

"I'm not a fighter," Valentin bit out. "I'm a fucking torturer. I'm an assassin. I don't dance in a ring for entertainment. I extract pain slowly, until they scream."

Zaal stepped back. I knew it was to distance himself from the male that held his sister's heart. The male that, before he loved her, had tortured her. Had exacted the pain he talked of so excitedly.

Valentin's chest worked up and down as he tried to gain control. I had turned to speak to Zaal when Viktor came running through the back door of the Dungeon.

He rapped his hand on the office door as he passed. My father and Kirill walked out from doing business and moved toward us in the training ring. Viktor stopped and tried to catch his breath.

"What?" Kirill asked, adjusting the cuff links on his shirt. His eyes moved to Valentin, and I saw the flash of pride he had for our new brother. Valentin was a monster from your nightmares. And now he was a potential Red King of the Bratva. My father-in-law couldn't wait for the day he could introduce the new Bratva/Kostava circle to the other crime bosses of New York.

He knew exactly what seeing the three of us would inspire— pure fear.

Viktor inhaled deep, and, looking me dead in the eye, said, "I know how we get you into the pit."

The moment his words reached my ears, my heart started thundering in my chest. "How?" I pushed. Zaal came to stand at my right; Valentin, also eager to hear my old trainer, stood at my left.

Viktor looked at the three of us and explained. "I've just heard from my contact in Georgia that Arziani is holding a death-match tournament in the Blood Pit. He holds regular matches, but he has a group of champions that cannot be defeated. The investors, the crime bosses that go there regularly to gamble and pit their fighters against his, were becoming frustrated with Arziani's men never losing. To prove Arziani doesn't rig his matches, he is giving other gulags he's invested in, and bosses outside his network, a chance to pit fighters against his men and the others entered. It's an ultimate tournament." He looked to Kirill and Ivan, then said with emphasis, "Big stakes. The money to be won is in the tens of millions."

"But how do we get in?" I asked, confused.

Viktor glanced nervously to my father, then to the Pakhan. My father frowned, but answering my question said, "Each gulag can enter up to three of its champions to fight in the tournament." He swallowed. "I was contacted by an old colleague to ask if I had any fighters I wanted to enter."

Pure adrenaline surged through my body. I stepped forward, my fingers twitching, and asked, "And you said 'yes,' yes?"

Viktor slowly nodded. "Yes, but better still"—he paused—"my contact, him and his three brothers work for Arziani. His brothers are guards in the pit."

Valentin began rocking beside me and hissed, "Wraiths."

Viktor paled but shook his head. "No. They were taken and made to work there to repay their father's gambling debts. Just as I was." Viktor faced me again. "Only Abel was repaying the debt as a driver, like me. He has told me that because he couldn't pay the money back in time, they took his brothers, too. They made them Wraiths and made Abel move to their officer ranks." Excitement flared in Viktor's eyes. "They all hate Master Arziani and want out. I'm sure they can help us once we're inside, if we make it worth their while." Viktor paused, then flicking a frustrated look to Valentin, he added, "Not all of the guards are there because they believe in Arziani's cause. In fact, Abel told me he believes a good thirty percent or more are there to repay gambling debts—their own or someone in their family's."

"So that's our way in?" I queried, and crossed my arms over my chest. "We go in as fighters." I glanced behind me to Valentin and Zaal. "We fight in the tournament and find a way to kill Arziani from inside?"

"We can't get in any other way," Viktor said. Valentin walked beside me; a new energy seemed to be running through his veins. "He's right. We won't get in the pit ourselves." He glanced to me, and I could see his need for blood shining back at me. "But we can fight. We can go in as gulag warriors."

"You're not a fighter," Zaal said from behind. When I glanced back, Zaal was frowning. He was glaring at Valentin. Valentin was seething on the spot as he glared right back.

"I can fucking fight," Valentin snapped.

Zaal stepped forward and pointed at me. "Luka was the champion of his gulag. I fought as a prototype of Jakhua. We are fighters like those in the pit. We were raised to do nothing else. You were raised to torture and kill. You are different. You're not a death-match fighter."

Valentin's lips rolled back from his teeth as he squared up to Zaal. "I can kill in more inventive ways than you, Kostava. I can kill you in ways you can't even imagine." He looked to me and said, "I'm going."

"He'll be a liability," Zaal argued, as Valentin practically radiated death on the spot.

"That's my sister in there! She's that dick's whore, and you expect to go without me? Not happening."

"He knows you," I said, then looked to Zaal. "He knows you, too."

They both looked to each other, then at me. "I'm going," they said in unison. I exhaled deeply.

Facing Viktor, I stated, "He doesn't know me. No one in that pit will know me. My gulag was in Alaska. From what we can tell, once it was emptied when I escaped, it never reopened. I'm the one they don't know."

"Luka," my father spoke. I turned toward him. His face was red with frustration. I knew why. He didn't want me to go.

Viktor stepped forward. "We need to submit three fighters or none at all, Luka." He waved his hand in Zaal and Valentin's direction. "I've thought of how to get them in."

"How?" Zaal asked.

Shrugging, Viktor said, "We enter under a fake name. Not the Volkov or Tolstoi dungeon, but a decoy. Abel and his brothers will ensure we get on the list without being checked." He explained, "We can say that our men bought these two from the males that used to guard them. Zaal from one of Jakhua's and Valentin from the Mistress."

"The Mistress was his sister," I argued. "He'll kill Valentin the minute he sees him."

"I'm going!" Valentin thundered. I held out my hand for him to be quiet. He silenced, but his lips curled in annoyance.

"Arziani hated his sister. She was the bane of his existence. Abel said that when Arziani got word of her death, he laughed. He knew he was better off without her in his life." He flashed a worried look to Valentin, but continued. "Abel said that the only thing he cared about was the female *mona* being held by the Mistress." He nodded his head in Valentin's direction and clarified: "His sister. Now he has her, he doesn't care about the rest."

My pulse raced at the possibility of getting the opportunity to fight again. But more important, at killing Arziani and ending this ring of slavery once and for all. At putting an end to kids being sold like slabs of meat, being tested upon like rats, forced to fight and forget they're humans. Nothing more than killing machines.

My mind circled with the information. Looking to Valentin, I said, "If you come, we'll have to teach you how to fight for the pit. We'll have to get you trained with a weapon."

"I have my picanas," he replied.

"Guns and cattle prods aren't allowed in the rings," Zaal replied.

Valentin's eyebrow raised, and he said, "But short metal spears will be. I'm used to the feel of them in my hand through using the prods. They're a part of me. I can be just as efficient without their electrical charge as I am with it."

Zaal turned to me and nodded. Facing them both, I announced, "If we do this, if we all go in, we may not all make it out alive."

A shroud of silence descended around us. Valentin was the first to step forward and speak. "I'm going in. That asshole made me this . . . this *thing* I am today. And he has my sister. I'm going in. And I won't die. I won't die until his heart stops."

I nodded, then looked to Zaal. Arms crossed over his chest, he confided, "I don't want to fight again. I want my life to be with my Talia. But . . ." He sighed and I saw his inner demons shine through. "But Anri and I were tested upon there. Made to fight in the child- hood pits." He shook his head. "Until Arziani and this Blood Pit are destroyed, we'll never be truly free, will we? Everything each of us has been through stemmed from this enterprise." Zaal looked to my father and Kirill. "Arziani is bigger than even the Volkov Bratva. If we are to keep our standing here, if we are to give our females good lives, safe lives, we have to stop this male now. Before he comes for us. Let's take the fight to him." Zaal's face clouded with the need to kill, and he concluded, "before he comes for us."

Every word Zaal said hit my heart. I turned to Viktor. "When is the tournament?"

"Four weeks," he replied, "It lasts four days. Two-man matches until four fighters reach the final. No man will be paired with a gulag-mate unless they meet in the final. Then it's a four-man battle for the championship. Winner gets his freedom. Arziani's tournament prize is freedom." I raised my eyebrow at that. Freedom for males captured and forced to fight would make them fight that much harder. It would make them that much more difficult to beat.

"We all need to make it into the final battle," I said, and looked to Valentin and Zaal. They both nodded. "We can use the next few weeks to understand the pit and plan how to attack." I looked back to Viktor and said, "Contact your male. We need to be sure we have them as our allies, then use their influence when we're in there with those not committed to Arziani and his cause. Promise them whatever they want. Money, a life here in New York, anything, just get us into the Blood Pit. We'll take it from there."

Viktor nodded and rushed out the Dungeon's door. Zaal and Valentin came to stand beside me. Zaal laid his hand on my shoulder. When I met his eyes, he nodded his head, no words were necessary. I could see the conflict haunting his eyes—as much as I could feel my own.

We were different males now. Had different lives. Yet at the same time, until Arziani—the puppet master of our personal hells—was dead, we would always be the same captured males we had been for most of our lives. We would be forever imprisoned by our pasts. We would never truly move on.

Addressing Valentin, I said, "We need to use the four weeks to train you." I then spoke to Zaal. "We need to train ourselves again, too. Ask Viktor to get us ready. We have no choice but to come back to our females. To do that we need to defeat every fighter that gets in our way. It's the only way we can go—we go to win."

Zaal held out his hand and I shook it. Valentin did the same. As we looked to one another, a surge of excitement welled up in my heart. In four weeks' time, for four days, I would once again be Raze.

I had missed being Raze. I had missed and craved the blood I would shed. For two weeks, I could be the gulag champion again; then I would forever leave him in the past.

Turning on my heel, I jumped from the cage, and my father stepped in my path. Kirill fell in behind him, a look of serious concern on his face. But it was my papa to whom I gave my attention. The sad yet stubborn expression on his face was hard to ignore.

"I won't allow it," he said, and shook his head. "Your mama and Kisa won't want this, Luka. What the hell are you thinking?"

Glancing down to the floor, I then looked back and said, "How many more kids are in gulags around the world? How many are stolen from group homes or the streets and being forced to fight?" I held on to my father's arm and said, "How many papas are searching for their lost sons? Not knowing, never believing they could be under the control of some fucked-up psychopath who has a delusion of being a sadistic Caesar from ancient Rome?" My father paled, but I kept going. "It's not over, Papa. Even though I've been back here in New York with you, Kirill, Mama, Talia, and Kisa, I've never been fully present."

I searched for a way to make him understand. Kisa's face filled my mind's eye. I pictured my hand on her stomach, which punctured a hole in my heart when our baby had kicked. Pushing the lump from my throat, I said, "Kisa is due to have our baby soon. I can't live in a world with my child while being haunted by the past. To be the father I want to be, the father you are, I need to end this once and for all. The Arziani empire must fall. And I must be the one to do it." This time I looked to Kirill and said, "To be the Pakhan of our Bratva, I have to rid myself of all the pain I still carry with me. Arziani is the root of all of this evil. He's the snake. And I'm going to rip off his fucking head."

"Luka," my papa rasped, and placed his hand on the nape of my neck. He brought my forehead to his and said, "I'm proud of you, son. But I cannot rest until you have taken this bastard down and returned home safe. For good this time."

"Thank you," I hushed back. Lifting my head, I met his worried gaze and said, "I'm Raze. I'm the champion. I don't lose." I thought of my beautiful wife and our child. I thought of Zaal and Talia, Valentin and Zoya, and I knew I wouldn't fail. This was my family now. And we would all survive. We had to, there was no other choice.

Kirill walked around my father and kissed my head. He didn't speak, but I didn't need words to see the pride on his face. Kirill had been the Pakhan for decades. He knew that leaders sometimes had to sacrifice a part of themselves for the greater good. And killing Arziani was for the greater good.

I had four weeks to recall and embrace the savage killer I had pushed down deep.

As I made my way home, I flexed my hands, staring at the fingers that would soon be reacquainted with the bladed knuckle-dusters they knew so well.

And with every mile driven toward my home, the identity tattoo on my chest burned hotter and hotter. 818 was breaking back through, pushing Luka Tolstoi aside.

Temporarily, I had to embrace the monster within.

I'd let him take the reins.

Then when I arrived at the Blood Pit, I'd let him unleash hell.

For one very last time.

Before I laid him to rest, for good.

9

901

Two weeks later . . .

I stood in the center of my cell, waiting for my time to be called. Tonight was the first show fight Master had planned for his tournament investors. He had told me over the past two weeks that these matches were important to secure money for the spectators. He impressed on me that these investors will gamble on the fighters, and some more important bosses might enter their own.

And he had told me in no uncertain terms that I was to take my time with my opponents. Draw out the kill. Obey his every command. He even offered me a bribe: If I did as he instructed, he would continue sending 152 to me every night.

This was exactly why I intended to kill my opponent in three seconds flat.

My gut clenched as I thought of the past two weeks. Then I thought of what my nights would become after tonight. She'd be gone. It was what I needed. Though I was starting to think it wasn't what I wanted.

Since that night two weeks ago when she had pleaded with me to let her die and she had spoken to me in Russian after I had called her a whore, we had barely spoken. That night I had let myself get too close. I had asked her too much. Listened to her too much.

Felt too much.

I squeezed my eyes shut, trying to block out the memory—of how she had told me to get a guard instead, of how much that pissed me off, the repulsive thought of her under a Wraith. Something inside of me had broken when she'd pleaded for that version of hell.

She wasn't a whore. I hadn't meant what I had said. I was pissed, lashing out. I hadn't known she was Russian. Her dark hair and features made her appear Georgian. It only made me want her more.

She was like me.

Master still sent her every night. I released inside her when the drugs made her need me, but we never spoke. She slept in the corner of the room, and I stayed on my bed. She knew I didn't want more. She never asked for more. I gave only as much as I was willing to give.

Master's plan to fuck with my mind wouldn't work, I couldn't let it. I'd defy him tonight, and he'd punish me by taking 152 away. I glanced down at my hands wrapped around my Kindjals' handles at that thought. They shook.

My mind clogged, it stabbed with the sound of 152's moans as I took her as mine. Her touch was sensuous as her hands scraped on my back. The look in her eyes as they cleared from the drug in the aftermath of our releases was so welcome. It was when her true self came through. The look that showed me her gratitude. The look that seared me on the spot.

Krasivaya.

Footsteps on stone outside the cell made me walk to the door. 667 was walking past. He was dripping with sweat, marked in slashes from what looked like a bladed chain. He flicked his chin as he walked by.

His *mona* arrived only minutes after he had. She swiftly moved into his cell. As she passed by, I studied her for the first time. She was attractive, nothing like 152, yet pretty enough. But it was the look of worry on her face as she ran after 667 that made my stomach flip over. She cared about him enough to run to his aid after he had been injured. I frowned. I couldn't remember a time, ever in my life, when someone comforted me. Then again, the only times I had been injured were as a child figuring out the run of the cage. Learning what weapons to choose, and hardest of all—learning how to kill. I had been alone ever since.

Seeing 667's *mona* run to him, her affection for him was obvious and unapologetic. For a moment, it made me regret the decision I had already made.

Another cell door opened. 140 pounded past, his expression one of a male that was minutes away from sending a soul to hell. In a flash, my regret for losing 152 tonight was gone. Because here was a male that was a shadow of his former self. He had allowed himself to want and need a *mona*. That had been his ruin.

The crowd outside roared. Just as I was about to move from the doors, someone stepped out of the shadows. A guard stopped before me and flicked his chin in my direction. "Master has sent a message. He said that your opponent belongs to one of the biggest investors. He has bought several shares in many gulags from Master over the years and is planning to enter many fighters in the tournament. Master has demanded that you slow the kill and not simply slaughter." The guard stepped closer, holding his gun toward me. "Master said that if you don't obey, there will be consequences."

My top lip hooked in amusement. His taking 152 from me was the best punishment I would receive.

The guard backed away, shaking his head.

My legs moved from side to side as I warmed up my feet. I envisioned the kill in my head. I would duck right, then left, strike left, then plunge my Kindjal into him. The blade would pierce his heart and he would fall to the floor. I opened my eyes. Just as I did, 140 came walking through, covered in blood spatter and with the wide, staring eyes of bloodlust.

He rushed past, panting and high from the kill. My adrenaline spiked; I'd be up next. When the guard walked down the hallway, I cracked my neck from side to side. When the cell door opened, I sprinted down the tunnel to the pit. With every step I envisioned my opponent's blood hitting my chest and the thrill I'd feel at disobeying Master. The crowd roared as I ran forward, Kindjals at the ready. Then something from the crowd caught my attention. As I fended off my opponent's strike, his bladed pickax narrowly missing my head, I looked up at the crowd. A flash of light caught my eye again. At the very back, directly behind Master's seat, was a guard . . . and in his arms was 152.

It took me a moment to realize what I was seeing. Then it made perfect sense. A guard had a knife to 152's throat. The light was the blade glinting off the pit's lights.

Immediately, rage ignited inside me. My eyes next dropped to Master, as I ducked under my opponent's swing. When I saw him, he was smiling, victory in his dark gaze. His hands gripping the arms of his seat was the only indication that he harbored doubt that I would let her die.

Feeling my opponent approach, I crouched down. The wind from his ax passed, blowing through my hair. Turning, I drove the blunt end of my handle into his kidney, the huge dark-skinned man bending over at the hit. I backed away, steeling my emotions. I narrowed my eyes on my opponent, forcing myself to turn off my concerns about the *mona*.

Ignore her. She means nothing. Let her die, I told myself, turning my Kindjals in my hands, readying to strike. My opponent turned, his close-shaved black hair and sheer height coming into view, almost matching mine. His teeth were bared as he faced me, gripping his ax as he prepared to strike. Replaying my plan in my head, I ducked left as he charged, then made a quick right. But as I approached and the bladed tip of his ax rose high, I did not use the anticipated gap to my advantage. Instead, I let the blade's sharp edge slash my upper arm.

The crowd roared as 419, my opponent, drew first blood. Unable to stop myself, I glanced up at 152, who was still as night in the guard's arms. Even from this distance I could see her eyes shining in pure terror.

Just let me die, I heard in my head, 152's soft voice from two weeks ago. I shook my head, trying to forget about her up there, with a knife at her throat. I tried not to care. But just as I couldn't let her die on the floor of my cell before, I wouldn't let her die now. Something inside me, feeling like a dull ache in my chest, wouldn't let me.

Sighing deeply, I ran at my opponent, smashing the Kindjal's blunt handle to his face. He responded with a punch to my cheek. And I put on a fucking show. I gave Master what he wanted. Hit after hit, blow after blow. 419 and I were both cut, bleeding and bruised. I had gashes on my arms, gashes on my torso, and swelling on my cheeks. But I knew, without a shadow of a doubt, that I could have beaten him in seconds if Master hadn't forced me to submit. 419 was nothing. As a contender, he was a joke. Yet I made this fight look like I'd barely hung on.

Enraged at what I'd been forced to do—at what I'd *allowed* myself to do—I stood and gripped my Kindjals. Enough was enough. I'd toyed with this fighter too long. It was beneath me to play with this male any longer.

It was time for him to die.

419 swayed on his feet, on the brink of passing out. His ax hung by his side, his slackening fingers barely able to hold the heavy steel. Needing to see him fall, see this male breathe his last, I charged

forward, and in a double movement of my blades, I sliced across his stomach and stabbed a Kindjal down and through his skull. My blade cut through him like butter, and the feel of his large body submitting to death sent the best drugs to my veins.

The crowd jumped to their feet as 419 hit the bloodied sand beneath our feet. It was the loudest response I had ever received in the pit. And when I looked to 152 in the stands, the guard slowly removed the knife from her throat. I snarled, abruptly wrapped in a cocoon of pure hate, when I saw a faint bloodied line on her skin.

And I knew. In that moment, I knew Master hadn't been faking this threat. If I had failed to obey, he would have slit the High Mona's throat. He was crazed and unstable, but he was obsessed with the female. Yet to break me, to see me bow down to his feet, he would have slit her throat without a second thought.

A mixture of anger and some cavernous feeling I couldn't describe swirled in my stomach. Because I knew, by this match, that I had given Master a hold over my mind. The realization hit home. He hadn't sent 152 to me weeks ago to make me want her, then hurt me by taking her away. He had given me her to threaten her life. His High Mona, the female he stared at like he wanted to completely possess her soul. He had given her to me to force me to yield to his control.

And it had worked. As furious as that made me, I couldn't deny the truth: I had played right into his hands. Even as I stood here now, seething, almost splintering apart with the most intense rage, my eyes kept drifting to 152, dressed in a sheer deep purple dress. She was frozen to the spot, but she watched me, too. Her eyes were a mixture of confusion and pain, but they were fixed on me. Solely on me.

Her attention only made me break more.

I hated myself for submitting like a mewling bitch.

And despite myself, I hated her for being the cause of this truth.

Snapping my eyes away, I ranged my gaze over the crowd. I wanted nothing more than to jump into the fray and tear them all apart. I wanted to shred their limbs and snap their bloodthirsty necks. Then my eyes found Master, still sitting in his seat, staring down at me, looking every inch the Blood Pit King.

Focusing on me, *his* champion.

The one he now controlled . . . in every way possible.

As if knowing what I was thinking, a slow victorious grin pulled on his lips. My legs physically shook as I tried to keep from sacrificing my life just to take his life first. But as his wide, glittering eyes looked up to 152, standing like a broken child behind him, I planted my feet into the sand.

A wave of protectiveness washed over me when I saw who 152 was looking at: me. And I saw Master's livid reaction to who held her gaze. This time when he looked at me, there was a new fire in his stare. He had given his *mona* to me—but he didn't want her to want me. He wanted her affection all to himself.

My cheek twitched as I fought the smirk threatening on my lips. Master caught it, though. His knuckles became white as he gripped the arms of his seat. He leaned forward, his hard face showing how much he wanted to order my death. For a moment, when he rose to his feet and the crowd quieted down, I thought he would see through his biggest wish.

Then a darker man, dressed in strange clothing, stood beside him and shook his hand. The male was smiling wide, nodding his head at something Master said. As I glanced to the dead male beside me in the pit, I saw the similarities to him and the strangely dressed male. It was his Master. The one my Master had needed me to win over.

I had done as Master planned.

The crowd grew restless as the males talked. When Master finally looked back my way, he dismissed me from the pit with a quick flick of his wrist. Turning on my heel, I jogged out of the ring and down the warriors' tunnel. I forced myself to look unaffected. But when the tunnel darkened and I knew I was out of the spectators' view, I drew to a stop and clenched my teeth at the pain stabbing at my body. I glanced behind me and saw my bloodied footprints on the sand. I raked my gaze over my body and growled low when I saw I was littered with gashes, deep slices showing more than a few hints of open flesh.

I hadn't been touched in five years. Hadn't sustained a scratch since I became champion and simply decided that no opponent would ever touch me again. I knew this match had just made the excitement for Master's sick spectators that much stronger. The champion, the Arziani Pit Bull, had just been wounded in the show rounds.

It would raise expectations. More investors would join, eager to have their champions bring me down once and for all.

I heard the guards beginning to move in behind me. I kept going, struggling to walk all the way to my cell. As I passed 667's cell, I heard a high-pitched giggle drifting into the hallway. I stopped dead as his *mona* laughed again. The sound cut through me like a knife. Not because I couldn't stand the sound, but because I'd rarely heard that sound in my entire life.

As his *mona* laughed again, 152's beautiful face came into my head. I saw her tears, I saw her fear . . . I didn't see her laugh. My heart stuttered as I envisioned her smiling at me or laughing at something I'd said. I couldn't breathe as I was trapped in that dream.

It fell apart when I caught 140 moving to his cell door. He stared at me with his vacant, lifeless eyes, as his arms threaded through the bars and hung across the horizontal bar.

When 667's *mona* laughed again, 140 moved his attention to the other champion's cell door. He spoke without looking at me. "It's only a question of time," he said coldly, his body still bathed in his opponent's blood. "When Master feels like it, needs something, or simply wants to fuck with his mind, he'll kill her." 140 pointed at 667's cell. "He'll start by taking her away from him every now and again. He'll expect her and she won't arrive. When she does, she'll be hurt and bruised. She'll be quiet. He'll bring her to his cell door or have him brought to the *mona* quarters. Then, with 667 restrained, Master will take her or stand by as he orders another warrior or guard to do it for him. 667 will slowly begin to break, seeing his female being forced to take another male's cock." His hands moved to tighten on the bars, then he bit out, "He'll kill her in front of him. And he'll die along with her." He looked to me, but I knew his eyes were still locked in the past. "Only he'll be forced to still live in this pit, waking each day and fighting some other man-made animal he doesn't give a shit about in the ring. And the worst part is, Master won't even think of it again. He'll move on to play with another warrior's head. Because that's what he does. He created this empire to toy with us, his slaves."

667's laughs came from his cell, and my eyes drifted to fix on his door. "I have been here since I was ten. I don't know how many years have passed—Master makes sure we don't know, doesn't he? But I guess that I am in my twenties. I got my *mona,* I think, about two years ago." I glanced back to 140. Now he was staring at me. "In all of the years I have been here, I only remember those days I spent with her. They are the only memories I have. I don't remember much of my childhood, because of the drugs. I don't remember my fights, because I have killed too many, too often. But I remember every second spent with her." His face flushed red. "And I remember the gleam in Master's eyes when he slit her throat as my punishment for not being effective enough in the pit. I received a blow to my arm that the Master thought made his warrior—me— look inefficient. So he killed my heart."

"He is an unworthy male," I responded.

140 laughed a humorless laugh. Then his face hardened back to a deathly expression. "Since my *mona* died, I have been thinking every night: Why are we here? Where did we all come from? Why did Master create this Blood Pit?" His face contorted. "And why the hell are we all obeying? We are all warriors. We kill. That is *all* we do. We kill every day. As children, we killed. As males, we kill. Yet we do not kill *them*." He meant the Wraiths. "We don't ask questions about anything, we don't rise up. We only know this life. And we accept it."

"Most of the male fighters are drugged more than we are. We are on special privileges because we are champions," I said.

"The *chiri* give us our drugs every day. Every person in this pit. The *monebi*, the *Ubiytsy*, the fighters, us. Why? Why do we all do it? If the *chiri* were to stop the injections, the males would fight with clear heads. We could save the *monebi*, whose only purpose is to spread their legs and then be killed. We could be free."

"You want to be free?" I asked, his words circling my head. I couldn't stop his questions from becoming my own.

He shook his head. "No. I want to die. I want to leave this life." I frowned. 140 leaned forward as much as he could out the cell door and said, "But I'll take out as many of these fuckers as I can as I go. Master, if possible; his investors, at the very least. Since he killed my *mona*, I have nothing left to live for. Once I get my chance, I will take it with eyes wide open. And I'll die with a smile on my face, knowing I have taken some of the Wraiths down with me."

"How will you do it?" I asked, my heart beating faster. I was siding with his plan. My body celebrated the thought of his vision.

He shrugged. "I don't know yet. But a time will come. I'm praying all of us slaves will finally rise up and take them all down. But if that never happens, I'll die doing it myself."

I was quiet after he had spoken. 140 began backing away. But before he disappeared into the privacy of his cell, he said, "You, 667, and I have been in these quarters almost the same amount of time. In all of those days, I have never seen you even gain a scratch in battle." His eyes narrowed, then widened, clearly realizing something important. Moving closer again, he guessed correctly. "The *mona*. The High Mona that you have been servicing each night. He used her, didn't he?"

My lips rubbed together, and a sense of failure took me in its hold. 140 shook his head slowly and sighed. "You want her." He stared at me and added, "I thought you felt nothing for her. I have walked past the cell and seen her in the corner, alone, afraid." His head tipped to the side as he searched my hard expression. "But you do. And he now knows it." His hands took hold of the bars. "Am I right?"

My silence said everything.

"How did he threaten her? Did he threaten to take her back? Did he hit her? Starve her? Give her to another warrior?"

I vibrated on the spot as I thought of the guard holding a knife to her throat. I held my Kindjals tighter, as I replayed the wide look in her eyes. Opening them, I hissed, "He was going to cut her throat. He had a guard stand behind her. He ordered me to make more of the fight. To draw out the kill." I glanced away in annoyance, then added, "I was going to just let her die. I needed to let her die . . ."

". . . But you couldn't," 140 finished. I wanted to snarl back that he didn't know what he was talking about. That I didn't care for the *mona* that had been forced upon me.

But the words wouldn't come from my mouth.

I couldn't get them out, no matter what I tried.

"He was going to kill her?" 140 prompted, and stepped back. His hard expression turned to sympathy.

"What?" I spat, edging forward toward his cell.

140 stopped. Then, running his hand over his face, he said,

"Then you're fucked. He tested you. He normally starts slow. But with you and his *mona,* he put everything on the line." He crossed his arms. "We've all seen him parading the High Mona through the pits, holding her close, owning her, possessing her." His eyebrow raised. "Even though he has given her to you, he hasn't truly given her to you. And if he was willing to kill her for your submission, it means he will risk it all for you to break. It makes you the most sorry son of a bitch in this place."

As 140 walked away, he said, "I didn't even know her name. I knew her number but not her name. Fuck, I don't even know my own. I know nothing. None of us know anything, outside of how we live and exist in here. But without the drugs, the privilege we earn as champions, it means that we can think. For ourselves. I don't know what the world outside is like, but I know that this place of blood and pain is *wrong.* I feel it in my heart. I feel it with everything I am."

The sound of the guards approaching made me move forward. With every step I took, the fire inside rose higher and higher, until I felt like I was burning from the inside out.

When I reached my cell, I slammed the door shut and leaned my heavy body against the nearest wall. My legs gave way as I slumped to the floor. My arms fell down, the injuries making them weak. My Kindjals clattered on the stone floor. Trickles of blood ran over my cut skin and onto the floor beside me.

I stared straight ahead, unable to move. 140 was right. All of the years here in the pit I had spent alone. Untouched and untouchable. And now they were gone. All because of Master's whore.

I'd put my dick before my strength; now *I* was as much Master's toy as 152. I had given him my pride. I had nothing left.

I didn't know how long I sat there, but the sound of light quick feet approaching my cell pulled my attention to the door. My chest constricted when 152 appeared. A guard opened the door, then slammed it in her wake.

Her blue eyes were huge as she watched me sitting in the floor. Rather than be glad that she'd survived, it only fueled the fire in my blood.

Nervously, she stepped closer, then began to bend down to where I sat. Before she could, I threw my Kindjals across the cell, the noise thundering on the floor. She flinched and staggered back. Meeting her gaze to show her how much I wanted her gone, I snapped, "Get in the corner and out of my fucking sight."

I heard her suck in a deep breath. A stab of some unknown feeling rumbled around my stomach. I pushed it aside when she scurried past me and crouched down. I felt her watchful gaze, but I didn't look her way. My skin felt on fire, my muscles twitching in agitation. The air in the cell seemed too thick, too hot. I fought to draw in a simple breath.

Movement outside my cell door caused my head to turn. A guard let in a *chiri,* who had arrived to stitch my wounds. She carried a bowl of water in her hands, the needles and threads in a small bag hanging from a string around her fingers.

The *chiri* bent to work on my wounds. I pulled my arm away when she tried to clean off the blood. "Get off," I hissed. "I'll do it myself."

The *chiri* bowed her head at my harshness and immediately got to her feet. She rocked from side to side like she didn't know what to do. I looked up and saw her eyes widen as she stared at the stone floor. Her face was pale, and when I looked to her clasped hands at her waist, they were trembling.

140's words about all of us in this pit played on my mind. About where we all came from. About how we all do what Master says without question. All the *chiri* wore the tattoo 000. *I didn't even know her name. I don't even know my own . . .*

"Leave them here," I said, less harshly this time. "I'll fix it myself."

The *chiri* turned for the door, and I saw her shoulders slump in relief. She was scared of me. I risked a quick glance to 152 in the corner. She was huddled down, her body facing toward the wall.

She was scared of me, too.

For the first time since becoming the Arziani Pit Bull, Master's cold and ruthless champion, it unsettled me. Everyone was scared of me. Even the guards never came too close to the cell for fear I'd snap their necks. It was a well-founded fear, I'd done it to them many times before. Opponents had even pissed themselves when I'd run into the pit from the darkness of the tunnel. Everyone stayed clear. It was something I'd ensured was the case.

667 had told me that we—all under Master's rule—were the same. We had to protect one another.

I had only ever taken care of myself.

The clanging of the cell door shutting echoed off the stone walls. And then we were in silence. My head fell back against the cold wall and I closed my eyes, simply breathing.

I wanted to black out. Just fall asleep and wake up with 152 gone and my life back to how it had always been. I felt the lines crease on my forehead when I thought about my life before the past couple of weeks. It was the same thing every day: wake, eat, be injected, train. Then on match days, kill. It was an endless cycle.

A hole caved in the pit of my stomach. 140 had told me the privilege we got from being champions was being free from the drugs. We could think. Think for ourselves. For so much of my life I had no memory of how I had lived, of how I was taken.

I didn't even know my *name.*

Once I was off the drugs and moved into these quarters, I quickly fell into my routine. But now 140 had implanted a seed inside my head—one of free thought. Opening my eyes, I looked down at my cut arms and legs. I saw the blood washing over my stomach, drying over my identity tattoo.

901. I was 901, nothing more, nothing less. I was Arziani's Pit Bull. The most efficient and successful killer the Blood Pit had ever known. I wondered if I was ever something more. If I was freed from this place, could I be more? The squeeze of my chest told me I was and I could.

I tried to envision what the world was like aboveground. I couldn't. My only memory of being out there was when the Wraiths had taken me. When they had arrived in the night and taken me from my bed.

There was nothing else.

I thought of the thousands of investors. I thought of the spectators that sat in the crowd at the matches. They were not from the pit. They were from outside. They had lives. They were free.

So why weren't we? Why wasn't I?

The skin began twitching around my wounds. I knew I had no choice but to tend to them. If I was to be okay for the tournament, I had to seal the wounds so they wouldn't get infected.

Taking the bag off the floor, I ripped it open, the thread already hanging through the needle. Holding out my arm, I picked up the needle and brought it to my first wound. I didn't even flinch as the needle punctured my skin. I was used to more than this level of pain. Though I grunted when I reached halfway. I couldn't reach the top of the wound at this angle.

Dropping my arm, I sighed. My jaw clenched in frustration.

"Why?" My head snapped to the corner of the cell at the soft question coming from 152.

As I met her blue eyes, her cheeks flushed. Her arms were wrapped around her bent legs. Bent legs that were tucked as close as possible to her chest.

My eyes narrowed, not knowing what she meant. Seeing my confusion, she swallowed then explained, "Why did you do it?" She glanced away, then added, "Why didn't you just let me die?"

I shifted on the floor. Then a pain hit my chest so hard, I thought it might cave in. She sounded so sad, so defeated. I couldn't stand it. The red line over the front of her neck caught my eye. I realized just how close the guard had been from slitting it open. When my attention dropped back to her face, she was staring at me. I couldn't understand her expression, but I noticed how beautiful she was.

So damn beautiful.

The metal bracelet on her wrist reflected the light hanging from the wall. As my vision became lost in my thoughts, I said, "I couldn't see him kill you."

There was a long pause. "But why? I don't understand. You . . . you don't want me." Her head fell forward, her dark hair shielding her face. I thought she had stopped speaking, but then she whispered, "You should have let me go."

That pain in my chest grew to a deep ache. "No one should die by the hand of a Wraith."

She lifted her head and a lump built in my throat on seeing tears tracking down her smooth cheeks. She laughed a humorless laugh and asked, "Not even Master's whore?"

My eyes fell to her bracelet again. I hated hearing how sad she sounded. My fingers curled into a fist. I took three deep breaths. On the fourth, I forced myself to meet her eyes. "You're not a whore."

She frowned. "You don't believe that. You think I belong to Master, that I want him." Her bottom lip trembled when she added, "He hurts me, you know. He makes me bleed and bruises my face."

I stilled. The flames of hatred circled my heart, heating its blood. Then her head tipped to the side. "But you do not," she added almost mutely. "You do not want me, but you give me your release to save me from pain. You do not want me, but you cause yourself pain to save my life." The blush on her cheeks turned to a scarlet red. "And when you take me, you do not hurt me. You are gentle, although you are big in size. You could end this game that Master is playing with your mind. You are kind, and soft . . . you give me your care."

I had nothing to say in response. 152 glanced away to stare at the far wall. "You are the Arziani Pit Bull. You are feared. But to me, you are safety."

A low growl slipped from my throat at her words. Yet again the unknown feeling settled within my heart, chasing away the heat. I tried to look away from this *mona,* curling against the wall, but I couldn't. She had me trapped.

A cold snap of air drifted through the cell, slapping against my wounds. Hissing at the feel of the breeze on my torn and exposed flesh, I glanced down at my open sores and picked up the needle. I tried to angle my body so I could sew up this wound, but no matter how I positioned myself, I couldn't reach.

"Fuck," I spat, about to rip the damn thing from my arm, when I felt a small, soft hand cover the back of my own. I looked up. 152 was kneeling before me. Her blue eyes were huge as she nervously looked down at me.

Her hand jumped as it lay over mine, and I felt her fingers shaking. Her face was flushed. Inhaling deep, and with a strength I would never have imagined, she took the needle from my hand and held it in hers. Wordlessly, she moved around where I sat. Sitting on the floor, she leaned in to my wound and commenced threading the needle through my skin. I watched her hands as she worked quickly and gently. When I moved my eyes to her face, my heat rose.

She wasn't a whore. And I felt my stomach cramp when I thought of her being Master's. She wasn't his. He didn't deserve her.

The feel of warm water trickled over my arm. 152 was cleaning the wound she had been working on, the wound that she had now sewn shut. Her touch was so light it felt like it almost wasn't there.

Without looking up, she moved to the wound on my shoulder

and began to work. I couldn't speak as I watched her. My pulse was thundering in my ears, my blood was rushing through my heart at a rapid speed. I had never been this way with a female. This close. Feeling these strange things. The idea had repulsed me. Nothing about this was repulsive.

As 152 reached the halfway point on my wound, her bottom lip began to tremble. I didn't know why, but it made me suddenly feel cold. When a tear trickled down her cheek only to splash on her arm, I reached for her arm and stilled her hand with my wrist.

I wanted her to look at me. When she finally did, she whispered, "I do not like that you are this wounded." She lifted her hand to her chest. "It pains me in here that you are hurt." She blinked, her long dark lashes brushing her upper cheek. "That you are hurt because of me." She turned her head away. "I made you weak, after all. Your greatest fear realized."

I didn't know what to say. I didn't like to see her cry. My hand clenched and unclenched. I raised my hand, fighting against my instinct to stop, and placed it on her cheek. 152 froze under my touch.

I went to pull it away, feeling too much pain at the fact that she didn't want my hand on her skin. But as my arm dropped, she quickly lifted her hand and laid it over mine. She was keeping it in place.

I breathed, and she breathed in unison as we stayed still in the moment. When her eyes met mine, she said, "I was the cause of your fall. I am a whore and made you submit."

Clearing my throat, I rasped, "You're more than a whore. You're more than a *mona*." I shook my head. "We all are. All of us slaves."

"Slaves?" she questioned, her pretty face screwed up in confusion.

"The *monebi*, warriors, *chiri*. All of us are under Master's control."

She nodded at my words, but I could see she still didn't understand.

"We are alike," she said finally, and my heart melted when a small smile pulled on her lips. A smile. Something I had rarely seen given so freely.

"Yes," I whispered in response.

"His champion and his whore." This time her voice shook with sadness. "Not free."

Not free.

152 sighed, and with her eyes narrowed, she continued, "I . . . I think I would like to be free." Her hand slipped from her chest and lay over mine. My skin jumped at her touch. "Would you?" she questioned. "Would you wish to be free, too?"

I thought about what she had asked me. I had never wished for freedom before. I never believed I would get it. Never wanted it. "901?" she pushed. Something about her calling me by my number caused annoyance to spike in my blood. 152's hand drifted slightly to my tattoo, and she asked, "Would you?"

Using my free hand, this time I laid it over hers on my chest. Her full lips parted slightly and she sucked in a gasp. "What is your name?" I asked, and saw her cheeks pale.

"My name?" I watched her as she thought hard. When her shoulders slumped, I knew she had not found an answer. "I can't remember," she said quietly. "I don't know my name."

"Neither do I," I replied. "I know I'm Russian and I think I'm age around twenty-four."

She flicked up her head and said excitedly, "I'm twenty-one."

As I looked up at her slightly smiling mouth, the wall lamp on the far wall haloing her head, she looked perfect.

"Near my age."

Her cheeks burst with redness and she ducked her eyes. When she looked back up, her face had become serious once more. Her gaze wandered to take in my cuts, slashes, and bruises. "You saved me," she whispered. "You saved me from death."

My teeth ground together at the relief in her tone. "I couldn't do anything else. I saw you in that guard's hands." I paused to raise my head and run my fingertip over the faint knife mark on her throat. "I saw his knife and the mark it had created. I saw in Master's eyes that he would order your throat to be slit." I stilled, then on a sigh, admitted, "I couldn't let it happen." I tapped the spot over my heart again. "In here. It hurt too much in here."

152 didn't react to what I had said. She didn't move. For a minute I believed she had sincerely wanted me to let her die. Then she shifted her knees closer to mine and, leaning forward, pressed her lips to my forehead. My breathing came quick and fast.

Her unique scent drifted up my nose. Filling my lungs, I had to force my hands not to reach up and pull her closer to me. When 152 moved back, I instead ran my finger down her face and said, "You are beautiful."

Her eyes widened, as if she could not believe those words had come from my mouth. When my eyebrows dragged down in confusion, she revealed, "I didn't think you liked me. I didn't think I appealed to you."

I reared back in shock, my shoulders hitting the cold wall behind me. My hand fell to the floor. 152 shifted closer and implored me to answer with her blue stare.

Fighting against my instinct to push her away, I replied, "I want you. I . . . like you. Too much. I wish I did not."

A small gasp left her mouth. Reaching down, she picked up my hand in hers. I watched, rapt, as she brought it to her mouth and pressed three long kisses to my broken skin. I sucked in a sharp breath, waiting for what she would do next.

She lowered our joined hands until they had fallen to her knees. She said, "I want you, too. I like you, too. Very much."

With those spoken words, I knew something within me had broken. I could feel the wall around my heart crumble. And I also knew that there would be no more hiding, no more fooling myself that I could be unaffected by her.

My want for her was as real as any match I had ever fought. It was as dangerous, too. 140 was right. Master had me exactly where he wanted me. His plan had worked perfectly. It should have fueled my constant rage. Instead it filled me with light.

Her eyes fluttered to stare at me, and she said, "And I also think you are beautiful." The blush from her cheeks spread to her neck and down over her chest. "I am not sure if a female declares that to a male, but I think it nonetheless."

152 picked up the needle and thread from the floor. She tried to pull our joined hands apart, but I held on. She looked up at me, confused that I wasn't letting go. I wasn't sure. I just didn't want to.

Clearly seeing this in my expression, she smiled and said, "Let me tend to your wounds. You need to close the harmed flesh, then you need to bathe."

I reluctantly let go. 152 shifted to my side and cleaned my gashes with the warm, wet towel. She moved to every cut and sealed them shut, cleaning the blood from my skin.

When she was done, I walked to the shower to wash the remnants of the fight away. As the water hit my head, all I could think of was 152 caring for me, cleaning me . . . smiling at me.

I wanted to smile at her, too.

Turing off the shower, I dried myself off, then entered the sleeping room. When I searched for 152, I found her sitting back in the corner of the room, her knees tucked against her chest.

My heart fell. She was so small and delicate huddled on the floor. She watched me move to the bed. As I slumped down, I took a deep breath. Then I held out my hand. 152's eyes widened.

It was several seconds before she timidly got to her feet and made her way to where I sat. Her hand landed in mine, and she froze. I shifted back on the narrow mattress and guided her down. She lay beside me, still looking at me in surprise.

Finding myself suddenly racked with nerves, I said gruffly, "No more sleeping in the corner for you. If you're in this cell, then you're in my bed. You'll be sleeping right next to me."

Tears filled 152's eyes, but none fell. I waited for what she would say. But she simply squeezed my hand. My eyes were heavy, pulled under by sleep. When I woke later that night, 152 thrashing from the drugs, I rolled her onto her back and rid us of our clothes. As I pushed forward, wrapped in her heat, her eyes dilated with need, I wished that she wasn't under the influence of the drug.

For the first time in my life, I wished that she were beneath me of her own accord. Wanting me inside her, taking her as a male takes a female.

Making her mine.

No drugs.

No mind games.

Just her and me, lost to the feelings. Two slaves, for one night freed from their Master's chains.

10

152

"You're smiling."

I blinked, clearing myself from the trance I had become lost in. The steam from the heat of the water rose from my hot skin and bubbles surrounded every inch around me. When I looked to Maya, she was studying me.

Bringing my hand to my lips, I asked, "I am?"

She nodded suspiciously. "In fact, you've been different for the past few days." She stared off into space as though racking her brain. When she looked back to me again, she added, "Since 901's match."

Instinctively, I raised my hand to my throat. The knife mark was fading, but the skin was still broken, still sore to the touch.

Maya's face fell on seeing the mark. She had been worried about my throat since I had told her what they had made 901 do. I hadn't told her of how he held me close as we slept. Of how he told me that he liked me, how he wanted me. How he thought I was more than Master's whore. I didn't know why I had kept that to myself. But I didn't want to share it. It was sealed in my heart for only me to enjoy.

Maya's head tipped to the side as she brought the sponge along my arm. "Did something happen over the past few days, miss? With 901?"

"What makes you say that?"

Maya sat back on her haunches. "You are acting different. Less closed in. More at peace, if such a thing can be achieved here." She paused, then said, "You are like the champions' *monebi*. The ones weaned off their drugs. They smile like you. They own a peace the others can't gain. Just like you."

Over the past few nights, 901 had healed. He had been excused from fighting, from leaving his cell. But I was still delivered to him every night. It was later than usual and I was collected first thing in the morning. There wasn't much time for talking, but when I walked in the cell, he would immediately hold out his hand. I would take it as he guided me to his bed. We would fall asleep facing each other, until the drugs struck my veins and pulled me under. I would always wake later, flush against his chest.

Safe.

"Miss?" Maya pushed, and I cleared my head once again. She was watching me expectantly. Maya's shoulders sagged. "You like him." It wasn't a question. She knew it to be the truth.

Dropping my head to run the water through my fingers, I said, "I like him very much. More than I fear I should."

"Miss, you cannot pursue anything with 901."

My stomach fell at the urgency in her quiet but hurried tone. "Why?"

"Master," she whispered, then glanced back to the door. When she faced me again, the blood had drained from her face. "Master can't think you have feelings for 901, or 901 has them for you." I sat patiently, waiting for her to continue. "He has given you to 901 because 901 showed interest in you. I watch Master, miss. I watch his every move, to protect you." Her small hands gripped the edge of the tub. "He is obsessed, miss. I don't think you realize the extent." She looked down, then took a long breath. "I . . . I have followed him sometimes. To see where he goes at night when you are with 901."

"And where does he go?"

"To the champions' quarters, miss. He watches you being taken by 901." She looked away, a sad expression spreading on her face.

"What are you not telling me?" I questioned.

Maya slumped back. "He often goes to the *monebi* quarters afterward."

I stilled.

"He takes a *mona,* one with dark hair and preferably blue eyes." She stopped talking after that. I stood from the tub and wrapped myself in the towel. I sat down opposite Maya and took hold of her shaking hand.

"What, Maya? Tell me."

"He hurts them," she said almost inaudibly. "He punishes them as he takes them. Beats them, lashes them, all while calling your name."

Every muscle in my body drained of energy. "He does what?"

Maya suddenly leaned forward, gripping my hand tightly. "You can't like 901, miss. Master wouldn't tolerate it. The last High Mona—"

"What?" I pushed, jerking her hand. "What have you discovered?"

"I asked around, miss. I asked the other *chiri.* One of them confided in me that the High Mona, the one before you, the one Master never looked at like he does you, he had her killed. He hurt her for days and days before she died, because she had affection for a warrior, a warrior Master made her visit . . . just like you and 901." Maya's fingers shook. "She risked her life to visit him in secret. Her *chiri* helped her in leading the way. She was killed, too."

"No," I said in a hushed voice. My heart thudded too loud and too fast at the thought of the female before me. My heart squeezed in understanding. She had found a male she wanted to be with, one he forced her to be with, then killed her. It was too cruel.

"And the warrior?" I questioned. "What happened to the male?"

"The next night Master entered him in a championship match." Maya's dark eyes never moved from mine. A cold trickle dripped down my spine, a stark realization hitting home. "901," I whispered. "He fought 901. 901 killed him."

Maya nodded. "He wouldn't have known. To him he would have been just another opponent."

"But 901 is undefeated," I concluded. "Master knew he had sentenced him to die."

Maya nodded slowly. "Miss, you must keep your emotional distance from 901 until Master believes there is no threat. If he believes you have feelings for each other"—she shook her head, her face paling—"there is no telling what he would do. Master is unpredictable, and he is deadly. I fear that the way he feels toward you, the compete fascination, the obsession he has for you, will make him that much more cruel."

"I understand," I said. And I did. Maya checked the time and got to her feet. "Miss, I have to get you ready. You are to attend the second and final show fight with Master tonight."

As her words left her lips, my legs grew numb. Maya crouched down. "What, miss?"

"901 is fighting again tonight," I said, and watched Maya's expression reflect one of worry like mine. "I can't," I said, shaking my head. "I can't see him hurt like that again."

"You must," Maya said, and cupped my face, wiping away tears I didn't know had fallen. "You must act as though he means nothing to you."

The sound of guards approaching pulled my attention. I had just risen from the floor, guided by Maya, when the door to my room slammed open. Fear ran through my veins like ice, sluggish and slow, when Master walked through. He was impeccably dressed, not a hair out of place. But the hard glint to his eyes told me that tonight I was dealing with the Master that liked to cause pain. The Master that liked to be cruel. The one that liked to make you scream.

I froze when his eyes collided with mine. Master, cool and controlled as always, made his way to me. But I saw his cheek twitch with each step; it betrayed the anger simmering beneath.

Maya's hand tightened on my arm. Master stood before me. Like batting away a fly, he gripped her by her hair and threw her to the floor.

Maya fell with a thud. I instinctively called out and went to help her. But Master was there first, gripping my arm in a painful hold, spinning me around as he dragged me to the bed. My body was bared as he threw the towel to the floor. Without speaking, he pushed my chest down over the side of the bed. I cried out when his feet kicked my feet apart. I heard the zipper on his pants rip down. Then he was over me, slamming inside with all the cruelty I knew he harbored within.

My hands grasped at the bedsheets as his chest pressed flush to my bare back, keeping me in place. And he was relentless. He wasn't slow, didn't ease me into the taking. He took me hard and fast. He took me unprepared. The pain was great, but the hurt blazing in my chest was worse. He moved my head, shifting its direction on the mattress. I faced the room, my eyes colliding with Maya as she still lay hurt and afraid on the floor.

I squeezed my eyes shut, not wanting to see her witnesses this. As I did, I felt Master's breathing pant in harsh breaths over my cheek. He groaned as the speed of his thrusts increased. Then, leaning down farther, he placed his mouth at my ear and said, "You are mine, 152. *My* High Mona." Possession laced each of his words. His free hand reached down to grasp my hip. I bit back a scream as his fingers dug into my flesh, the hold bruising.

Master called out as his length twitched inside me. I prayed it was over, but Master fought back his release. His hips rolled, making sure I felt every stab of pain within. "You tended him," he hissed, my eyes snapping open in alert. "My guards watched you. They watched you kiss his forehead. They watched you wash him. They heard you speaking to him in Russian." Master gripped my head and forced me to arch my back. I held back from making a sound. He would like that. I didn't want to give him the satisfaction. "But worse, you slept beside that monster, in his bed. He fucked you in his bed then held you close." Master's mouth moved from my ear, and pulling my neck to the side, he bit into my shoulder. This time I had no choice but to scream out in pain. Just as I did, Master shouted out in pleasure.

He thrust into me four more times, then released me. My cheek fell to the bed, my body aching. Master pulled from my channel, moving to stand to the side. "Get her dressed," he ordered Maya. Maya pushed to her feet. Her hair was pulled from her neat bun. Doing as instructed, Maya came to where I lay and helped get me to my feet.

I winced as I walked. Master was still as night at the end of the bed. "You have fifteen minutes." Master's harsh command made me jump, then he added, "Don't clean away my release. Leave it there." Maya quickly ushered me into the side room and began fixing my hair and face. As I looked into the mirror, tears built in my eyes. The bite mark was bloodied and deep, my hair was in disarray. Worse was Master's seed running down my legs, the thing he had ordered Maya to leave.

Nausea clawed up my throat, but I held it back. Maya was silent as she readied me even quicker than Master had demanded. I stood as she draped me in a dark blue High Mona dress. The material was beautiful but sullied by the seed dripping down my thighs and the bite mark sitting garishly on my skin.

As Maya threaded long earrings in my ears, our eyes met and I saw the fear in their dark depths. And I understood what that look meant. He knew. He knew, or at least suspected, that I had feelings for 901.

As much as I feared the male waiting in the other room, as much as I knew he would hurt me in the most horrific ways if he knew just how much I cared for 901, I couldn't find the strength to care.

Maya stepped back and nodded her head. Taking that as my sign to exit the room, I did so, my head hanging low as Master liked.

"Ah," I heard him whisper aloud. "You look beautiful." My heart skipped a beat, but not in happiness. It was in complete confusion. Master's finger came under my chin and lifted my head until my eyes met his. He was smiling, but there was still residual anger in his stare. "So so beautiful," he murmured, and leaned forward to press a long, single kiss on my cheek.

I trembled. I had strived to not show my anger, but it couldn't be held back. "Shh," Master soothed as he drew back. His lips tightened, then he said, "You're a whore, it's what you were made for, what I made you be. It isn't your fault that you want that beast to mount you." He stepped closer and closer until her towered over me. "Or is it?" he questioned, his tone flat and threatening. "Do you want him to screw you, petal? You want him more than me?"

I was too scared to speak, so I didn't. That was the wrong decision. Master's hand gripped my upper arm and squeezed until I cried out. "Answer me," he hissed.

"No, Master," I replied quickly. "I don't want him." Master's grip loosened. When he looked at me, the widest, most genuine smile was on his lips. In a flash, his anger had vanished and I felt stunned. His ever-changing personality had softened to the male that looked at me like I was the most important female of all in the pit. Which I was, I realized. I was on his arm, not 901's.

That thought caused me more pain than I could bear.

Slipping my arm through his, he turned to the door. "Come. Our investors await us." It wasn't lost on me that he called them "our." I knew that in his mind I was again his property. But when we walked out the door and Master began leading me toward the fighters' tunnel, a sense of foreboding settled over me. It wasn't the way we usually walked to the pit and Master's seat; this hallway led to 901. It led us to the champions' quarters.

I stumbled as Master pulled me forward. I had unintentionally slowed down. I tried to keep my composure as we entered the champions' quarters, but my legs felt weak and I couldn't keep my hands from shaking.

Master did not speak. As we passed the other two champions' cell doors, they appeared, to see who had arrived. The champion 140, when he viewed Master, reddened in the face. His hands were gripping the bar with incredible strength. If looks could kill, Master would be drawing his last breath.

When we arrived at 901's cell, he was already waiting beyond the door, blades in hand, ready for battle. As it did every night, my heart skipped a beat when I saw him. He was wearing his black pants, his feet bare. His chest glistened in a sheen of sweat. I knew it was from the exercises he did to warm up his muscles for the fight. His blond hair was in a messy disarray, but his blue eyes were bright.

They immediately dulled when he saw me on Master's arm.

Master appeared cool and collected, but his arm linking with mine tensed to the point that he hurt me. My nostrils flared at the pain.

"901," Master said smugly, stepping closer to the cell door. I had noticed in the past few weeks that the guards kept a safe distance from 901 when he was at his cell door. Maya had told me how everyone feared him, how he had killed several guards just for killing's sake. But Master got so close that if he wanted, 901 could have hurt him very badly. Master didn't even seem threatened.

Master pushed me in front of him, my back at his chest. His hands lifted to grip my upper arms. His hold was unyielding.

When I looked up, 901's cheek twitched. It was the only sign that he was affected by our presence. Master stayed silent for a long second, until he drew back my hair, baring my shoulder. The shoulder he had bitten, the one that was already red, bruised, and swollen.

A low growl rumbled in 901's chest. He was staring at my new wound. I ducked my eyes in embarrassment. Master tensed at 901's reaction, then leaned down and ran his nose along the side of my neck. I squeezed my eyes shut in repulsion. I didn't want him to touch me. He hurt me. But more than that, I didn't want 901 to see Master with me this way. If I could help it, he would never know that Master had just taken me, brutally and raw. I wanted to keep 901 safe.

But that was shattered when, wordlessly, Master bent down and lifted my dress. With every revealed inch of my legs bared, I became more and more breathless. My chest ached when he bared my core for 901's viewing. Master's release was still on my thighs. He was showing 901 what he'd done.

The air in the champions' quarters thickened until I felt caged and hot. When I finally opened my eyes, unable to stand the tension crackling between us, it was too see 901 radiating with rage. His muscles were taut, protruding with veins. His teeth were gritted together. I could see he was about to explode.

I tried to capture his attention. I implored him to meet my eyes, but his gaze was transfixed on my thighs. It was only seconds later when 901 released a livid roar and charged the cell door that I shouted out as his shoulder slammed into the rigid metal bars. But

Master didn't move. He didn't even flinch. When I glanced back to see Master's face, it was lit with triumph. My heart stuttered in its beat. He wanted this. He was breaking his champion.

He had used me to achieve it.

I hated myself at this moment. But not as much as I hated Master.

901 reared back and hit the bars again. "No!" I called out. "Stop!" 901 immediately stilled, his chest rising and falling in rapid movements. He met my pleading eyes.

But Master's smile had fallen. In its place was the male that had taken me only a short while ago. Dread infused me. By my plea I had shown that I cared.

"Get off her," 901 snarled when Master moved to the side of me. My arms fell to my sides as I waited for what he would do. When Master reacted, I was unprepared. In a flash, Master balled his hand into a fist and rammed it into my stomach. White-hot pain splintered throughout my body. I leaned forward, gasping at this sudden loss of breath. I heard 901 shaking the metal bars, but I couldn't straighten to ask him to calm.

That was quickly resolved when Master took me by my hair and forced me to stand straight. I bit my lip to hold back my cry. Just as my eyes collided with 901's, Master's hand swung out and slapped me across my face. My cheek burned at the feel of his strong backhand. This time I did cry out. The injury on my cheek pulsed, but Master wasn't done.

Moving in front of me, his back to 901, he struck me again in my stomach with his fist, then again in my ribs. My legs gave way and I started to fall. Master's arms caught me before I hit the floor, and he wrapped me in his arms. "Shh, petal," he murmured, seeming to comfort me by stroking his hand gently through my hair. He acted as though he hadn't just been the deliverer of my pain.

Over his shoulder, I saw 901 lift his blades. I watched in horror as 901 went to strike Master's back. Sheer terror held me in its grip. 901 would die if he killed Master. As the blades readied to plunge through the metal bars, I pulled Master back and shouted, "No!"

Master moved with me, and I saw 901's blades stop at my demand. The tip of the Kindjal froze halfway through the bar. Master turned his head to view his champion.

Master lost his footing as he held me but quickly regained his ground. I lifted my head in disbelief. In this moment, seeing how close he had come to death, Master was shaken.

In this brief loss of composure, I saw how much *he* feared 901.

Master straightened and pulled me back. He took me in his arms and smiled so wide when he looked at me. "*Mona*," he whispered, "You saved me." The expression on his face, the glint in his eyes was something knew. Something unexpected.

It was gratitude. It was pure affection.

Then it was gone. Whipping around, Master faced 901. 901 had lowered his blades. He too wore an unreadable expression on his handsome face. "You dare to strike out against me?" 901 ignored him and stared over Master's head at me.

Master followed 901's gaze and let out a harsh, mocking laugh. "You are nothing, 901. My *mona* saved me." When he turned back around, Master stepped closer to the bars and said, "If you want to see her again, if you want to touch her again, you extend this match until I give you the signal." Master slipped his hands into his pockets and said, "In fact, if you don't comply, you'll never see her again."

I tried to capture 901's attention, to tell him that I wasn't saving Master, but I was saving him from certain death. But he wouldn't look my way.

Master walked to me. He stood in front of me, pride clear in his eyes. He cupped my cheeks with the most gentle of touches and said, "You know I didn't *want* to hurt you, but you *made* me. I had to test that you wanted me above all else. You proved to me that you do, petal. That you're all mine."

I whimpered as Master's lips came down on mine. Master groaned in response. But he had mistaken my meaning. I kept my eyes open and stared at 901 to show him I was his. His eyes met mine as Master kept my head locked in place. My vision blurred with the tears building in my eyes, but I knew that 901 could see my discomfort. As Master's back was turned, I discreetly held out my hand in 901's direction. I blinked to clear my vision and watched his face lose color.

His light eyebrows pulled down as he edged closer to the bars. I stretched out my hand an inch farther and saw the moment 901 realized what I wanted, what I was trying to say.

I was saving him.

All his anger fell away; slowly and nervously, 901 held his blades in one hand. He reached his free hand through the bars and wrapped his fingers in mine. As Master's kiss grew harder and deeper, I squeezed 901's fingers tighter, never once breaking from our locked stare.

901's raw and open expression was almost my undoing. It was as if the final barriers surrounding his heart had fallen away; he was letting me in. He was opening himself up to me. He was opening his heart.

Feeling Master beginning to pull away, I reluctantly broke 901's hold. I panicked as he left his hand outstretched, unwilling to let go of me. The cutting look of pain and insecurity was fading. As Master's mouth moved from mine, 901 drew his arm back into the cell and replaced my hand with his blade.

Refocusing on Master, I paled seeing my blood from a cut lip on his mouth. Clearly feeling the warm drop of liquid, Master licked it with his tongue, excitement showing on his face as he tasted it.

Pressing his forehead to mine, he lifted his thumb and wiped away the remnants of my blood. I flinched at the pain it brought, trying my best to ignore the ache in my stomach and the tenderness of my ribs. My cheek pulsed in the wake of Master's strike, but I held myself together. I didn't want 901 to be punished because he liked me.

"Come," Master said, taking my arm and linking it through his. He led me away from 901's cell without another word.

Master walked us to the stand and up onto his seat. The stands were packed, and several males came up to talk to Master. A male with an unusual accent came up to Master and shook his hand. I didn't listen to what they said as I tried to breathe through the pain from Master's strikes. But I heard that 901's opponent belonged to this male. He owned a gulag somewhere named Prague. 901's opponent was also undefeated.

Nerves racked my body on hearing that fact. Fear and trepidation were wrapping me in their embrace. I knew that Master was not going to make this match easy for 901. He wanted to assert his dominance. He wanted his champion to obey.

Master moved to his seat and pointed to the floor at his feet. I sat down, lowering my eyes from the looks I was receiving from the male spectators. Master rested his hand on my head and lazily combed through my hair. A guard moved into the pit and Master signaled for the match to begin.

I heard the pounding of feet carrying through the tunnel. When a male broke through, my heart fell. This male was bigger than 901. He was covered in black tattoos and was dark skinned. As he ran around the pit, two daggers in his hands, I balked when I saw his back. Lash scars marred every inch of skin. The warrior drew to a halt. When he looked to his master in the stands, there was nothing in his stare. It was blank, devoid of life.

Like he had nothing left to live for.

Master signaled again to the guard. When the guard disappeared, it was only seconds before 901 came running out. My heart beat in a heady rhythm as his perfectly toned body entered the pit. His blades were drawn, and for a moment I feared he would slay 175, his opponent, in seconds. But as 175 ran at 901, he ducked left but left himself open to be struck. I winced as 175 sliced the edge of his dagger across 901's chest. Master's hand had stilled on my hair as 901 entered the pit, but seeing him complying with his demands, Master relaxed. I could do no such thing.

901 toyed with his opponent, circling the pit. His opponent didn't move as quickly, nor was he as agile. But just as Master commanded, 901 took blows from 175. He gave serious, but not lethal, blows back.

With every slice and every cut gained, I waited with bated breath for Master to give 901 the signal to kill. But the minutes dragged on and Master remained relaxed in his seat.

175 suddenly charged 901, obviously tired of the charade. His hard expression showed his want and need to kill. But as 175 struck out with his dagger, stabbing through 901's thigh, 901's eyes drifted to Master in the stands. I froze, along with 901, waiting for Master's order. None came. Just before he looked away, 901 met my eyes. My heart broke when I saw this tender stare.

More minutes passed, both fighters dripping blood. I had to distance myself mentally from the excited roar of the crowd. Just when I feared Master was going to allow 901 to die waiting for his sign, he sat forward in his seat. I looked to the pit just in time to see 901 catch Master's flick of the wrist. 901's entire demeanor changed in an instant. He slid to the sandy floor, slicing the back of 175's thighs. 175 dropped to the sand, his ability to stand stripped away. 901 stood to tower over him and finished 175 with one final stab into his throat, 901's blades running him through.

Blood ran freely from the wound as 175 drained of life. 901 panted heavily on the spot, glaring down at his kill. The crowd jumped to their feet in celebration, but their cries were muted to my ears. I watched as 901 took hold of his Kindjals' handles and wrenched them from 175's throat. 901 then wiped his blades clean on 175's lifeless torso.

901 turned to stare up at Master. He had a bloodthirsty look in his eyes as he stared the older male down. His legs and arms twitched. For a spilt second, I felt he was about to fight his way up the stands to end Master's reign. Fortunately, 901 planted his feet into the sand and waited to be dismissed. He was covered head to toe in blood, a mixture of 175's and his own. His blue eyes were wild, and he looked every inch the killer his reputation boasted.

Eventually, Master stood and flicked his wrist in dismissal. 901 turned to run down the tunnel, but not before glancing back and staring at me with desperate eyes. He was silently telling me that he had done this for me. He had taken this beating, endured these injuries, for me.

My heart almost leapt from my body. The feelings rushing through me, knowing he had done this for me, were filling me with the brightest of lights.

Master stood and congregated with some of the crowd. A few minutes later a guard came to me and ordered me to stand. I winced as I did. My pulse raced when I was led in the direction of the champions' quarters. With each step I gasped for breath at the bruising on my stomach, cheek, and ribs. But that pain was overridden the closer I came to 901's cell.

As we made our way through the narrow hallways, I wondered why Master was doing this. I believed I wouldn't be given back to 901, no matter the outcome of the match. But from the minute the match ended, Master had ignored me just like he did when I was first given to 901. Like he had to distance himself from what he was about to let happen.

I racked my brain for answers, but when I arrived at 901's cell, those questions fled my mind. Right then, I didn't care about the consequences. I was here with 901. He had fought for me. Obeyed for me.

I wanted this with all my heart.

When the guard opened the door, a *chiri* was just finishing sewing up 901's wounds. The blood that had been covering his skin was now covering the towels on the floor.

901 looked up at me in the doorway. Just as the *chiri* made the final stitch to the wound on his chest, 901 knocked her hand away and got to his feet. His large body swayed and his face screwed up in pain. Then his eyes fell on mine and never moved.

The *chiri* gathered her things and quickly fled the room. The guard slammed the door shut behind her. We simply continued to stare. The ragged wounds from days ago and today had ravaged his muscled body. His hair was slick with the remnants of the bloody fight and sweat. He looked beaten and torn.

901 suddenly stepped forward. My heart leapt into my throat as he approached. With a gentleness I wasn't expecting, 901 lifted his hand and ran his finger softly beside the sprouting bruise on my cheek and the broken cut on my bottom lip. "You are hurt," he whispered, a deep pain to his rough voice.

And he spoke to me in Russian. He spoke in our language.

Reaching out, I placed my hand on his shoulder, the only nontainted area on his body. "So are you," I whispered in response.

He swallowed, and a swooping feeling looped in my stomach. Standing here with him now felt different. Something had shifted between us. It was indescribable. It was raw, but it made me feel alive.

Something 901 thought had immediately changed his mood. His head fell forward and his shoulders slumped in defeat. "Master took you," he said plainly. I tensed.

His fingertip ran down to the bite mark on my shoulder, and I winced at the tenderness of my skin. 901's jaw clenched and he bit out savagely, "One day I'll fucking slaughter him. And I'll make him pay for everything he's ever done."

"Shh," I soothed, moving even closer. 901's body was like an open flame, radiating a searing heat.

His skin twitched when I got to my tiptoes and placed my hands on his face. His blue eyes were wide, solely focused on me. I smiled as I felt his rough stubble under my fingers. My smile faded seeing a large cut to his face. 901 raised his hands to wrap around my wrists.

"What?" he questioned hoarsely.

"You keep hurting yourself to save me."

His eyes dropped to look at the ground. When he looked back up, he said, "This time you were hurt trying to save me, too."

I fought back the lump in my throat and said, "I couldn't . . . I couldn't bear . . . I didn't want Master to kill you. I want you to live."

901's forehead fell forward to press against mine. I didn't care that he was covered in blood. All that mattered was that he was alive, breathing and before me. Wanting me as much as I did him.

We stayed that way for minutes. Eventually, I slid my hand in his and guided him toward the washing area of his cell. A shower was fixed to the far wall. Releasing his hand, I walked over and turned the handle. I backed away to where 901 stood. Reaching up to the clips that kept some of my hair off my face, I released them, letting my long hair fall forward. 901 watched me the entire time with a focused intensity to his eyes.

Next, I moved my hands to the clasp at my shoulder, the one that held up my dress. When the clasp released, my dress pooled on the floor, leaving me completely bared to his eyes.

901's nostrils flared as his gaze dropped to my breasts. Then a harsh gasp tore from his lips and he snarled, anger contorting his face. When I glanced down to see what had him so mad, I saw large bruises forming on my stomach and ribs. I briefly closed my eyes, then forced any bad thoughts away.

901 looked down to my face when I stepped closer to him. Silently, I raised my hands until they lay on the waistband of his pants, and slowly pulled them down.

901 hissed, his muscles taut as I dragged the fabric over his hips and down over his legs. I swallowed back my nerves as 901 stepped away from the gathered material at his feet. Feeling the heat of warm water from the shower billowing around the room, I reached down and took his hand in mine.

901 stared at our joined hands. Leading him forward, I guided him under the spray. 901 followed me without complaint. Second by second, the blood fell from his skin. I watched as he shut his eyes and tipped his head back under the stream.

He was so beautiful. When I was close to him, his incredible height and width made me feel so safe. I hadn't experienced that before. At least, I didn't think I had. And I definitely hadn't experienced that since I had awoken as Master's High Mona.

Shaking those thoughts away, I smiled as 901's head fell forward. He sighed as the remnants of the match washed away.

Seeing a bar of soap on the ledge beside the shower, I picked it up and stepped under the spray. Sensing me close in, 901 opened his eyes. He never once looked away. Lifting the soap to his chest, I ran it over his identity tattoo, tracing each number slowly and with care.

901's skin bumped even though the water was warm. Smiling, I looked up to his eyes and my heart skipped a beat at the look upon his face. 901 lifted a hand and stopped my hand on his chest, then he lifted his fingers to my mouth.

I didn't dare move as his fingertips grazed over my lips. With water sluicing down his face, he said, "You smile at me. No one ever smiles at me."

I took his hand on my lips and brought it to lie over my heart. "You make me want to smile."

"Why?" At his question, his eyes searched mine deeply for the answer.

"Why do you make me smile?" I clarified. He nodded. I almost cried at the look of desperation on his face. For why he needed the answer. Stepping as close as I possibly could, I said, "Because you never hurt me. When I was forced into your cell. Even when you tried to keep me away, you still kept me close. You took me when I needed you, and you speak to me. Speak to *me,* like I am not a whore."

"You are more," he told me roughly. "My more. 152, my more."

Tears filled my eyes and I said, "I wish I knew your name."

901's shoulders sagged. "I wish I knew yours."

I smiled again, unable to do anything else with the sudden lightness that had filled my soul. Moving the soap along his chest and down to his stomach, I said, "Let me clean you. Let me erase today."

"Only if I then do it to you," he said. A flash of pain crossed over his face. His attention dropped to my thighs, and I saw anger stealing the brief happiness that we had found.

"No," I said, and he shook his head. "Don't think of it."

"He took you," he said. "I can't stand that he took you. And hurt you . . . and has you whenever he wants." His breathing increased in speed, and I saw his neck tense the more he thought of our reality.

"Stop," I urged. He inhaled deep and long. Leaning forward, I pressed my lips against his chest, right over his tattoo.

901 sucked in a quick breath at my touch. Stepping back, I made sure he met my eyes. "When it is me and you alone, there is no Master. When we are here, in your cell, there is no Blood Pit." A smile tugged on my lips. "There are no matches to the death. There

are no quarters where I am held captive all day. There is your heart beating in sync with mine. Speaking the language of our old home, in the company of the male that is becoming my *new* home."

"*Moy prekrasnyy,*" he whispered, and I closed my eyes as the words attached to my soul. *My beautiful,* he had called me. *My beautiful . . .*

His.

Inhaling deeply, I murmured, "*Moy voin,*" in return.

My warrior.

Any residual anger fell from 901's face, and I began moving the soap over his skin. He was silent and unmoving as I cleansed him of his fight. But his eyes never left mine. When I had finished, he took the soap from my hands and brushed the wet hair from my face.

"*Krasivaya devushka,*" he said softly as he ran the soap gently over my arms. I closed my eyes, enjoying his touch. He moved around me, savoring the moment. He stopped only when he reached my thighs. I opened my eyes to see him on his knees, reaching out to run his finger where Master had made me wear his seed.

I placed my palm on the side of his face and guided him to look at my face. "He isn't here with us," I reminded. 901 nodded. He remained on his knees, and I wondered what he was about to do. My heart swelled when he moved his head forward and tentatively pressed a kiss on my hip. When he pulled back, he pressed his hand to his mouth.

Then I understood. I thought of his hand holding mine as Master kissed me in front of 901's cell. And I remembered his face as he watched Master's mouth attached to mine, taking what wasn't freely given. There was devastation in his stare, the usual glare of anger in his eyes . . . but there had been something else there too, something I hadn't recognized—envy, curiosity . . . *want.*

"You've never been kissed before," I realized. I already knew why. 901's head fell forward in embarrassment. I made sure he lifted his head once again with my hand below his chin.

I saw something new in 901's eyes as he looked up at me from his knees: shyness.

It was by far the most beautiful he had ever looked to me.

Stepping back, I held out my hand. 901 got to his feet. He hesitated as he looked at my hand. I stayed strong and never pulled it back. Finally, after several long seconds, he slid his hand in mine. Reaching behind him, I turned the handle on the shower and switched off the water.

I led him to a small pile of worn, faded towels. Releasing his hand, I picked up two. Handing him one, 901 quickly dried off the water. I did the same. I ran it over my wet hair, separating the thick strands with my fingers. When I dropped the towel, so did 901.

I took his hand again and led him to the bed. I sat down first, 901 following quickly after. Our hands remained clasped on the mattress between us, until I lay down. 901 did the same. I faced him.

Now that he was clean, the stitches keeping his wounds together were more prominent on his skin. A stab pierced my stomach as I looked at the large one across his chest and the new slash across his face. For some reason the scarred male from my dreams flashed across my mind. I always thought that I was imagining him. But something about how 901 was watching me, was here for me, open and raw, made me confide, "I see a male in my head sometimes." My eyebrows pulled down as I tried to hold on to the image of his face. "I don't know who he is, but I think he is from my past." I covered my heart with my hand and said, "In here, I feel he was someone special to me. But I don't . . . I can't remember who he is."

Swallowing, I asked, "Do you ever have memories like that? You are a champion, have been for a long time. Maya tells me that with the lesser dose of drugs we get, my memories will start returning, but they haven't yet."

"Maya?" 901 questioned.

I realized my mistake, but trusted 901 enough to reveal, "My *chiri*. Her name is Maya."

His eyes widened. "You talk to her, you use her name?"

I nodded my head. "She is more than just a number." I breathed deep and said, "The male from my dreams told me that I am more than just a number."

"We are," 901 said, and I heard the hard edge to his statement. "We are," he said again. "I had never thought about anything until recently. You are right, I have not been on the heavy drugs for years, but I never changed from what I was." He took a fallen strand of my hair between his fingers. "I never thought about anything but winning in the pit. And the male that would one day finally kill me. The one that would take the championship from me and free me from this hell. From being under Master's control."

"And now?"

"Now," he began, and then paused. He stayed quiet, then a red blush coated his cheeks. "Now I think about a lot of things. Why are we here? How I now want to be free." He sighed and brought my hair to his nose. He inhaled, dropped it, then added, "And you. I think about you. I didn't want to. But I do, and now I don't fight it."

"Why?" I whispered.

This time, he placed his hand over his heart and said, "You have made me feel, in here. You have made me want things I never dare let myself want. You have made me want to fight for survival, not pride. I no longer want to die on the pit's sand, like a warrior. I no longer want to die at all." I held my breath, exhaling only when he said, "You make me want to live."

I shifted closer, and closer still, until my face hovered only a fraction from his. 901's eyes immediately focused on my lips. *"Krasivaya?"* he questioned, using the word "beautiful" instead of my number.

I smoothed the damp hair from his head. "You have never been kissed. And while I have been kissed many times, probably by many different men, I have never given a kiss freely. Although I remember none but those Master stole from my mouth." 901 rolled onto his back. His skin was still slightly damp from the shower. "It may seem like I am different from you in that regard, but I am not."

"I know," 901 agreed, and waited for what I would do next.

My heart raced as I licked my lips, and then without giving myself a chance to overthink what I was about to do, I lowered my mouth until my lips pressed against his.

901 tensed beneath me. I froze, thinking I had pushed too far, but when his hand slid into my hair and he pulled me even closer, I knew this was what he wanted, too. Our lips were slow moving and shy, but as the seconds passed, 901 deepened the kiss. And it was unlike anything I had felt before. Where Master was hard and cruel, 901 was gentle and caring. He was a contradiction: soft and kind, but possessive and certainly took what he wanted.

I moaned against his lips, and when we broke away, we were both breathing hard. I didn't say anything; neither did 901.

Glancing down, I saw my hand had splayed upon his chest. His skin was warm. I could see that he had hardened at my touch. Compelled to explore, of my own free will, I let my hand drift down his abdomen and felt his scarred skin. 901 hissed as my hand moved toward his hard length. His hand suddenly covered mine, and my eyes snapped to meet his.

"Don't," he said quietly. He looked away. I leaned over him until his face turned toward mine. Before I could ask what was wrong, he said, "The drugs make you need my release. Master takes you when he wants." He shook his head. "I don't want you to do this if you don't want to. You have no duty to serve me." Releasing his hand from mine, he placed it at the side of my neck. I closed my eyes at the comforting feeling, then opened them when he said,

"You are more than what you are forced to do. You are more than a *mona*. You are free from the drugs right now, able to choose. Us, just like this . . . is enough."

A lump clogged my throat. When I chased it back down, I pressed a kiss to his cheek and said, "I have never lain with a male of my own free will. I have never had that choice available to me." I sighed, the weight of those words truly settling in my heart. Rearing back just a fraction, I added, "But I am choosing to be with you. I am choosing you as my first. Despite the other males I was forced to be with. Despite Master. You will be the first in my heart. The only one I have given myself to freely . . . with no drug forcing my hand."

The emotion staring back at me from 901's eyes undid me. I lowered my mouth and took his in a soft kiss. I let my hand retrace its steps, until 901 broke away. Pushing my hair from my face, he confessed, "You are already the first that I chose."

I blinked as the realization of what he was saying sank in. "I was your first . . . ever?" I questioned in disbelief. This male was formidable. Maya had told me that the champions were gifted with *monebi*. 901 had been a champion for a very long time.

"You are the champion. Master must have gifted you *monebi* often."

He looked away. "Yes, but I never took them. I had the guard take them away."

A sudden rush of disappointment and guilt panged in my stomach. I shifted back, gaining some space. 901 stopped me by wrapping a large, muscled arm around my waist. "What?" he pushed, concern written on his face. "Do you not think me a worthy male, knowing you were my first?"

I shook my head, emotion welling in my chest. "No, that's not it," I whispered.

901 searched my face. "Then what?"

"That night," I divulged, thinking back to being thrown in this cell. "You didn't want me. You called for the guard to take me away, but Master had ordered that I stay. When the drugs flooded my veins, the other champions told you to take me . . ." I shut my eyes in humiliation. When I opened them again, I hushed out, "You were forced to take me. I took your choice away."

A tear slipped down my cheek, but then 901 was above me, his hands jailing mine at my sides. "Stop," he snapped, and I saw the famed Pit Bull shining through. I relaxed, knowing he wouldn't hurt me. 901 lowered his head and said, "From the first time I saw you on Master's arm, I wanted you. I have never looked at a female the way I looked at you. And I have never wanted a female like I want you."

"But the drugs made you react to me. You had no choice."

"I had a choice," he argued. Then, with a surprising tenderness, he pressed three light kisses along my neck. When he raised his head, he said, "I chose to take you. I chose to hold you close." He inhaled. "I chose to make you mine."

My skin broke out in shivers at his words. 901 released my hands, and I wrapped them around his neck. His hard chest brushed against my own, and I said, "I wish I knew your name. I want so much to know the name of the male who has brought me home to his heart."

"*Krasivaya,*" he murmured, his voice thick with need. 901 crushed his mouth to mine. Unlike the previous kisses, there was nothing possessive about this. 901's lips covered mine with a gentle yet consuming intensity. I moaned in surprise when I felt his tongue pushing into my mouth. I tensed at first, unsure what to do, but when my tongue brushed against his, it troubled me no more.

901's heavy body smothered mine, and my hands slipped from his neck and down along the breadth of his back. 901 groaned low, the sound traveling straight to my core. I gasped at the feel of him above me, needing this as much as I did. 901 moved his head back, and staring in my eyes, he slipped his hand down between us, his fingers reaching between my legs.

I cried out, holding on to his shoulders when his fingers drifted along my core. My back arched and my skin scalded with heat. But this time there were no drugs causing me to need this moment. This was me and this was him. This was us choosing this act for ourselves, taking this pleasure because we wanted each other freely. In a world of iron cages and bars, we were taking something of our own.

901's warm breath ghosted across my face. He was breathing hard, not so different from me. I cried out when a teasing burst of pleasure arrived due to his gentle touch. 901 stilled and looked down at me. I could see the concern on his face. "Is this okay?" he asked, his hardness pressing against my thigh.

"Yes," I replied breathlessly. "More. Touch me some more." I felt my face heat at my brazen words, but when 901 growled low and began moving his fingers again, I was lost to his touch.

901 teased and he played, and when his finger slowly entered my channel, I broke apart on a loud shout, blistering light and pure pleasure splintering me apart.

901 pulled his hand away, and just as he did, I opened my eyes. His handsome face was stern and anxious as he watched for my reaction. When I eventually smiled, he exhaled a relieved breath and covered my body again. Showing him what I wanted, what I was *choosing,* I wrapped my legs around his hips and reached down to take his length in my hand. He hissed out in pleasure and gritted his teeth as my fingers wrapped around him. As I guided him to my channel, he paused to drop the sweetest soft kiss on my forehead, before pushing forward and filling me to the hilt.

901's head snapped back and a low groan slipped from his tensed lips. My eyes rolled back as he sat within me so perfectly. Before moving again, 901 hooked his thick arms under my shoulders and slowly began to rock. With every movement, I felt the darkness in my soul lift, and with every kiss on my face from his soft mouth, my heart beat louder and louder.

"*Moy prekrasnyy,*" he whispered as his breathing increased in speed.

"*Moy voin,*" I whispered back. We didn't have names. Our numbers weren't welcome in this moment. Right now I was his beautiful, and he was my brave warrior.

901's thrusts grew faster and faster as the minutes passed by. I moaned loud when tingles spread on my thighs. 901's length twitched within me, and I knew we were both getting close.

901's arms kept me close to his chest, and just before my body filled with the brightest of light, he brought his mouth to take mine, swallowing my cries.

My body arched as 901 roared out his release. His head drew back as his neck corded from the strain. His wounded body was flushed and damp. It was perfect, this moment was perfect, as was he.

The billowed warm air from the shower's heat was sticking to our skin. It bumped when a cold draft from the cell door circled around us. 901's head fell onto my shoulder. I stroked at his back, feeling a strange lightness in my heart.

Just as I tried to think what this sensation was, 901 lifted his head. "I feel different." He pulled his arm from under mine. He placed his hand over his chest and said, "In my heart. It feels different. Changed."

My stomach flipped knowing he was feeling this, too. Taking in a much-needed breath, I asked, "Does it feel light, like at any moment it might combust?" 901 nodded his head, his understanding expression telling me I had described it completely correct.

"What is it?" he asked, lines of confusion creasing on his forehead.

Following what my heart was telling me to say, I replied, "I think it means we have found a peace within each other's arms. I think it means . . ." I trailed off, unsure if it was the right word to use.

"What?" he pushed. "Tell me."

Combing my hand through his hair, just so I could touch him once more, I nervously said, "Happy?" I lost my breath when 901 stilled. Finding the last of my courage, I added, "I think it means we are . . . *happy*."

901 froze, then with watery eyes, he repeated. "Happy. Together, we make happiness."

I smiled. I smiled freely and uncaged. And when 901 moved beside me and wrapped me in his strong arms, I fell asleep with my hand over his chest, with the heady feeling of this newfound happiness in my heart.

11

LUKA

Undisclosed Location

Georgia

Eastern Europe

My leg bounced as the plane began its descent. Viktor was at the front of the plane getting the documents in order. Abel, his contact, had come through for him. Zaal and Valentine sat opposite me. Zaal was the picture of calm as he sat stoically in his seat. Valentin was the complete opposite. His eyes were wild and his body twitched like he was still on the drugs they'd pumped into our bodies for so many years.

Over the past few weeks, Valentin had thrown himself into the practice of death-match fighting. His focus was solely on using his rage to his advantage. As he had promised, his skill with the unpowered picanas was astounding. His strength and ability to kill with efficiency were no less than Zaal's and mine. But the best part of Valentin's arsenal was his unwavering belief and drive to get his sister back. That desire would override any lack of training he might have in combat. As an *Ubiytsa*, his ability to kill was unrivaled. He would be fine.

Seeing the land of Georgia coming into view from Kirill's private plane, I leaned forward, Valentin and Zaal meeting my eyes. Placing my hand on the table between us, I asked, "You're sure you're clear with the plan?"

Zaal nodded, and Valentin spat out, "Yes."

Needing to make sure, I said, "Viktor is the manager of a New York gulag. Not the Volkovs. Abel has already approved us without question, so to Master we are simply another underground fight ring. Nothing of importance." Zaal and Valentin listened hard. "I am the ultimate champion, retrieved from escape." A rush of sadness spread in my chest. I was using what had happened to Anri in my story. It was plausible. Clearing my throat, I pointed at Zaal. "You were bought from the Volkov Russians. You were too feral and untamed. Viktor bought you to fight in his gulag."

Zaal nodded.

I next pointed to Valentin. "After your collar malfunctioned, you killed Mistress and her Wraiths. You have no memory of this. One of the Wraiths survived and knew of Viktor's gulag. He sold you and fled the U.S."

Valentin's lip curled in disgust, but he nodded. Keeping his attention, I said, "We've talked this through a thousand times, but if and when you see your sister, you mustn't react. Hold yourself together until the opportunity to strike arrives. If she is still alive after all this time, she will survive for a further few days."

"Then the Master is mine," he growled, and I nodded in agreement.

"Then he is yours. But for that to happen, you must stick to the plan. If one of us fucks up and reveals who we truly are, they will kill us on the spot."

A sudden flash of fear passed over Valentin's face. "I can't leave my Zoya," he said, an almost gentle edge to his harsh-sounding voice. It was strange hearing such sentiment from such a brutal male.

Zaal lifted his hand and put it on Valentin's shoulder. A peace had settled between them over the past few weeks. Zaal had seen himself as Valentin trained in the cage. He was fighting for his sister's return, just as Zaal had fought so hard for his. "We won't fuck up. We will destroy this place, then return home to our females."

Valentin's wide shoulders relaxed. Kisa's tearful face entered my head. Her good-bye to me this morning. Zaal, Talia, Valentin, and Zoya had arrived at my father's house to leave for the airfield. From the night I told Kisa what I was to do, she had said nothing in response. She knew I had to do this. It didn't mean I couldn't see the terror and concern every time she looked at me over the past few weeks.

She held my hand longer, she kissed me softer, and she made love to me every chance she got. I glanced down at my hand, and I could still feel her kiss on my palm as I said good-bye to her this morning. Talia and Zoya had proved themselves to be just as strong as my wife. They had supported their males. If this all went according to plan, after this battle there would be no more war to fight.

Blinking away the memory and emotion on Kisa's face, I looked to my brothers and said, "We will win. There is no other choice."

"And the fourth warrior in the champion round?" Zaal questioned.

"He gets on board or we take him out first. Whatever we have to do." My hands clenched into fists on the table, and the old surge of adrenaline flooded my veins. "We will kill many. That includes fighters that are too far gone or any that stand in our way. We do not give second chances, we do not hesitate to strike those that try to stop us. We kill quickly. We kill without mercy."

Zaal and Valentin nodded.

I sat back in my seat as the plane descended. "How far is the pit from the airfield?" I asked Valentin.

"No more than twenty minutes," Valentin replied. "The airfield is Arziani's. Wraiths will guide our van to the loading door."

Nodding, I reached for the hem of my sweater and pulled it over my head. When my bare torso was on display, I retrieved my worn but trusted knuckle-dusters from my bag. I stared at the metal, felt the bladed tips with my finger to make sure they were sharp. When a bud of blood formed on my finger, I felt the excitement of being back in this place spark inside me. The old Raze stirring inside, waking from the sleep I had kept him in for months.

With a deep breath, I slipped the knuckle-dusters in place. I bent my fingers, feeling the weight of them once again in my hands.

When I looked up, I saw Zaal had followed my lead. He looked every inch a gulag fighter, bare chested and wearing only the standard black pants. And in his hands were his black sais. From this vantage point, as Zaal's eyes remained cast down to stare at his weapons, I felt like I was here with Anri once again.

I fought a smirk at how my best friend would have relished in this moment. He would have stormed into this fight like a hurricane of rage, taking Master and his Wraiths out with a smile on his face. When Zaal looked up at me, he asked, "You think of my brother?"

My chest tightened, but I replied truthfully, "Yes."

Zaal nodded sadly. I knew it still bothered him that his memories were almost gone of his twin. Only fragments of their childhood remained. "This is the moment he wished for," I said, thinking of our parting in Alaska. "He was coming back to find you and destroy this place. He didn't quite remember, but he knew his heart was being called here."

Zaal's green eyes brightened.

"I was just thinking of how he would have rejoiced in this moment. Finally getting to meet the male that created this hell. Getting to return to the slave factory where you were experimented on like rats." I huffed a laugh. "He would have burned it to the ground with a laugh bursting from his chest."

Zaal didn't say anything in response.

"And we will. In his memory, we will do as he would." My eyes darted to Valentin, who was sitting bare chested with his sharp picanas in his hand. Zaal looked to his new brother. Valentin looked to him. "Every move we make in this pit will be in Anri's honor. We will attack and survive as he would . . . then we will burn it to the ground, just as he would."

Several long seconds passed before Zaal nodded. "Yes," he agreed in a husky voice. "We will do this for Anri."

Zaal's eyes drifted to look out the window as the ground approached. When Valentin looked to me, I nodded my head in thanks. Hope sprouted in my heart at Valentin's unexpected words. He was sitting stoic, like I had told him to be. His moods were unpredictable and his rage uncontained. But here, seated before me, was a male that met the story Viktor would tell. A savage male captured and made into a brutal killer.

I knew the male underneath, the one seething with rage. The one willing to risk anything for his sister.

The plane bumped as we landed. Viktor looked back from his seat at the front. Four of Zaal's males had been brought along. They would play the part of Viktor's Georgian gulag's guards.

When the plane drew to a stop, several cars and vans stopped beside us. Wraiths.

Valentin growled low in his throat when males dressed all in black left the cars. Flicking my wrist, I gestured for Zaal and Valentin to take their places. Three of Zaal's males came toward us and attached rope around our necks. My muscles tensed at being back in this position. The male that was holding my rope sent me an apologetic look. It helped calm the flames sparking in my chest.

When I glanced to Zaal, he was calm and quiet. Valentin, at

having something back around his neck, wasn't faring so well. But he held it together.

The sound of the plane door opening cut through the cabin, and my heart slammed against my chest. Viktor disappeared down the steps. We were all quiet in the plane as we listened to Viktor discussing his "cargo" with the Wraiths. Ten minutes later, Viktor shouted for us to disembark.

Zaal's *byki* led us forward by our rope collars. I went first, Zaal following behind. Valentin was at the rear.

The night was black. As I was led down the steps, I glanced up through a fallen strand of hair and saw miles and miles of what appeared to be barren wasteland. The perfect disguise, I thought, knowing that beneath the ground was a slave city.

The Wraiths were gathered in a perfect formation. Their guns were loaded and aimed at us, just in case we charged. They stared at me as I stopped to stand next to Viktor. A few of them murmured in quiet whispers when Zaal stopped, too. But their reaction to Valentin trudging down the steps was clear to anyone with eyes. The guards tensed and stared at the monstrous scarred male as he descended to the tarmac.

The Wraith in charge stared at Valenin in shock. Moving closer to Viktor, he said, "So you weren't lying, you truly have 194 in your gulag."

Viktor nodded. A fake prideful smile on his face. He too was acting the part of the perfect gulag owner. "We do. And he is one of the best fighters I have ever seen. He will give your champions a challenge like no other." He pointed to us all when Valentin came to stand by our sides. "They all will."

I could see by the Wraith's expression that he believed Viktor. I could also see that he was impressed by us. Relief settled in my bones. If the Wraiths thought us strong and viable males, in comparison to their own, then we had a chance for our plan to work.

The head Wraith pointed to the van. "Load them in there," he said to our *byki*. Zaal's males did as ordered and placed us in the back of the van. We were all silent as we were plunged into darkness. I knew it was Valentin who sat beside me. The male's body was pulsing with aggression.

"Calm," I whispered in Russian.

"Wraiths," he snarled low and almost unheard.

"Calm," I repeated just as the van began to move. Valentin took long, deep breaths.

The tension thickened the farther we drove. Until we came to a stop. In seconds the back doors were opened and our *byki* reached for our roped necks. When we got out of the van, I took in what was before us. We were standing in the center of a large compound, enclosed by high, dark fences. There was barbed wire covering the tops. Two large watchtowers were in sight, but I couldn't see the others; the wall stretched too far. Each tower was manned by at least three guards.

When the other cars stopped beside us, I saw Zaal and Valentin scanning the perimeter. They were recording all this for future use. But other than the walls and the towers, there was nothing. Nothing but a steep set of steps descending into the earth. No buildings, no life, just barren land and these stairs.

The head Wraith jumped from a blacked-out jeep, followed by several of his males. He indicated for us to follow and began walking down the steps. Our *byki* guided us down, Viktor walking out in front.

The steps were many, then at last we came to a large set of steel doors. The head Wraith banged on the metal. The heavy doors creaked open, revealing a dank, wide tunnel beyond.

After we entered the tunnel, the doors slammed behind us. The Wraiths' heavy boots echoed off the stone floor. We walked for what felt like miles, until we arrived at another large set of doors. Beyond these doors were more steps, followed by many hallways. The head Wraith paused just before leading us down the left tunnel. "You have been privileged, Viktor," he said proudly. "Master wants to see you and your fighters." His gaze then fixed on Valentin, and ice filled my muscles. "He wants to meet the monster that slayed his sister."

Valentin tensed beside me. But Viktor played into the role. "I'd be honored," he replied, and the head Wraith smiled.

"Come," the head Wraith ordered. We followed him down the narrow hallway. With every step, my mind raced with what we would do if Master wanted to punish Valentin. I prayed that Valentin wouldn't react first when coming eye to eye with the male that had called his sister back to his pit. The male that had become Master to his sister. The male that was using her for sex.

The hallways were winding and long, but eventually we entered a large hall, the size of it surprising. A table stood at the end of the space, and around it were three males. I immediately sought out Arziani. He carried himself like many of the crime bosses in New York did—arrogantly, like he was the most powerful male in the world. I supposed here, in this underground town, he was.

His expensive shoes tapped on the floor as he approached us, his two guards following closely behind. I stood between Zaal and Valentin. I almost choked on the hate pulsing from their bodies.

Master stopped before us, and I got a good look at his face. I hadn't been sure what to expect, but he was nothing special. It was the glint he had in his eyes that betrayed the true nature of his black soul. The glint that showed his ruthlessness was underneath, the male that took enjoyment from others' pain.

Arziani's eyebrows rose as he roved his excited gaze over us all. His lip hooked into the briefest smile when he saw Zaal. He stepped closer to Zaal and lifted his hand to trace his tattoo—221.

Zaal's teeth ground together as Master's fingers dropped down to his torso. When he looked back into Zaal's eyes, he said, "One of the Kostava twins. We had long imagined you dead."

Arziani looked to Viktor. "The Volkovs gave him to you?"

Viktor nodded. "Yes, Master. They wanted to use him to kill for them, but he was unsalvageable. Too far gone in the head."

Arziani stared back at Zaal. "He appears docile enough now."

"It is the drugs, Master. We bought the Type A from you. We use it to keep him obedient."

Arziani nodded his head, then looked to me. "And him?"

"Our gulag's ultimate champion. A Russian. Known as Raze. The previous Alaskan champion. We bought him after he was found by a smaller Georgian organization that knew of our gulag in New York."

"Is he good?"

"Unrivaled."

Arziani smiled and said, "Good. My champion is a Russian, too. Taken as a child from an orphanage and raised to be exactly the kind of killer I dreamed about." His face then flashed with annoyance. "Though he has lost my favor of late." He stepped back, eyes bright. "This 818 seems he could perhaps give him a challenge. I will look forward to seeing it."

Master then moved to Valentin and his lost his humor. Valentin stared straight ahead, frozen to the spot. Master lifted his hand and brushed his fingertip over the scar on Valentin's neck, but he didn't stop there. He moved to his scarred face and traced the lashes that Valentin's Mistress had meted out for his disobedience, permanently disfiguring his face.

Master stepped back and regarded Valentin coldly. "So this is the mutant that slaughtered my sister?" Silence. The air pulsed with electricity as we waited for what would come next.

I could feel our *byki* loosening their holds on our ropes. They expected a fight. So did I.

But when Arziani's lips spread into a wide grin and a booming laugh came from his mouth, that expectation fell away. Arziani slapped Valentin on the shoulder. "That woman was the bane of my life. You did me a favor by killing her." He looked to Zaal. "And her asshole of a lover. The one you killed. You did me a favor. Jakhua had thought himself higher than his station. I had already issued his death warrant. You just beat me to it."

I waited as Arziani's eyes fell back to Valentin. I waited for him to mention his sister. I waited for him to taunt him with the fact that he had her under his control and in his bed. But Arziani didn't say a thing. I wondered why, then thought that maybe he didn't know. Maybe he didn't know Inessa was Valentin's blood. Maybe his sister had never told him.

Arziani looked to Viktor. "Your gulag must be strong. You are the last fighters to arrive, and none have males to rival yours. After the tournament we should talk." He smiled. "We Georgians need to keep our business close to home, no?"

"Of course, Master," Viktor replied. Relief trickled down my spine.

"We have quarters for you and your fighters. The tournament begins tomorrow. You will receive good fights. I'm interested how your males will stand up to my champions, but maybe they are matches for the later rounds. If they make it to the final round, they will be awarded the champions' quarters, and you will be given better accommodations, too. We honor our victors here in the Blood Pit."

"Thank you," Viktor said. Arziani flicked his wrist in dismissal. The head Wraith led us out of the hall and down the hallway. With every step, my blood pumped faster and faster around my body. *This could actually work,* I thought to myself.

We walked through three long hallways, then arrived at a section filled with several large rooms. When I looked through the open doorways, fighters of all nationalities sat inside. They glared as we passed, holding their weapons or sitting drugged on the floor.

We arrived at an empty room, its walls and floors made of dark stone. Several beds lay on the floor, with a side room at the back that was probably for washing. The head Wraith pointed for us to enter. Viktor hung back and was told, "Your food will be brought to you. You don't leave these quarters until training. The fighters will be taken to the training pits and will be there all day. If they win, *monas* will be provided for relief."

Valentin growled beside me at that news. Zaal discreetly put his hand on his arm to shut him up. He did, but his body shook as he held back his need to kill.

"No *monebi*," Viktor said. "They don't get females in our gulag."

The head Wraith's eyes narrowed, then he shrugged his shoulders. "Your choice." He stepped away and continued, "You'll be told of your scheduled fights soon. There will be a viewing cage for your fighters to watch the other matches. We find that the fighters who watch the other men perform better when they enter the pit. The bloodlust makes for a more interesting battle."

Viktor nodded and the head Wraith walked away. Viktor hovered near the door until the coast was clear. The *byki* released our ropes, but we stayed sitting against the wall of the room, just in case we were being watched.

Viktor sat opposite. Not looking at me, he said, "I have never seen anything like this place. Who would ever believe something like this existed?"

"Me," the three of us replied in unison.

Viktor's head turned to face us, and he nodded sadly. He sighed and said, "We should all get some sleep. We have to be focused tomorrow, in case you are announced as a first match."

"Agreed," I said quietly. Before we all moved to our beds, I said,

"No matter what happens in these few days, even if one of us falls, we carry on. We bring this place down."

"Agreed," Zaal and Valentin said in unison.

I moved to a bed without another word, slipping off my 'dusters and laying them at my side. The sound of fighters practicing echoed off the walls. A constant dripping from a leaky pipe splashed repeatedly on the floor. Hearing Zaal and Valentin moving to the beds near me, an image of Kisa's beautiful face filled my head.

I wondered if Zaal and Valentin were thinking of their females, too.

Because if they were, if they were fighting to return home with everything they had, we couldn't possibly lose.

We had been thrust back into hell.

But this time the only way out was to burn it in our wake.

And we had only limited days to see it through.

12

901

Everything about today felt different. I had awoken with 152 in my arms, like every other day. But today wasn't like every other day. We had changed. Things between 152 and me had changed.

I was changed.

I had taken her every night for weeks because she'd needed me for the drugs. Last night I had taken her because she wanted me to. The most beautiful *mona* in the pit had wanted me.

She had been taken to her quarters by the guard this morning, but before she left, she had pulled me out of view and given me a slow kiss on my lips.

Even now I could taste her on my mouth.

A guard came to the door and I stepped out. I walked to the hallway and, like every day, received my drugs. There was only me in the line, then 667 and 140 fell in behind me.

"First day of tournament," 667 said. "The rest of the fighters are being moved to another part of the pit. The training pits are just for the champions and tournament fighters."

The *chiri* injected me and I walked forward toward the pits. I held my Kindjals in my hands. Noises of males training hit my ears.

When I entered through the open doorway, I roved my eyes around the mass of movement. 667 and 140 arrived behind me, and I knew they were looking, too.

Males of all sizes were sparring with their trainers. Every kind of weapon was being used: swords, daggers, chains, axes, hammers, sais, spears, knuckle-dusters.

I watched a few of the males in action. None seemed threatening. I moved to my usual pit, 667 and 140 jumping into theirs beside me. Only three other males were in this section with me. Three males that, when I watched them train, instantly pulled my attention. One was darker in skin with long black hair. I stared at another and my eyes widened. He was huge, tall with broad shoulders. He had severely scarred skin, the most severe lash scars on his face. But around his neck was the red remnant, evidence he had once worn a collar.

His hair was black, and in his hands he held two unpowered picanas, similar to what some of the guards held. When he turned his head, snarling in his sparring, I got a clear view of his face. His eyes were blue.

A third male suddenly slapped him on his back. My attention then went to him. He had blond hair and brown eyes. He was broad and tall. He didn't look as severe as the other two males, yet there was something in the way he stood that made me think he would be the most threatening of them all. He had a calmness that betrayed his comfort at being inside a pit. The way he led the other two males he trained with told me he was used to taking control. Attributes like this always made the hardest warriors. The ones that could effectively stop the beating of your heart when you least expected it.

As if feeling my stare, the male turned around. His dark eyes watched me, and they narrowed. I watched him clench his fists. He wore bladed knuckle-dusters as his weapon of choice. I had fought many with them on before. They could be just as deadly as a dagger if you knew how to wield them correctly.

"Our biggest competition," 667 said, arms folded across his chest.

140 flanked my other side. "They wouldn't have been given this space if Master hadn't found them worthy."

"He is right. They are worthy. They move better than any other fighter in this pit. They are seasoned and effective."

818, the male that looked to be in charge, was suddenly joined by the other two: 221 and 194. The three of them stared at us, we three stared back.

I tried to show I was unaffected, but my eyes kept drifting to the heavy scarred male. Not because he caused me fear or worry, but because of his eyes. His eyes were too similar, too familiar. The same color as 152's. I turned away. I had to get her from my mind. She had no place in this pit. She would be a distraction, one I couldn't afford to have.

A short male came toward the three fighters and pulled them away. My trainer arrived, and as was routine, I followed him to the pit. We began slowly, warming up my muscles. Before long, I was in the zone, smashing my Kindjals against my trainer's shield.

Hours passed, and my body dripped with sweat. Movement caught my eye from the walkway that circled the training pit. My heart slammed against my chest when I looked up and saw 152 approaching. My blood instantly boiled when I saw her being paraded on Master's arm. Her face was blank. She stared straight ahead. Master was holding her close, a smug smile on his fucking face.

I growled low and used my anger to strike out at my trainer. I smashed my blades with rapid force. I heard 140 snarl. He turned to see Master watching us train. He eyes casually left his three champions and landed on the three new fighters under the control of the short Georgian.

Seeing he was distracted, I used this moment to look to 152. I expected her to be looking back, stealing a glance. But instead, she stared at the three new fighters. A strange expression crossed over her face, one I couldn't read. Her cheeks had drained of color. When I followed the path of what held her attention, it was to arrive on the scarred male. He was training hard, his huge body attacking the trainer's pads with perfect form. He was relentless as his powerful strikes almost knocked the trainer from his feet.

He turned in the pit, his position now directly facing Master. His eyes were still focused on the task. But when the trainer called for him to halt, 194 glanced up, and his gaze collided with 152's.

And it never left her.

Possessive shivers broke out along my skin when I looked to 152 and saw that she was trapped in his stare. Master watched the other two males sparring with an excited glint in his eyes. He hadn't noticed the scarred male watching his *mona*.

Watching what was *mine*.

152's eyes were narrowed, the same action she made when confused. When I looked to 194, a strange expression set on his face.

My hands shook against my Kindjals, jealousy ripping through me like a fever. My feet braced to move. I looked to 152 once more, and this time saw Master following her gaze. His jaw clenched when he saw that her attention wasn't solely on him.

Turning on his heel, Master flicked his wrist to the guard. The guard stepped forward. "Move!" he commanded and pointed to the center pit. 152, still caught up in 194's stare, was dragged to follow him. I moved to get him to remove his hands, when 667 gripped my arm.

I spun around, ready to attack, when 140 stepped in between us. "He was saving you from fucking up and putting your female in danger. You go after Master in this pit, and you'll find yourself waking up in hell."

My muscles tensed, knowing he was right. They watched me, ready to stop me again, when I reluctantly nodded. 140 slapped me on the shoulder, and we moved to the center pit. The three other males followed, standing slightly behind us. The other competitors gathered, too. But I had no time to take notice of them. 194 had all my attention now. The fresh meat that had his eyes on my female.

The sound of Master climbing to his podium made me look up. When I did, he took his place, towering above us all. But this time he brought 152 with him.

Her head remained lowered as Master paraded her in a dark red dress in front of his males. She stood to his left, timid and meek.

My heart swelled on seeing her looking so beautiful. I focused on her face and saw that her bruises and cuts had been covered with makeup. That angered me. Master had hurt her, then disguised it.

"Warriors!" Master shouted, and held out his arms with a smile on his face. "Welcome to the Blood Pit!" Males around me rocked from side to side as they stared up at Master, fueled by his words.

Master dropped his arms. "As you know, the tournament begins tonight. If you are to fight first, you will have already been told by your trainer." Master paused for effect, then said, "It is a four-day-long battle. You win, you will progress to the next round. If you don't . . ." Master trailed off and shrugged. The males muttered and growled around me, bloodthirsty for the kill.

Master drank it in, getting high from the tension in the room. "You will be paired for all fights but the final. Four males will reach the end stage of the championship and will battle it out in a winner-takes-all war." Nodding, he added, "Then the male that wins, that slaughters the three left in his path, wins the ultimate prize." Master walked farther forward, peering down, and said slowly, "He wins his freedom."

Louder voices cut through the pit this time, males pushed to their limits. They wanted freedom. As I cast my eyes over the tens of males, I could see that this chance to be freed from their chains was everything. This tournament was their chance to become more than they were—killers, animals bred for slaughter.

Master's gaze then landed on his three champions and the males that had been beside us in the pits. "Tomorrow will be your turn. The champions with the lowest odds will take to the arena." My blood's temperature spiked at the thought of taking on any one of them. Master then looked to another six males at the opposite side of the center pit. He pointed to them and declared, "And you will be their opponents."

My lips rolled back over my teeth in frustration. I glanced to the side to glare at the scarred champion, only to find him staring up at the podium. I knew what I would find when I followed the path. I was right—it was 152 that held his attention. When I saw a possessiveness flash across his face, my stomach cramped with the need to rid him of his head. But when 152 lifted her head, and stared back at the male, an equal interest in her blue eyes, I felt my anger overrun my resistance.

Why the fuck was she staring at him? Why was he staring at *her*?

I didn't hear Master dismiss us. My blood was too loud in my eyes as it rushed like torrents in my ears. I didn't notice the fighters returning to their pits. All I could see was a red haze, the need to stake my claim on 152.

Storming forward, my shoulder crashed against 194's. The large male growled low at the contact and whipped to face me. Before he could react, I threw my Kindjals to the ground, seeing him doing the same with his picanas. I charged, I ran to where he stood, and plowed my fist across his jaw. His head snapped back like I hadn't even made a mark.

In seconds he had hit me too, his crazed blue eyes boring into mine. Slamming my chest into his, I warned, "Keep the fuck away from her. Don't you ever dare look at her again."

He pushed against my chest. "Get back."

"She's mine," I hissed, and struck out again. I smashed my fist into his lip, immediately drawing blood. He lifted his hand to his lip, and his already fucked-up face contorted with rage. His muscles tensed until they shook with the effort. But just as I braced for him to strike, a firm hand landed on my chest and pushed me. I stumbled back, before righting myself. The blond champion in his party was pushing the scarred one away. The scarred fighter tried to push past him to get at me.

"Retreat," the blond male ordered 194. I was surprised when I heard them speaking in Russian.

"I'm going to kill him," 194 snarled, and glared at me over the blond's shoulder. "He called her his. He fucking called her *his*."

At his words, I rushed forward just as the one with long black hair wrenched the scarred Russian out of my path. Instead, the blond leader turned on me and swung. His heavy fist collided with my cheek. I swung back, striking him in return. Blood dripped from his mouth, and he smiled. Blood coated his white teeth, as I tasted blood on my tongue.

"*He* doesn't look at her," I ordered in Russian. The blond blinked, then stepped closer.

"He does whatever the fuck he wants," he answered back.

"She's mine," I shouted, and took the fucker to the ground. I struck and struck, any chance I got. He fought back. Rage took its hold when this male didn't break under my fist.

He gave as good as he got, slamming his blows into my ribs and stomach, matching my every move. I panted as the Russian champion didn't submit. He sweated when I didn't give.

But my drive kept strong. When my eyes met his, I could see he was livid. I rolled him on his back and plowed my head against his, but as soon as our heads connected, he flipped me onto my back and smashed the back of my head into the ground.

Finally, a guard's whistle blew and hands were tearing us apart. I tried to fight off whoever grabbed me, craving this fight, needing to show them she was mine, but the arms were too strong.

667 and 140 wrenched me back, caging my arms. When I looked to the two new champions, they were pulling their leader back. His brown eyes were locked on mine, and his face was filled with fury.

"Impressive," Master's voice called out from above, as he clapped slowly. My gaze shot to his. He was grinning in excitement as he watched us brawl. His eyes narrowed on mine. "901, it seems we may have found a fighter to rival you, after all." He then looked to the new champions and added, "Or maybe all three could." When he faced me again, he said, "You may be the champion here in the pit, but that may be a limited title."

My eyes next found 152, who was watching me, tears filling her eyes. My stomach turned on seeing her look so upset. She appeared in distress. Her hand lifted toward her forehead, but she quickly dropped it back to her side. Her skin was still pale. She broke her gaze from mine and looked to the scarred male. She shook her head, then turned away.

Master picked up 152's hand to link her arm back through his own. She went with him, and it took all I had not to run after her and ask her why she stared at the new male so much.

A guard appeared at my back and pushed me with the nose of his gun. I reached down and picked up my Kindjals. I headed for the tunnel, followed by 667 and 140. 140 pulled me around by my arm. "Don't do anything to fuck up your chances in the pits. You make it to the final, you get to take those fuckers down."

I wrenched my arm back, then pounded to my cell. I sat on my bed for hours, until the guards arrived to tell us we could watch the opening fights from the observation cage. I left my cell. 140 and 667 walked beside me. I entered the cell that gave us a clear view of the pit. As I looked to the stands, every seat was full and money was changing hands. My lips curled in disgust.

"Cocksuckers, every one of them," 140 hissed from beside me, as the other fighters moved aside to let us to the front. 140 rested his hands on the bars, and we watched as Master moved to sit on his seat, guiding 152 to sit on the floor in front of him.

My pulse raced at how beautiful she looked. Her hair was up on her head, and long curled tendrils hung to the sides of her face. She was dressed in a shouldered white dress, and long earrings draped from her ears. I couldn't move my eyes from her as she sat looking sad and uncomfortable at Master's feet.

She shouldn't be here.

This shouldn't be her life.

Low mutters came from behind us. When I turned around, the three new champions were cutting through the weaker fighters. My back bristled when they came to stand beside us. 667 and 140 closed in on me. They didn't need to. I had heard the scarred male just fine. He was right. I would destroy him in the pit.

I focused back on the arena in front of me. This was my domain. They would be the ones to fall.

Master stood to signal the guard for the match to begin. Two males ran out, their weapons held in front of them—a sword and a spear. It was a slow match, neither male gaining the upper hand. Eventually the male with the spear caught a perfect shot to the other's heart. The mortally wounded male immediately fell to the sand.

I would have slaughtered both in seconds.

The remainder of the fights passed in a similar way. With every match, I was convinced that I would get to the final. As I glanced across to the three new males, I thought that most, if not all of them, would make it, too. A strange regretful feeling spread inside when I thought of the fact that 667 and 140 would not make it there.

Talking to them over the past several weeks had not been bad.

In fact, I found myself liking talking to the warriors. They understood this life. They understood what 152 meant to me.

With that thought, my attention drifted to where she sat. She wasn't watching the match. Her eyes were downcast, her thoughts elsewhere. I frowned, seeing the confused expression on her face. I wanted to ask her what was wrong. I wanted to press my lips to hers and make her smile.

152 suddenly flinched. I immediately knew why, when Master pressed his hand to the back of her neck. He wore a severe look on his face as another fight passed without much excitement. He was hurting her. He was pissed that his fighters were not making their kills exciting.

152 was bearing the brunt of his anger.

A low curse came from my side. When I looked across the caged cell, the scarred Russian was watching Master holding 152 with obvious fury in his eyes. Unable to stand here and watch it, stand next to this ugly fucker gawking at my female, I turned and headed back to my cell.

When I arrived, I sat on my bed and waited. I waited and waited for 152 to come to me. But as the night dragged on, and the guards didn't arrive, I frowned. Footsteps sounded from outside, and I stood waiting for her to enter. But she didn't. Master stood in the hallway.

Alone.

"Champions," he called. We all walked to our cell doors. I saw 667 and 140 glaring. He met each of our eyes and said, "Tomorrow you will face fighters that are no match to you. But as my champions, I expect you to give my crowd what they want."

"Where's my *mona*?" 667 asked.

Master looked to his face. "She won't be joining you tonight." He next looked to me, and I noted the victory in his expression. "None of them will."

Disappointment ripped through me, but I didn't let it show.

667's jaw clenched and his hands tightened on the bars. "Perform well tomorrow and you will be rewarded her in return," Master said. He left our quarters and I moved back to my bed. I slumped down on the mattress, forcing myself to get some sleep. But all I could think of was 152. Of her metal bracelet that would inject her with drugs. Drugs that would make her need my release when I wasn't there to ease her pain.

My eyes snapped open and I made myself stay still. The anger was thick and hot as I thought of that prick taking her in his bed. Thought of her cries as he was brutal and raw. Possession burned bright in my mind. No matter how much I tried to sleep, very little came.

But the embers of anger remained.

They intensified and increased until they were all I was. I welcomed tomorrow's fight. A fight I would drag out as long as I could. Because the reward would be worth it. Just to have 152 in my bed once more.

Even if it meant forfeiting my free will.

Even if it meant giving Master everything I had left.

"They're good," 667 said as the scarred male walked away from the pit into the tunnel. We had been watching the long-haired Georgian and the scarred Russian. Both had slain their opponents within seconds of entering the ring. The Georgian had pierced his opponent in the eyes with his sais. The scarred Russian had sliced his picana through the skull of his. Neither had even broken a sweat.

A guard arrived and pointed at 667. 667 took his weapons in hand and turned to go and wait in the tunnel. The tournament fights were a quick turnaround. No sooner had one match ended than another had begun. I had watched last night and the matches so far today. The crowd loved it. Was bloodthirsty. But Master had sat stoically throughout. 152 remained at his feet, rarely looking up.

I could tell Master wanted more from the fights. His teeth had been grinding together as the Georgian and the Russian easily defeated their opponents. Master wanted the theater. In his pit, it wasn't the death that he treasured; it was the fight to live.

The crowd roared as a male jogged out into the pit. He had a closely shaved head and pale skin. His number read 289. He was big and carried a hammer as a weapon, but from the minute the blond Russian champion, 818, ran out into the pit, you could see who was about to come out of this alive. The blond's knuckle-dusters were ready in his hands.

He jogged forward, increasing his speed as he approached. The large male swung his hammer. But with perfect accuracy, the blond laid three punches on his opponent. 818 ran past him, leaving his opponent in shock but still on his feet. The male glanced down. I followed his gaze. The blond Russian stood still, not even looking back. Suddenly, his opponent dropped to his knees. I saw that he had two blade punctures in his stomach and one right over his heart. On cue, he keeled over and his heavy body thudded to the ground.

Turning on his heel, the blond ran out of the pit and straight into the tunnel.

140 sighed. When I looked to his face, he looked at me, too. Shaking his head, he said, "They will test us in skill."

I agreed. Master could get exactly what he wanted from this tournament—a new champion. And me, dead.

The guard appeared and signaled for 140 to wait in the tunnel. He left, and I held my Kindjals tighter, knowing my turn was coming soon. The guard closed the door to the cell, and I watched the pit, waiting for 667 to come out. Movement from the back of the stands caught my attention. I narrowed my eyes, seeing 667's *mona* in the arms of a guard. Just like 152 a few days ago, the guard had a knife to her throat. He was standing directly in front of the tunnel, directly in 667's sight as he ran out.

I watched as the fighter ran to the pit, stumbling in his step when he circled the ring. He had seen her, seen his female in the guard's arms. His face contorted in rage as he glared at Master. Master barely reacted, but for a small smirk pulling on his mouth.

I rocked on my feet in agitation. That fuck should not be able to get away with this. 152 looked up when 667 began grunting in anger, waiting for his opponent. She stared at the champion, then tracked his gaze to the back of the stands. I watched as her eyes widened and her mouth dropped in shock. Then, as I hoped she would, she looked to the cage that held me. I could see the plea in her eyes.

She wanted me to do as Master demanded. She wanted me to live.

The sound of feet running up the tunnel drew my attention. 667 held his daggers in hand and took the first blow of his opponent's spiked club. With his shoulder beaded by tens and tens of holes from the spikes, I knew he was doing as Master commanded.

He was giving the people a show.

I moved closer to the bars as 667 turned on the fighter. But just as he did, the fighter swung his club at 667's head. It happened almost in slow motion before my eyes. 667, instinctively defending himself from the blow, ducked and struck out his daggers. Both long blades slipped like butter through the chest of his opponent.

667's face blanched as he turned to watch the male fall, headfirst to the sand. The once excited crowd now groaned in disappointment. 667 turned his body to the stands just in time to see Master flick his wrist to the guard holding 667's *mona*. A loud, pained roar left 667's mouth as the guard, with no time to lose, sliced his blade across 667's *mona*'s throat. Blood immediately burst free from the blond female's neck and her eyes widened in a mixture of fear and shock.

The guard threw her crumbling body to the ground, leaning down to wipe his blade on her quickly soiling dress. My attention fixed back on 667 just as he jerked forward, a war cry wailing from his mouth. With only one focus in his eyes, he leapt into the lower levels of the stands, slaying anyone in his path as he fought to reach Master's seat.

The crowd began to rush from their seats when, from the tunnel, 140 came sprinting out, axes held high. He charged across the bloodied sand, jumping over the slain fighter's corpse.

My heart thudded in excitement at seeing the spectators running for the exits, my brothers spilling blood as they raced toward Master. Needing to help them, wanting to join them in taking the fucker down, I began roaring out in frustration. I turned and slammed my shoulder against the cell door. It didn't move, and guards ran past my metal prison. Running toward the pit. Turning to face the bars showcasing the pit, I hit them with my blades. "Get me out!" I demanded, and looked up. When I did, fear wrapped around me. 667 was staggering, still rows from where Master sat . . . where he held 152 before him like a shield. A gunshot sounded. I realized that 667 had already been shot and was fighting to stay alive.

140, however, was still charging toward Master, the guards' bullets missing his every move.

"No!" I screamed, seeing Master holding 152 toward where 140 approached. I was wild as I charged against the bars, sparks flying as metal clashed against metal. I wanted to take Master down. I wanted to punish him for using my female as a shield and for slaying 667's *mona*.

667 staggered to his feet, riddled with bullets. But just as he did, a guard moved behind him and sent a bullet straight through his head. 140 never heard the shot that came for him. He raised his weapon, ready to strike Master, when another guard fired a bullet into the back of his skull. 140's body stiffened as his skull splintered, and his body collapsed on the row of chairs beneath him.

The cacophony of fearful voices and the crowd's screams were nothing compared to the roars pouring from my throat. The guards moved quickly, rounding up the crowd. Master's spectators were forced back toward their seats. The head guard appeared seconds later with a mass of *chiri*. He hit them with batons as he commanded them to retrieve the slain bodies and remove them from the ring.

But my eyes stayed locked on Master as he released 152 to dust off his jacket like nothing had even happened. 152 was shaking, white in pallor as she swayed faintly on the spot.

Rushing down to the middle of the pit, Master held up his hands as his guards raised their guns high and forced the shaken crowd to listen. When they did, Master spoke. "Ladies and gentlemen, I apologize for that small accident." He forced a smile that I could see straight through and said, "This is the Blood Pit. It is a death ring. Occasionally the fighters forget their place."

He tried to speak again, but I clanged my blades louder on the bars, pacing back and forth as I shouted to let me the fuck out. Master didn't look back at me. He continued talking, informing the crowd there would be a slight break before the final match: mine.

Movement from behind me made me turn, and I saw several guards at the cell door. "Shut the hell up!" one snarled, but that only poured fuel on my fury.

Clutching my blades, I charged the door. The guards jumped back, their guns held high. One of them held an unfamiliar gun toward my chest. When I backed away to charge again, something shot out from the gun and lodged inside my chest. I looked down to see that a small pellet had hit my skin. I looked back up, incensed at being shot. I moved my feet so I could lean and strike out at the guard, but my legs were suddenly leaden and my vision began to blur.

"Direct hit!" one of them shouted, as the world flipped to the side and I staggered until I hit the wall of the cell. I heard the sound of the lock sliding open. I saw the blur of several guards dressed in black filling the cell. Hands grabbed at my arms and dragged me from the cell and out into the hallway. My feet tried to find purchase on the sand beneath me, but my muscles struggled to work.

The guards dropped me to the floor. I hit the floor with a thud and blinked my eyes. My vision cleared some, but my movements were delayed, my limbs moving a second later than when I'd ordered them to.

The guards circled me, guns raised. I managed to push myself to a sitting position, just as two feet came into view. Two feet wearing black shoes.

It belatedly sank into my mind who those feet belonged to, as they struck out, slamming into my ribs. I fell to the sand, the coarse grains flicking inside my mouth. I spat out the sand and tried to sit up, but as I did, those feet kicked across my face. The taste of blood burst onto my tongue.

"You pathetic pieces of shit!" a voice snarled down to where I lay. It was Master's voice. Fingers gripped my hair and ripped back my head. Master's face swam in and out of focus as he glared at my face. "You all thought you could revolt?" he snapped lowly. "You thought you could best me in my own fucking pit?"

I tried to tell him to fuck off. That he dared hurt 152, dared put her in his fucking way, but nothing came out. Master's hands let go of my head. It wanted to flop to the floor, but I fought to keep it held high. Master laughed down at where I lay, drugged and losing strength. "You think you can fight?" he asked sardonically. Master then looked at the guards. "Get the *chiri* to finish cleaning the stands and pit quickly." He kicked me on the ground, then said, "Then get him into the tunnel. He will fight. And tonight, he will finally die."

Master walked away and I lay on the hard sandy floor replaying his words in my head. *Then get him into the tunnel. He will fight.*

And tonight, he will finally die . . . 152's terrified face blasted to the front of my mind. Even drugged, I pushed my hands onto the floor and forced myself to sit up. My arms shook with the strain, but I held on as I saw 152 screaming when Master pushed her in front of him as 667 and 140 charged. Anger swirled in my stomach. I reached out my hands, feeling my blades lying beside me. Wrapping my hands around the handles, I felt better knowing I held cold steel in my hands. I had fought with these Kindjals for so long that I prayed my body would remember how to fight.

I had to make it to the final. I had to live for 152.

Moving my legs, I managed to push myself to stand, swaying as my legs almost gave way. I gritted my teeth as my head swam. Snickering and laugher rang out around me. The guards jeered as I stood, their voices sounding like tinny bells in my ears.

A whistle sounded from somewhere far away, and a hand was pushing me forward as I stumbled until I reached a tunnel. The tunnel was dark. My vision pulsed and shimmered with black spots when the light at the end scalded my eyes.

"Go!" a voice commanded. I kept my female's face in my mind as I pushed my leaden feet forward. My shoulders banged off the walls as I staggered into the pit. The crowd was quiet when I walked through. I lifted my head, but the spectators were a blurred line in the darkness.

I tried to search for her, but I couldn't pin her down. I stilled, trying to listen to my opponent. I heard it late, but I heard it. The grunt of someone lifting something heavy. A light breeze bristled at the back of my head and I ducked, just as what looked like chain swung where my head had just been. Holding my Kindjals, I turned and swung, feeling the shift in weight as I connected with something. I knew I had hit my opponent, but I hadn't struck him deeply enough.

I shook my head as I stumbled back a few steps. I blinked away the fuzziness in my eyes just in time to see a tall male running toward me, chain circling above his head, something round attached to the end.

I dived to the ground as the ball on the end of the chain smashed into the sand beside my head. I kicked out my leg as the fighter passed, bringing the tall male to the ground. My legs weren't strong enough to hold me up. I needed to take this kill to the floor. It was my only chance.

The crowd's volume increased. Shifting to my knees, I searched around me. I couldn't place where my opponent was. Suddenly, a thick chain around my throat cut off my breathing. Dropping my blades, I reached up and tried to pull it away, but my opponent's grip was too tight. I clawed at his hands, forcing my fingers to work, but he didn't move. Praying it would work, I leaned forward. With a sudden lift, I rammed the back of my head into what I hoped was his nose.

I heard the crunch of bone breaking. I used the brief slackening of his grip on the chain to wrench the metal from his hands and throw it across the pit. I wasn't sure how far it went, but I didn't have a chance to check as my opponent flipped me onto my back and straddled my waist. His hands circled my throat. He squeezed, again cutting off my air supply. I kicked my legs to try to throw him off. He held fast.

Black spots began filling the limited vision I had. My eyes began to close. I wanted to let go. I wanted, in that moment, to give in to the darkness. But as my mind cleared, on the brink of death, my female's pretty smiling face filled the void. Her face as I took her, both of us choosing to join because we wanted it. Then I pictured her being hit by Master, him throwing her in front of him to protect his sorry ass.

I couldn't leave her alone.

Blinking my eyes open, I moved my limp hand that was lying

beside me. I began dragging close to try to fight my opponent off, when my palm ran over cold steel. My heart thundered with hope as I managed to grip the handle. Hand shaking, I trusted my muscles to help me end this match.

I searched for a deep breath, but it was impossible to breathe. Knowing I was on the verge of blacking out, I used the remainder of my strength to lift my Kindjal and aim for my opponent's head. The blade jammed against something hard, and when his fingers released my neck and warm liquid sprayed over my face, I knew I had sliced through his skull.

The fighter's body slumped to the side, and the roar of the crowd became deafening. I gasped for breath, my throat burning as I dragged in much-needed air. But I couldn't move. My muscles were exhausted, the drug finally taking control.

I wasn't sure how long I lay there, but arms wrapped around me, lifted me from the floor, and began dragging me from the pit. Before I reached the tunnel, I found enough strength to turn my head to the stands, to where Master sat. He was watching me go with fury in his stare, but 152 was staring at me in relief. I thought I had smiled at her, but as the drugs took me under, I couldn't be sure.

But my female had.

She had gifted me her secret smile away from the watchful eye of our Master.

One given freely.

Only for me.

Only ever me.

13

152

I hadn't been sure before this moment that a heart could beat so fast yet almost break apart at the very same time. As I had watched 901 collapse into the pit, bloodied and unable to find strength, I knew that Master had hurt him, drugged him somehow. Hurt him because he had tried to save me, save me from the two champions that had attacked.

Nausea built in my throat when I thought back to the moment that Master had ordered the guard to slit 667's *mona*'s throat. Her lifeless eyes as the body fell to the floor, the floor swimming in her blood. And 901 had charged the bars to reach me, reach me as Master had used me as a shield.

All to protect himself.

Master stood from his seat as 901 was dragged out of the pit by four guards. My heart swelled and burst, then regained a lost beat when a hint of a smile had pulled on his split lips.

He was so handsome. I cared for him so much, it seemed an almost impossible sensation to endure.

Master walked into a throng of people, all fussing and panicking over the champions' attack. Master was trying his best to calm them all down, but I could see the strain and anger on his face.

A hand gripped my arm, and I found myself being forced to my feet by a guard. He guided me roughly to the beginning of a tunnel where Maya waited to take me back to my room. Her eyes were facing the floor in submission as I met her. She fell into step beside me and we hurried to follow the guard. I rushed as fast as I could through the hallways. I was glad that the guard was quick, clearly needing to return to the pit. I wanted to be alone with Maya. I needed to work out a way to get to 901.

As soon as we arrived at the door, the guard threw both Maya and me into the room. He slammed the door shut, and silence descended on us when we were left in our own company.

Maya's head raised, and she moved to lock the bolt on the inside. When she did, I gestured with my hand to the side room to be sure we couldn't be overheard.

As soon as the curtain was closed, sectioning us off from the rest of the room, she said, "Miss? What is happening? The entire place is in a fluster!"

I pressed my hand over my forehead and sat down on the couch. Maya crouched before me. I shook my head in disbelief at the actions of today. Maya took hold of my hand for support. I cast her a grateful smile. Meeting Maya's eyes, I confided, "The champions revolted."

Maya's eyes grew as wide as saucers. "901?" she questioned in concern.

I shook my head. "He was trapped in the waiting cell. It was the other two males." I quickly explained the rest.

Maya got to her feet and guided me to the chair in the center of the room. I sat on the vanity seat, and I sighed as she released the pins that were keeping up my hair. I groaned as her fingers raked over my scalp, and I heard Maya sigh.

"What?" I asked, feeling a nervous energy flowing from where she stood.

She walked around me slowly. "Miss," she said softly, and I watched as a small smile spread on her lips.

"What?"

Maya took my hand. "I discovered your name."

In a split second, my pulse raced at a heady speed. "What?" I whispered in disbelief.

Maya nodded her head and squeezed my hand. "And I know 901's, too."

"How?"

Maya shrugged. "I have been asking the *chiri* to help me." She raised one shoulder. "We are a close community. We help one another." Meeting my eyes, she said, "One of the *chiri* cleans the offices where the files for all slaves are kept. I asked her for yours and 901's."

My body was tense as I waited for her to reveal the biggest mystery to me. "You are Inessa Belrova, miss. From Russia."

As she told me my name, it felt as though the invisible chains that kept me in darkness were breaking free from my soul. "Inessa . . . Belrova . . ." I repeated, and felt tears flow down my cheeks.

Maya wiped them away with her thumb, then said, "And 901 is named Ilya, Ilya Konev. He too is Russian."

A sob slipped from my lips as I thought of 901's, I meant *Ilya's*, handsome face against that beautiful name. "Ilya," I whispered, treasuring the sound of those letters on my tongue. "Inessa and Ilya."

I laughed this time, the sound strained through my hoarse throat. I blinked to clear my vision. "We have names," I said to Maya. She nodded her head. "Names," I repeated, and this time, she laughed, too.

Leaning forward, I wrapped Maya in my arms. "How can I ever thank you?" I asked. Maya tensed. I immediately pulled back.

Her eyes dipped and she said, "Since I was sent to serve you, you have treated me as though I were alive, that I am somebody. This is worth more than I could ever give you, miss."

"You're wrong," I said as my heart warmed. Maya shook her head. A sudden seriousness set in her expression. I waited patiently for her to speak.

"Miss, I found something else, too." I held my breath as she revealed, "You had a brother, too. He was named Valentin, Valentin Belrov."

At this moment I felt as if I were a cracked vase, taken back in time. I was the broken pieces, shattered and seeming irreparable, suddenly fixed and re-forming into a normal state.

"Valentin," I said, and immediately saw a young boy holding me in his arms as we traveled in a small cage. I was crying, but he held me close, kissing me and making me feel safe. The boy that I waved to.

I pressed my hand over my lips. My eyes fluttered, when I whispered, *"I'll miss you."* Maya didn't react to my words, didn't ask why I had said it, but I explained, "When I was taken from him, when he was fighting to get me back . . ." A sudden image of high walls and towers flooded my mind. Snow and steep dark steps. "But I waved from far away and told him, 'I'll miss you.'"

My heart felt like it was cracking as an onslaught of images raced through my mind. Him as a young boy, training in the pits. Then him slightly older, near Maya's age, with a metal collar around his neck. My hand lifted to my neck and I let my fingertips drift over the skin.

"He wore a collar," I said, seeing a female dressed in all black using me to make him yield. "Mistress," I said, and it was said harshly. I barely remembered the female, yet something told me that I hated her with all my being.

"Yes," Maya clarified. "Master's sister. She was the one who took both you and your brother away with her."

"But I came back," I clarified. Maya nodded sadly.

Sadly.

"What?" I questioned.

Maya sighed, then revealed, "Mistress was killed. Not too long ago. We don't know how or by whom or even where, but she *is* dead."

"And my brother?"

Maya shook her head. They didn't know.

I pushed my brain to remember more, but nothing else would come. I was tired and confused. And Ilya . . .

"I want to see Ilya," I told Maya.

She nodded sympathetically but said, "Master will not allow it, miss. If you go against his orders, you will be punished." She glanced away, then faced me again. I knew that look. It wasn't anything good that she was about to reveal.

She hesitated, but I urged, "Just tell me."

Maya exhaled, then said, "Master never intends to give you to Ilya ever again. I overheard him telling his high guard that he achieved what he wanted with his gifting of you to him."

Maya paused, but I pushed. "Tell me. Everything. Please."

Maya closed her eyes. "He said that you are too beautiful, and he won't have a repeat of what happened with his last High Mona. Not with you. He said that once this tournament is over, he never intends for you to set foot out of this room. He wants you to himself and only to himself. He said that he knows you feel that way, too."

Repulsion rose in my throat. "I made him think that," I said in devastation. "At Ilya's cell, I made him believe that I was unaffected by Ilya. That I wanted Master."

Maya's eyes softened in sympathy. Her hand tightened on mine. She shook her head. "Miss, you can't disobey Master. If he believes you want him, and then you betray him, he will surely kill you.

What he did to his last High Mona was horrific. He likes you much, much more. Which means—"

"He would hurt me more," I finished for her. "The pain would be worse."

Maya nodded.

All I felt was sadness. Sadness and the impossibility of my situation. My hand covered my chest above my heart and I whispered, "Maya. The pain is so great in my heart when I think of not seeing Ilya again, that I feel like my heart is breaking."

Maya didn't say anything in response. How could she? What was there to say?

"Come, miss," she said eventually. "Let's get you in the bath for when Master comes back."

"Ilya," I said in a daze, as she led me to the main room. "His name is Ilya, I am Inessa, and I had a brother named Valentin."

"Yes, miss." My tears came thicker this time. Ilya didn't know his name. Wouldn't ever know his name if I never saw him again. And if I was confined to this room, I would never know what happened to my brother. For some strange reason, the fighter with the scarred face, 194, came to my mind. I had caught him watching me from the pits, but more disturbing than his attention was how I didn't mind. I knew it was because he reminded me of the male that was in my dreams.

As I looked to Maya's scarred face, I wondered if they had made him a *chiri*. Scars and disfigurements were nothing new in the pit— slaves were punished brutally for the smallest thing. Just like Maya. I wondered if he had somehow cared for me when I was under the drugs and didn't even know where or who I was.

I knew I might never find out the answers to these questions. After all, this was Master's domain and I was his favorite toy.

What Master wanted, he got.

And right now he wanted me, caged.

So I *would* be caged.

It was just that simple.

I shifted on the bed, trying to get comfortable. All I could think of was 901. No, *Ilya*. I still sometimes forgot to use his name. He *had* a name.

Ilya.

Inessa.

Valentin.

As I kicked the sheet off my legs, there was a loud knock on the door. I sat upright. Maya appeared from the side room and shuffled across to the door. When she opened it, a guard said something to her. Maya nodded, then shut the door again.

I sat up higher. "What?"

Maya approached me and said, "Master isn't coming to you tonight. He is entertaining his guests after the attack."

I nodded, about to lie back down, when I suddenly froze. "Maya," I said quietly, purposely keeping my voice low.

Maya tipped her head to the side as she listened. I threw back my sheet and slid to the end of the bed. "I need to see Ilya," I said, his name still sounding unfamiliar yet so perfect on my lips.

"No," Maya said, and rushed to where I sat.

"I have to," I said, and got to my feet.

Maya took hold of my arms and searched my gaze. "You can't, miss."

"Inessa," I whispered, and I felt my chest released from a weight I hadn't known I was even carrying. "Call me Inessa, by my *name*. I'm not 'Miss' to you. We aren't separate anymore."

Maya didn't reply. She was silent, but her glistening eyes informed me of how she felt. "Miss—Inessa," she quickly corrected, "it isn't safe, you know that."

I noted her concern, but Ilya's name circled my mind. Releasing

Maya's arms, I walked toward the door. "I'm going. I need to. Ilya has a name. He had a life before this pit. He is someone. I have to tell him." I lifted my hand to my heart. "Our names are part of our path to freedom. He *has* to know."

Maya searched my eyes. Shoulders sagging, she said, "Stay here."

Maya walked around me and opened the door. She looked back and said, "There are no guards. They are all guarding the guests, some are trying to leave after today."

"So we can get to Ilya easily?"

Maya frowned but said, "It won't be easy. But we can find an excuse if we need."

I shook my head. "No, I can't risk your life."

"You can't do this without me," she replied.

"Maya—" I went to speak, but she cut me off.

"My life is forfeit every day. Any of the guards could decide to kill me, or take me against my will on a whim. More *chiri* die in this pit than the warriors and *monebi* combined. We are nothing to these people. If my life is in danger anyway, I would rather die in the cause of something good than under the hand of someone's anger."

"Maya," I whispered, hating that this was her life.

Squeezing my hand, she slipped from the door and I followed behind. The hallway was unusually quiet. Keeping my feet as light as possible, I walked fast behind Maya. I kept my eyes alert, but there was barely a sound as we made our way to the champions' quarters.

Ilya's cell was dark when I approached. Maya opened the lock with the keys from her dress and she silently opened the door. A faint creak filled the barren hallway. I stilled, praying a guard had not been nearby. But there was nothing. Just silence.

I slipped through the doorway. Maya stood awkwardly behind. I reached back and pressed my hand against her scarred cheek. Her dark eyes looked up at me. "Go," I whispered, but she shook her head. "Go," I repeated. "Do not risk your life for me. I will say I left of my accord if caught."

It appeared that she wasn't going to move, but when I dropped my hand, she nodded in defeat and disappeared from the hallway. Steeling my nerves, I moved into the shadows of the room. I squinted my eyes, adjusting to the lack of light. One lamp was dimly lit on the far wall, blanketing the cell in a hazy yellow glow.

A quiet groan sounded from the direction of the far wall. I moved closer. On the floor sprawled a bloodied, naked Ilya. I rushed forward and bent down beside him.

My hands hovered over his huge body. I didn't know where to touch him. I didn't know where he was hurting. Sensing I was here, he rolled painfully onto his back. His blue eyes blinked up at me. His left eye was bruised and swollen. Dried blood stuck to his skin, and his hair was matted with blood and sweat.

Ilya inhaled, wheezing as he did so. My stomach dropped at how broken he appeared. This huge male, the undefeated champion, was now vulnerable. He stared at me. I wondered why, when his hand lifted and brushed down my cheek.

I lifted my hand and laid it over his to keep it in place. "*Moy prekrasnyy?*" he whispered, barely making a sound.

"Yes," I replied, and leaned down to press a kiss to his forehead. This close I could see that the pupils in his eyes were dilated. "They drugged you," I said, scanning his body to see where he was most injured.

Ilya moved his free hand to his chest, and I saw a small insertion. "They shot you with a drug pellet?" I asked. I suddenly frowned, wondering how I knew that the Wraiths did that. The vision of a young boy being shot with one came to mind. A black-haired boy. The one from my dreams.

"Yes," Ilya rasped out, pulling my attention back to him.

Ilya's hand twitched on my cheek, and he looked me straight in the eyes. "Last night . . . when you didn't come to me."

"He has forbidden any more contact with you."

His jaw clenched. Ilya looked away, and I saw handprint bruises on his neck. My stomach lurched at how close he had come to death. I shifted to my feet and reached for his hand. Ilya threaded his fingers through mine, trusting me completely.

I helped him up and led him to the shower. I turned the handle and the spray came on. I shed my dress and proceeded to wash him down with soap. My hands ran over every inch of hard muscle; Ilya's huge body was still uncoordinated with the aftereffects of the drug. I pressed kiss after kiss to his back and his shoulders, then moved to stand at his front.

Ilya's head was bowed, and he watched me as I washed him. My hands smoothed over his torso and broad chest as Ilya's fingers stroked along my dampening hair. I smiled peacefully as I washed the blood from his chest, his number tattoo coming into view. My heart raced as I thought of his name, of how to tell him that he had a name. Ilya took a long, deep breath, and I quickly looked up. At first I believed it was simply the water from the shower cascading down his face. But when I truly looked into his eyes, when I saw the gutting expression of sadness and defeat on his face, I knew that it wasn't.

He was crying. Ilya, the Pit Bull, the champion of the Arziani death-match pit, was breaking down.

Reaching behind him, I switched off the shower. My stomach sank. Ilya's eyes were downcast, and his arms hung weakly by his sides. Rolling onto my tiptoes, I placed my hands on his cheeks. Ilya blinked and met my eyes. When he did, my heart splintered at the tears trickling down his pale cheeks. His blue eyes were dulled with pain, the whites bloodshot from his sorrow.

"*Moy voin,*" I whispered, throat tight. Ilya's drying skin bumped in the cool breeze that drifted around his dark cell. A tear ran over my thumb on his cheek. I wiped it away with a brush of my hand. A lump built in my throat at seeing a big male so broken. "What is it?" I asked, and searched his gaze for an answer. "Are you in pain? Do you hurt?"

He lightly shook his head. Ilya glanced away, then looked back in my eyes. His arms lifted and he placed one hand on the side of my neck. I momentarily closed my eyes at this feeling. His other hand skirted down my cheek. My eyes fluttered open under his touch. When he knew he had my attention, he rasped, "I thought I was going to lose you."

A pit caved in my stomach, hollow and deep. "No," I replied, but his eyes dropped and more tears fell.

I couldn't stand this sight. Couldn't stand this strong male feeling so torn. I opened my mouth to speak, when his gaze glazed over and he said sadly, "First he makes you want them. He makes you need them in your heart. Then he takes them away, he takes them away so that you'll do anything to get them back." I held my breath as the words kept pouring like razors from his mouth. "He uses your need for them to break you, to do anything he demands . . . then the minute you fail, the minute you don't do what he demands, he hurts them. He hurts them and makes you watch. Keeps you behind heavy bars where you cannot help, where you must watch and feel every hit like it was you that was receiving the pain." Ilya's hoarse voice cut off. He cleared his throat, then finished, "And finally, when you're desperate, when you'll do anything just to touch their face or hold them in your arms, he will end their life—slit their throat, put a bullet through their brain, stab them in the chest . . . and he makes you watch. Keeps you helpless, and through their death, takes your soul as his own."

Ilya's fingers chased the tears on my cheeks. I hadn't even known I'd been crying. "Please," I cried, and shook my head.

When I looked back into his eyes, he said, "He will take you from me, *moy prekrasnyy*. It has already begun. He gave you to me." Ilya stared at my face like he would never see it again. He studied my features like they were the most important thing in his world. Sighing, he added, "You became my heart."

Ilya's eyes squeezed shut and his heart contorted with pain. When they opened, he said, "He made me want you like I have never wanted anything else. Even my freedom doesn't compare. If I had to fight every day for the rest of my life here in this pit, I would do it gladly to have you with me." He swallowed, and his expression turned to one of grief. "But he won't do that. He wants me to pay for years of disobedience—by losing you. He will keep you away, or at the very worst . . ." He trailed off, then rasped, "He will kill you. Like he did 140's female. Like he did with 667's female today. The champion had not meant to kill so soon; it was instinct. He struck out in the way we had been trained to defend our whole lives." He shook his head. "But it did not make a difference. Master killed 667's female without a second thought. I watched from the waiting cell, and in that second, I saw the male die too . . . only his heart still beat and he still drew breath." Ilya swallowed. "But he was dead. I saw it in his eyes. There was nothing left to live for, so he attacked."

Ilya stepped closer to me, his body tired from the mixture of the drugs and the physical toll of the fight. He stared at me and I stared at him. I watched a large tear slip from the corner of his eye and roll down his cheek. "Master has already hurt you. He made me watch. His only move left is to take you from me for good." He winced at the thought. "To kill you . . . and that would kill me."

"Ilya." I choked on a sob when I heard the truth of his confession.

He froze, then with a hazy confusion in his eyes he questioned, "Il . . . Ilya?"

My stomach flipped when I realized what I had just revealed.

Ilya's hands tightened on my face. His fingers began to shake. Inhaling to calm my nerves, I said, "Ilya . . . it is your name."

Ilya's bowed head lifted and he searched my face for reassurance and an explanation of what I'd just revealed. I wasn't sure. "What?"

I nodded my head and smiled through my tears. "You heard me correctly." My hand drifted down off his cheek to run over his tattoo. I traced the numbers 901, then said, "You are Ilya Konev. You are from Russia. You were taken from an orphanage as a child by the Wraiths and brought here. You are twenty-four years old. I don't know more than that, but . . ." I laughed, unable to hold back my happiness. "You have a name. You *are* someone, *moy voin*."

"Ilya . . . Konev . . . ?" Ilya whispered, the words unfamiliar on his lips.

"Yes," I replied, and my smile grew wider.

Ilya's skin bumped even more as the temperature in the room dropped. Releasing him, I reached for a towel for each of us. When he took hold of my wrist, I turned to see him looking at me, his expression still one of deep surprise. "You . . . ?" he questioned. He looked at the back of my neck, where my tattoo was placed, and asked, "Do you know your name?"

Standing straight, I answered, "Inessa. My name is Inessa Belrova. From Russia. I also was taken by the Wraiths from an orphanage."

Ilya was silent in response. I could see this information had cost him more energy. Taking his hand, I brought him to stand beside the towels and quickly dried his wet skin. He stood there watching my every move. When I had dried myself, I walked us to the narrow bed and sat down on the edge. Ilya immediately followed my lead.

He still watched me. He was watching me with such intensity that I felt a self-conscious blush travel up my neck and bloom on my cheeks. I ducked my head, escaping his rapt attention, but he captured my chin before it tucked against my chest and guided it to meet his eyes.

"Inessa," he said quietly, like my name was a prayer on his lips. My heart skipped a beat, my lips parting in response. This close I noticed flecks of gray in his blue irises. "Inessa Belrova," he murmured, adding my surname.

Shifting his body beside me, he pushed my hair from my face. Inessa and Ilya."

I closed my eyes, savoring the sound of our names being uttered side by side. I squeezed the hand that still lay in mine. "Say it again," I asked.

Ilya sucked in a quick breath but complied. "Inessa and Ilya. Ilya and Inessa . . . more than just our numbers."

My eyes slammed open. A new kind of expression had taken root on Ilya's face. I determined it was due to the knowledge of who he was. But before I could think about it anymore, he slowly leaned in and pressed his mouth to mine. I moaned as our lips touched. Ilya's lips were tentative and gentle.

I wouldn't have wanted it any other way.

Ilya's mouth broke away, and he pressed his forehead to mine. I listened to his controlled breathing, then he said, "As much as I'm pleased I know my name, I think I like knowing yours more."

"Ilya," I whispered in reply, overcome by the confession.

Ilya opened his mouth to say something, but I shook my head. "Lie down," I commanded gently.

A stubbornness flitted over his face. "I'm not weak," he uttered coldly.

"I know," I said soothingly, "but I'm tired from today and want to lie beside you."

This seemed to work. Ilya carefully lay down, favoring the parts of his body that were hurting him. When his head hit the mattress, he turned to look at me. I mirrored his position. His hand lay on the patch of mattress between us. I covered his hand with my own.

Ilya watched me, but it wasn't in possession or want. He was looking at me as though our time was limited. Like I would be ripped from his side any second.

A surge of sadness rushed through me because I knew it could be true. Ilya's eyebrows pinched together as he watched me. I knew my sorrowful expression must be the cause. "I hate Master for forbidding me to come to you anymore."

Ilya's breathing paused. His fingers beneath my hand became rigid. Before he could speak, I continued. "He said that his work with you is done. He will keep me to himself. He is going to keep me in my quarters."

"He's going to cage you? Imprison you further?"

"Yes."

Ilya shifted toward me, his thick muscular leg lifting to cover my own. "How do you know all of this?"

"My *chiri*. She has become my friend. Her name is Maya."

His eyes widened in surprise. "She knows her name?"

"She knows everything that happens in this pit. She can move round undetected, without suspicion because of her lowly status." I glanced to his identity tattoo and explained, "One of her people was able to discover who we are."

Ilya stared in disbelief. As he did, another name circled my head: *Valentin*. A finger coasted down my cheek. I closed my eyes at the feel, then opened them again. Ilya was waiting for me to speak.

So I did. "She discovered something else, too," I confided. "She found that I had a brother. He was brought here to the pit."

"A brother?"

I nodded, then turned my hand over to grip his. I needed his hand tighter now. A pain had built in my chest, and my head ached as I tried to push myself to remember him. Something about him. All I got were broken images and fractured flashes flitting through my mind.

I squeezed my eyes tight shut when a pressure built behind them. I opened them, meeting Ilya's worried gaze. "He was called Valentin. Valentin Belrov." I sighed in frustration. I lifted my hand and rubbed it across my forehead. "But I can't really remember him . . . the drugs . . . the drugs have robbed me of a clear recognition of his face." I thought of Maya's face and said, "I see scars. I see Maya's scarred face, and something about it reminds me of a male. Then I dream. I dream of a boy holding me tightly, telling me he will come back for me. Other images sometimes break through, but I don't know if they are real or in my imagination."

"What do you see?"

"A larger male," I replied, trying my very best to hold on to the picture I saw in sleep most nights. I moved my hand to my cheek and neck. "Scars. He has scars that litter his skin." I then moved my hand to Ilya's chest and all the tattoos Master had forced upon his champion's skin. "He has tattoos, like yours, but at the same time not like yours. More like writing rather than pictures." I looked down at my bracelet and at the metal. "He also wears a collar, like my bracelet. And it makes him angry. It makes him change. He goes from being kind to being cold and brutal in a flash. Just like my bracelet makes me crave a male as soon as the drug hits my blood."

My eyes filled with tears, some unknown emotion making me very sad. Ilya moved closer still, his body heat warming my cold, shivering skin. Inhaling a long breath, I said. "But thinking of him makes me sad. Because I think this male . . . he was someone to me." I patted my chest over my heart. "I feel him here, like he is part of me." I blinked twice to clear the tears from my eyes. "I now believe he is my brother."

"Where is he now?"

"Maya couldn't find out. His information had been taken. I don't even know his number. I don't know if he was forced to fight or if he was a *chiri*." My throat clogged with a large lump, but I managed to say, "I don't even know if he still lives."

Ilya looked away. When he looked back, his eyes flashed with understanding. "194," he murmured, his voice indicating he had understood something in his mind. I frowned. He explained, "The Russian new champion fighter. 194. You were watching him in the training pits." Ilya nodded and said, "He has scars and words tattooed on his skin."

My stomach rolled at the thought of that frightening male. But Ilya was right. When I had seen him watching me, I couldn't help but watch him back. "Yes," I replied. "I am used to males staring at me. I am used to the fighters watching me on Master's arm, but when I saw that warrior, I couldn't help but stare. He has scars. The tattoos . . . the red mark around his neck." I shook my head, disappointment flooding my heart. "But the male wasn't clear to me. For a silly moment, I let myself wonder if that fighter could be the male from my dreams. But although similar, he also looked so different from what my dreams show me." I laughed a mirthless laugh. "I am being foolish. All fighters have scars and tattoos, many have collars or contraptions that Master forces upon them to inject them with his drugs." I sagged into the mattress. "For a moment, when I saw him watching me, I wondered if he knew me, if he could possibly explain why someone who looks like him is in my dreams. But I forgot it quickly. When Maya told me of my brother, the young boy I see at night made sense. But he looked nothing like the male in the pits. It was wishful thinking that I had anybody in this place. That I wasn't alone."

Silence stretched for a moment, before Ilya said hoarsely, "You have me."

My lips parted as a short breath left my mouth. Ilya's unwavering eyes never strayed from mine. And I felt it, I felt the truth of his words. I felt my heart beat louder and faster—a beat created just for him.

"You have me, too," I replied, and laid my hand on the side of his neck. Ilya took in a slow breath. Chest filling with light, I closed in and kissed his bruised mouth. But Ilya didn't seem to feel the pain. Instead his hand raced up my back to thread into my hair. I moaned as he pulled me closer against him, my breasts now flush with his chest.

And we kissed. We kissed and we kissed until I broke away on a gasp. But Ilya stayed close by, his hands traveling over my bare skin, making it bump in their wake. My eyes fluttered shut at the feel. Ilya groaned as my hand ran down his chest, my finger stroking his lower stomach. I opened my eyes just as Ilya rolled me onto my back. He moved to climb above me, but as he did, he hissed out a pained sound. I stilled, seeing his teeth gritting together. "What is it?" I asked.

Ilya flopped back to the mattress, his muscles tense with pain. "The fight today," he said in a low, husky voice. "It drained me." I roved my eyes along the expanse of his body. Severe wounds and large black bruises covered almost every inch of his skin. When I met Ilya's eyes, he confessed, "I want you." He swallowed and added, "I need you. I have to have you with your name on my lips and mine on yours. Us, together, each as someone." My lungs held in a breath as he added, "More than the numbers Master forced us to be."

Needing it too, I exhaled and moved above him. Ilya watched me with hunger in his eyes as my hand drifted to his hard length. His cut lips tightened when my fingers wrapped around him, and he hissed a guttural groan when I began moving my hand up and down.

My skin began to heat at the sight of this warrior as he closed his eyes and arched his back. I knew I had taken many males before, but never like this. I knew I hadn't, even though I had no memory. Because no one else could ever make me feel like this. No male could ever make my heart beat like Ilya.

I drank in his hard muscles and dark tattoos. Then I suddenly cried out when Ilya moved his hand to the apex of my thighs. I moaned as his fingers ran along my core. The pleasure he brought made my hand work faster on his length. Ilya growled a low, savage groan. I saw fire light in his eyes, and as I leaned down to kiss him, to join his lips with my own, he pushed his finger inside my channel and I burst apart with light.

My breathing was hard and heavy as my body jerked against his. When I raised my head, Ilya said, "I need you."

Acting on instinct, I released his length. Lifting my legs, I carefully straddled his waist. Ilya's hands immediately planted on my hips and his expression showed his possession, the approval of where I now sat.

I moved a hand to cover one of his own, and as I did, we both stilled. I met his eyes and he met mine, and I knew, without words, what was being said: *We had each other.*

Ilya and Inessa—the High Mona and the champion.

Forbidden.

Reaching behind me, I guided his length inside me, slowly leaning back until he had filled me so impossibly full. I gripped his hand as my head drew back at the feel. Shivers raced up my spine as Ilya began guiding my hips to move. I lifted up, then lowered back down, building speed in tandem with pleasure.

Ilya's hands roamed over my body. My eyes snapped open when Ilya palmed my breast and whispered, "Inessa."

I froze as I stared down at him. He was watching, waiting to hear my response. Moving my hips, seeing his nostrils flare, I replied, "Ilya . . . my Ilya . . ."

As his name left my lips, something in Ilya broke. His control snapped, unleashing a hungry snarl that ripped from his mouth. This time, despite his pain and injuries, Ilya lifted his torso. With strong, unyielding arms, he wrapped them around my waist and flipped me on my back. Ilya was over me in seconds. His body blanketed my own. His thick neck was corded with veined, tense muscles. Positioning himself between my legs, he pushed forward. We both cried out as he filled me again. As he braced above me, I turned my head and placed kiss after kiss on his wrist. I felt his racing pulse flutter beneath my lips. When I looked back up, Ilya was staring at me, his hips rolling, piercing me with pleasure. Reaching up, Ilya panting harshly above me, I ran my hands down his broad back. At my touch Ilya, groaned, head tipping back.

Pressure began building at the bottom of my spine. When Ilya looked back down, I whispered, "I'm close . . ."

Ilya's eyes glittered and his skin glistened with a sheen of sweat. "Yes," he groaned. I knew he was close, too.

Needing to see his face when I found pleasure. Needing to watch him come apart too, I slid my hands until they palmed his cheeks. Ilya lowered his head and pressed his chest against mine. His warm, quick breath washed over my face. His lower stomach pressed against my bud of nerves, and unable to hold off anymore, I felt my channel contract as pleasure took me in its hold, my scream of release echoing loudly off the cell's stone walls. "Ilya!" I moaned as the hedonistic feeling didn't fade.

Hearing his name usher from my lips, Ilya jerked in his movements and, with a final hard thrust, spilled inside me. His eyes squeezed shut as he gave in to his release. Then, like an answer to every wish I'd ever had, Ilya's mouth opened, and he called out, "Inessa!"

My vision blurred as he crushed his heavy body to mine. His lips found my cheeks and neck, and with every caress, he repeated, "Inessa, Inessa, my Inessa."

Ilya tucked his head into the crook between my neck and shoulder. I gripped hard and ran my hand through his blond hair. Ilya muttered something against my skin.

"What?" I asked breathlessly.

Ilya slowly lifted his head. When he met my eyes, he said, "I want this." He inhaled. "I want this every day. I . . ." His words cut off, but he forced himself to finish, "I want to be forever with you."

I blinked quickly to rid myself of tears. But my stomach still plummeted. Ilya's face dropped. "How would that be possible?" I questioned, the cave in my tunneling returning stronger and deeper. "Master will never allow it." I wrapped my arms around his neck, hanging on with everything I had. I wanted to freeze this moment so it would never end. I wanted to stay here, just like this.

"I don't know," he finally admitted. He was as defeated as I was. When I looked at his face, he said, "I thought having a female would make me weak. I thought wanting someone, being with someone, needing her, would destroy my place here in the pit." He paused, then said, "But since I let you into my heart, since I let you into my soul, you have made me stronger. I want more than fighting and death. I want more than this pit. And I want that with you. Only you."

"Ilya," I whispered. The only thing I could give him in response was, "I want all of that with you, too."

He ducked his head, then lifted it to ask shyly, "You do?"

I smiled and cherished the feel of his warm skin pressed against mine. "More than anything."

Ilya's lips twitched. I held in my breath when a full smile spread on his cut lips. I gasped at the beauty. Moving my fingers to his lips, I pressed my fingertips to them and said, "I don't want Master. I don't know what life looks like above this place, but with you I wouldn't care . . . as long as I could be with you. I would live in perpetual darkness if it meant I got to keep you by my side. We would be you and me. Then one day, we could maybe have more. Children. Laughter . . . happiness."

The tension around Ilya's eyes had softened at my confession. I waited with bated breath for how he would respond. But just then a cool, but angered, voice mused, "Well, this is interesting."

Ice shattered down my spine when I recognized *that* voice. I stilled in Ilya's arms. Ilya's cold killer expression filled me with dread. Ilya's arms shook at my sides. When the sound of the cell opening shattered the tense silence, Ilya jumped to his feet and charged for the door. I sat up on a scream as I saw guards run into the cell and push Ilya against a wall. Charged picanas were pressed against his skin, Ilya roaring out as the high-voltage charge ran through his body.

I stared at my warrior, but Ilya was glaring at Master. Master who, when I turned to face him, was storming toward me. His dark eyes were furious. He reached out and grabbed me by my hair.

A rage-filled bellow ripped from Ilya, but before I could even turn around, Master had pulled me from Ilya's cell, unclothed.

As I was dragged down the hallway, my feet slapping on the stone floor, I could still hear Ilya fighting to be free of the guards.

Tears streamed from my eyes, caused by the pain of Master's grip on my hair. He wrenched me around a corner and we began to descend some unfamiliar stairs.

Fear cut through me as I lost my footing and slammed against the wall. We landed on the floor of a narrower hallway and my knees gave out. But Master continued to drag me, my skin grazing on the rough stone. I cried out when he pulled harshly on my hair. My body fell forward, causing Master to stop.

Reaching down, he wrapped his hand around my arm and wrenched me to my feet. I cried out as he did, and I found myself being hurled against the wall. My back smacked against the stone, robbing me of my breath.

Then Master was in my face, his teeth gritted hard. "Bitch," he snarled, and released my hair to wrap his hand around the front of my throat. I struggled to breathe as he squeezed his hand tightly. Moving his face to mine, he bit out, "Bitch whore. Another unfaithful bitch whore."

I instinctively clawed at his hands. The second my nails dug into his skin, Master let go of my arm, keeping me in place by the hand on my neck. He sliced the back of his hand across my face. I had tried to move with the hit, but Master's other hand kept me still.

His dark eyes were wild as he glared at me. As he landed another smack across my face, I knew this was it. I had disobeyed the ruler of my life.

A life I knew he was going to take.

Leaning in closer, he spat, "You chose that savage animal over me!" His hand moved to my core and I closed my eyes. He used his hand on my throat to hit my head against the stone until my eyes opened again. When he knew he had my attention, he cupped my center harshly, then withdrew his hand and wiped it across the skin on my stomach.

Releasing my neck, he gripped my hair again and commenced dragging me down the hallway. The farther we got, the darker it became. We didn't walk for long before we came to a stop. Master opened a large metal door and threw me inside. He slammed the door behind us.

I forced myself to sit up, and when I did, I wished that I hadn't. I ranged my eyes around the room. It was empty but for two large beams that had ropes tied to them. And on the far wall were tools. Lots and lots of tools.

I felt Master close in behind me. Without speaking, he lifted me off the floor by my arm. I tried to protest when I saw he was taking me to the posts. Master dropped me in the center of the two masts and walked over to the first and took hold of the rope. My stomach fell when he walked back to me and tied a loop around my wrist. Master pulled hard on the rope until it tightened on my wrist. I cried out as the rope cut into my skin.

He didn't even flinch as he did the same with the rope on my right. He stepped back when he had attached them to my wrists. My hair was in front of my eyes, shielding me from his cold stare. But then the ropes pulled. They pulled so tightly that my body lifted up until only my tiptoes touched the floor. My arms were held high, suspended by the ropes.

I bit down on my tongue to stop my cries. The taste of coppery blood filled my mouth.

"Look up, slut," Master commanded. Forcing my head up, I could see Master glaring at me from a few feet away. My hair still covered my eyes, but I could see his rigid stance, I could see flashes of his fuming face. Annoyed by this, Master stepped forward and pushed my hair back until I could see him clearly.

He had taken off his jacket and vest. He had removed his tie and rolled up the sleeves of his shirt. His expression was severe as he glowered at me. His eyes tracked over my body. He shook his head. "So much potential," he muttered, and stepped away. I watched as he walked to the wall of tools and removed a leather lash. As he turned to me, he snapped it between his hands. The loud echo ricocheted around the bare room. Master stopped before me, making sure his words hit home.

Master took the end of the lash and ran it across my torso. "I sacrificed my High Mona to make 901 yield to me. To become the most ruthless champion there ever was. He would fight to get you back. You are a *mona,* a trained whore, your talents would make him fall in time. Fall hard."

He moved the lash to run over my lips. "But I never expected *you* to fall for him. *I* am Master of the pit. *I* created this world. *I* created you." The anger radiated off him in waves. "Why would you want him, an animal that knows nothing but killing, when you had me?" Master stilled. "My last High Mona chose a fighter, too. She fell for the animal that I had commanded to take her. Then she disobeyed my order of never seeing him again and crawled back to his cell."

His eyes were wild with rage and he drew back the lash. I watched it as he placed it at his side. "Just like you," he said coldly. "Just like you disobeyed me." Master stepped forward. Lifting his hand, he gently caressed my face. I flinched, expecting him to be cruel. But he wasn't; he was gentle and kind. His voice softened and he asked, "Why, petal? Why him?"

My lips trembled as I pictured Ilya's face in my mind. My heart swelled at the mercy thought of his smile and touch. My lips wore a small smile, and I said, "Because we are the same. With him I am someone. With me, he is someone, too. We make each other strong."

Master didn't move. A dark eyebrow rose at my answer, then he laughed. He laughed loud and true. He laughed in my face. My skin prickled as he sobered. Then, after a kiss to my cheek, he said, "You are not someone, pretty petal. You are a *mona*. I *own* you. My people took you from being someone, if you can call being an or-phan someone, and I put you to use. But I own you, make no mistake about that. Just like I own him. On your own you are nothing; to-gether you are nothing." Master shook his head in amusement. But I could see his ire at my choice of Ilya over him. It was killing him inside.

As I stared at Master, as I felt the ropes digging into my wrists, I knew this was it for me. I knew I would not come out of this alive. I knew he would murder Ilya, too. I didn't know how, but he would find a way to kill him in the final. It was two days away.

Knowing I had nothing left to lose, I found the courage to say, "There was no part of being with you that I enjoyed. You are a cruel and evil male. If you were to go toe-to-toe with any of the so-called animals you have created, they would tear you apart in seconds.

They don't hide behind Wraiths and guns. They don't need the heavy drugs; your champions prove that. You sit on your throne, making me grovel at your feet. In reality, you should be the one groveling for every life you have taken or sullied in this pit you call your empire. What the rest of us call *hell*."

My lips curled in distain. "I don't remember my life above the ground, but whatever it was, if it was good or bad, at least it would have been *mine*. I would have chosen my own path. And I would never have chosen a male like you. Your touch is repulsive to me. *You* are repulsive." I made sure I had his attention, and spat, "*You*, Master, are not worthy of *me*. It was *never* the other way around."

Master glared. I wasn't sure what he would do, how he would react. Then a smile pulled on his mouth, but it wasn't a good kind of smile. It was cruel. It was a smile he wore when he ordered someone's death.

Master's nose stroked down my cheek. "You may have had a choice aboveground, petal. But you would have always been a whore. Every woman is a whore. I just make sure there are no mind games with my *monebi*. They serve and they get fucked . . . the only thing they are good for."

Master stepped back, his hand tightening on the lash's handle. "I saw you, petal. I saw you watching 901 as he trained. I saw the look in your eyes. And I saw it with the scarred mutant the New Yorkers brought in. I saw you watch him too, and him watch you." He tapped his temple. "I stored it all away. Just in case you betrayed me, I kept note." He shook his head with incredulity. "901 is a champion. An animal, but a champion. The scarred fighter, 194? I don't understand the appeal of him, but you clearly did."

Master cracked the whip at his side, my body jumping at the action. He smiled again at my reaction and moved around the posts to stand directly behind me.

I closed my eyes, feeling his warm breath as he kissed the side

of my neck. "You held such promise. I thought I had picked well."
He tutted, then added, "But I was wrong. Your pretty face lured me
in, and every other man in this pit." Master kissed me again, and I
wanted to throw up. His touch was like poison to me now. There
was only Ilya who had me.

"You were my delicate flower, 152. My petal. And just like a
petal, you will wither when ripped apart."

My eyes opened. He stepped back. Three footsteps sounded on
the stone floor. I heard the crack of the whip and braced for the
punishment for my defiance.

"Just a few lashes," Master said flatly. My breathing came fast
as I prepared for the pain. "You seem to have a thing for scarred
mutants. So let's make you into one, hmm?"

It was several strained minutes before the first strip sliced along
my back. But as the pain ripped through my flesh and the screams
tore from my throat, I pictured Ilya in my mind.

I would die here in this room.

He would die in the final in the pit.

But I smiled as another strip hit, because we would each pass
knowing the other's name.

We would find each other again.

In whatever life came next.

14

ILYA

The room was covered in red as the mist of rage descended over my eyes. The guards struck, one after the other, the charge from their picanas singeing my skin. But I didn't stop. I swung and lashed out. The guards tried to stop me, but every crush of bone or spill of blood only fueled me more.

My wounds from the fight were forgotten as I replayed Inessa being ripped from my cell by her hair. I had seen the look in Master's face. He was going to hurt her.

He was going to kill her.

A loud roar spilled from my mouth, and I grabbed the nearest guard by his neck, lifting him clean off the floor. The others struck me with their picanas, bringing me to my knees. But I took the guard with me, using the last of my strength to slam him to the ground. The guard's spine cracked on the hard floor, eyes rolling back in his head as his life drained from his body.

Shaking my head from the aftereffects of the electrical charge, I didn't see the blow coming to the back of my head. I fought to keep awake, until my vision faded and I blacked out.

The next thing I knew, I woke with blistering pain throbbing throughout my skull. I forced my heavy eyes to open, my vision clearing to show me the wall of my cell. I frowned, unable to remember what had happened, when I suddenly remembered someone being dragged from my cell . . . Inessa!

"Inessa . . ." I growled low, my throat dry and sore.

Pushing off the floor, I staggered to my feet. The cell seemed to tip, and I fell against the wall. I focused on the cell door. Forcing myself to push forward, my hands felt along the wall, my muscles screaming for me to stop.

I ignored my aching body and wrapped my hands around the cell bars to keep upright. A guard stood on the opposite side of the champions' quarters, his gun raised and aimed at my head.

I didn't care.

"Let me out," I snarled. He shook his head, rocking nervously on his feet.

I could hear the distant sound of the crowd and knew I had slept long enough that the tournament had started. I was due to fight today if I wanted to get to the final. I squeezed my eyes shut when another harsh throb pounded my temples.

Incensed at the thought of where Inessa was, at what Master had been doing to her, I shook the cell doors. "Let me the fuck out!" I screamed.

The guard paled but otherwise didn't move.

I broke.

Bellow after bellow left my mouth. Even low on energy, I shook the bars until chips of stone began to break away above. I didn't stop. I kept going and going, until I saw another Wraith, one unfamiliar to this cell, put his hand on the other guard's shoulder.

"Go," he ordered. "I've been sent to cover these quarters. You are to go to the pit."

The guard that I had been screaming at relaxed. "Thank Christ!" he said in relief, and nodded his head toward me. "He's insane.

Master took his slut. He's just woken up and he's pissed." The other guard looked my way and nodded.

The previous guard left, and I began where I had left off. I shook the bars of the cell. "Inessa! Inessa. GET ME THE FUCK TO IN-ESSA!" I screamed relentlessly. The sound of footsteps approached, and I raised my voice as loud as I could. The bars creaked under the pressure of my strength.

The guard before me didn't show any emotion. Suddenly, people moved before me, and I growled louder seeing it was the fighters from the pit. The blond was in the lead, led by their short trainer. The long-haired Georgian followed behind, and the scarred Russian took up the rear.

They were dripping with sweat and coated in blood. Each held his weapons in his hands. They had been fighting today. I understood why they were here—they had made the final.

I had to make the final. It was my only way to *him*.

"Let me out!" I boomed out to the guard. The males stopped to watch me. 194 glared at me through the bars, and I saw scars on his face. My stomach lurched when I thought of Inessa and how she had said she dreamed of someone with scars. How this fighter reminded her of the male in her head.

I physically shook with rage and I roared, "Inessa! GET ME TO INESSA!"

The males that had commenced walking to their cells suddenly turned to stare at me. I noticed them from the corner of my eye, then looked at the guard. "Inessa! INESSA!"

I saw the males muttering to one another. When I screamed for Inessa again, 194 suddenly ran to my cell door and stared me down. "Who are you calling for, *hui*?"

My muscles tensed and my neck ached in his presence. He had called me a dick in Russian.

"Get out of my way," I warned.

He laughed coldly but lost that laugh when I screamed, "Inessa!"

At the call of Inessa's name, he slammed his hands against the cell, rocking the loosening metal. "I said why are *you* calling for *her*?"

I gritted my teeth, then noticed that the new guard wasn't doing anything to stop this piece of shit. He was watching the hallway like he was making sure no one was approaching.

194 slammed his hands against the cell door again. "Answer me, fucker! Or I'll tear your arms from their sockets right here, right now!"

Rage took hold. I was about to strike out when the blond Russian called, "Valentin, calm the hell down!"

My fist, which had been raised, ready to strike this asshole through the bars, stilled. My eyes collided with his . . . blue eyes . . . blue eyes the exact color of . . .

"Inessa," I whispered, and my heart began pounding too hard and too fast. 194 flinched like I had gone through with the threatened punch. Instead, I lowered my hand and dropped it to my side.

My eyes found the guard again. He was still not reacting. I watched as the trainer walked over to him and whispered something in his ear. The guard nodded. Heat rushed through my veins when the guard smiled back.

He was with them? A *Wraith* was under their command?

"Why did you say her name? *That* name?" I stared at 194's heavily scarred face and shorn black hair as he hissed out his harsh question.

"Valentin?" I questioned, but the male didn't react.

I met the blond Russian's eyes. "His name is Valentin?"

He folded his muscled arms over his chest. "Why? Why do you want to know?"

It was . . . it couldn't be . . .

Valentin pushed his broad chest against the bars and hissed,

"Tell me why you said her name? Don't, and I'll kill you." He pointed to the guard. "He's with us and won't stop me from slaughtering you slowly, painfully, until you've been stripped of your flesh."

The blond pressed his hand on Valentin's shoulder and then looked at me. "Answer him. He'll do what he promises. And I won't stop him if you don't speak."

I walked back to the bars. The long-haired Georgian moved closer, extra protection for the two males already confronting me.

I met Valentin's eyes and asked, "You are Valentin Belrov?"

His eyes widened a fraction before he asked, "Why?"

I inhaled deeply, then said, "Inessa is my female. Inessa Belrova."

"You lie," he snarled. His hard grip caused his palms to creak on the metal bars.

"I do not," I replied just as coldly. I pounded my hand over my chest. "Master needed to bring me under his control, so he gave me his High Mona. I didn't want her at first, but then . . ." I shook my head, unable to find the words to confess what Inessa meant to me.

"But you fell in love with her."

My head lifted as 818 spoke. I frowned. "Love?"

A flash of sympathy flooded his expression, when he explained, "You feel her in your heart. It hurts when you are away from her and you need her with you always."

The male perfectly described the feeling. I nodded. "Yes," I rasped. "Then I am in . . . love . . . with her."

"Where is she?" the Georgian asked from behind. I stared at the dark male with long black hair and replied, "Master forbade her to see me anymore, but Inessa came to me last night. I was wounded from the fight. Master killed a champion's *mona* and he attacked. So did 140, the other champion. They charged at Master in the stands, killing some of his guests. I was in the waiting cell and tried to fight alongside them."

The three males all looked to one another. When 818 faced me again, he asked, "Why? Why did he kill her?"

"Because it's what he does," I snapped, and felt my anger rising to boiling point.

"And Inessa?" the Georgian questioned. Valentin growled low, his crazed, piercing eyes never leaving mine as he waited for my answer.

I felt my heart turn black with hate as I replied, "He took her. She was here with me. She came to me. And he took her. He found us and took her as they pinned me back with picanas."

Valentin launched himself off the cell door and began to pace the hallway floor. His fists were balled at his sides. 221 moved to be near the guard. I knew it was to stop him from fleeing down the hallways.

"You knew his name." My eyes left Valentin and focused on the blond male.

I nodded. My stomach sank when I thought of what Inessa had discovered about us. *Ilya and Inessa, from Russia.*

"Inessa told me last night," I said, and watched Valentin pause. He kept his head down, eyes focused on the floor, but I knew he was listening. Gripping the bars, I said, "Neither of us knew our names. Inessa's *chiri* discovered that 152 is Inessa Belrova and I, 901, am Ilya Konev from Russia. We were both taken from orphanages as children."

Valentin's head snapped up and he muttered darkly, "Wraiths."

I nodded. "I don't remember much, but I remember them snatching me from my bed." I sighed and ran my hand down my face. "Inessa has been having dreams. She has been having dreams of a boy that held her tightly as they were taken by the Wraiths. She dreamed of a female all in black that made her feel fear. She dreamed of waving good-bye to a boy. It made her feel sad. But she couldn't remember more; only flashes, odd images came to her mind. A scarred man in a collar telling her to hold on. Telling her she was more than just a number. Telling her that one day he would come and set her free."

I looked to 818. "She was also told that she had a brother, Valentin Belrov. She didn't know where he was. If he was alive or dead." I looked to Valentin, who was now staring at me, a grief-stricken expression on his face. Directly addressing him, I said, "She had seen you in the pits and you made her think of the male in her mind. She doesn't know if the images are of her brother, because they are of an older male. She only remembers her brother as a child. But she saw you. For a moment she entertained the thought that you could be him, but you look different from her mental images."

Valentin stroked his hand over his neck, over the red scar. "I look different because I am free."

"But . . . ?" I trailed off.

"I am Valentin Belrov. I am Inessa's brother. I have been trying to free her for many years."

My heart raced and my eyes widened as he confided, "We are here to get her back. We are here to kill Arziani and burn this pit to the motherfucking ground."

I shook my head, convinced I hadn't heard right, when 818 held out his hand. "I'm Luka Tolstoi, *knayz* to the New York Volkov Bratva." I stared at his hand, then lifted my hand and threaded it through the bars to clasp his.

"I don't know what a Bratva is. Or a *knayz,* for that matter."

He smirked. "Neither did I when I escaped my gulag. I have learned a great deal since."

"You were in a gulag?" I questioned. Luka nodded and pointed to 221. "This is Zaal Kostava. He is the *Lideri* of the Kostava Clan, a Georgian crime family. He was held here as a child along with his twin. The drugs were tested and developed on him."

Zaal walked forward and offered his hand to me, too. "Georgian, but an enemy to Arziani. A rival crime family."

"He experimented on you and your brother?"

He nodded. "My brother died. I have a sister in New York." He pointed to Valentin, who was silently watching from behind. "Arziani sent Valentin to come and kill me and my family. He was Mistress Arziani's *Ubiytsa*."

"Mistress Arziani is dead," I stated.

A cold smile spread on Valentin's disfigured face. "I know. I killed her." Valentin stepped forward. "He took me and Inessa from an orphanage and made me her personal assassin. She used Inessa as bait to keep me submissive. I captured my Zoya, Zaal's sister. But we fell in love. When Mistress found out I had betrayed her, she told me she would send Inessa back here. But it was too late. Arziani had already seen her on a screen and demanded her return."

"To be his High Mona," I added, the unfolding picture making sense.

Valentin nodded. "We are all fighters. We entered this tournament to get her back."

"How?"

Luka spoke. "Not all of the Wraiths are loyal to Arziani; many are forced or sold to service as we all were." I glanced to the guard over Zaal's shoulder, and he flicked his chin. I faced Luka with a confused frown. "Selected *chiri,* the ones that administer the drugs to the males, have, from the beginning of this week, been injecting all fighters with the antidote my family have developed to counteract the Type A drug. They have been doing this every day. The guards on our side have been talking to the fighters. They have been preparing them."

"Preparing them for what?" I asked, my heart finding a new beat.

"For the riot," Luka said calmly. As I stared at his male, I knew that he was a born leader. Everything about how he spoke and the calmness that he kept showed to me it was the role he was made to fulfill.

"The riot?" I asked, my heart pumping my blood through my body like a torrent.

Valentin stepped closer to me and through gritted teeth said, "The final. We three are in the final. After we slaughter the fourth male, we will rush the crowd and cull every one of the sick bastards. Everything is in place." He smiled a cold smile. "Then we will go for Master."

"No," I hissed and hit at the cell door. "He's mine."

Valentin challenged my stare. But I would take that kill. Master was mine.

"You have a match today," Luka said. I nodded my head. He looked to Zaal and raised a brow. Zaal addressed me. "You are wounded."

"I will win."

"Even injured?" he questioned.

"I *will* win," I repeated, "I am the champion of the Blood Pit. The Arziani Pit Bull. I am undefeated on this sand. And until Master used my Inessa to control me, I never even gained a scratch in a match."

"You win," Luka said. "You win and you join us tomorrow." He glanced to Valentin, then back to me. "You will get Arziani."

"What?" Valentin hissed, and Luka faced him. "You got Mistress. This is Ilya's kill. We all had our closure with the males that ruined our lives." He pointed at me. "He deserves his, too."

Valentin shook his head, but then met my eyes and asked, "You love my sister?"

"Yes," I said truthfully, feeling this answer right down to my bones.

Valentin stared at me for a long minute, then nodded. The turn-coat guard suddenly held out his gun, and ordered, "Out!"

I stared to the hallway, as did Luka, Zaal, and Valentin. The three males prepared to strike, when a small female *chiri* walked through. Her head was bowed as the guard flicked his chin for her to stand before us. When she raised her head, and swallowed in pure fear, I noted the right side of her face.

It was scarred. Her hands trembled at her front. She was young, very young.

"Maya?" I guessed.

Maya's eyes widened when I addressed her by her name. Her eyes then filled with tears and rolled in thick drops down her face.

Valentin looked to Maya and asked, "Inessa's *chiri*? The one that told her about me?"

Maya watched Valentin, and questioned, "Valentin?" Valentin nodded his head in reply. "Then she was right?" Maya confirmed, and her hand flew to her mouth. She shook her head and then looked to me. "Ilya, Master took her to a torture room. He has her tied up with ropes and has lashed her back." Maya sniffed and wiped at her cheeks. "He retrieved me from her quarters. I have fed her and allowed her to drink. Master is keeping her alive. He wants to draw out her death as punishment for her betrayal with you."

Maya looked to the other males, then she stepped closer to reveal, "One of the *chiri* told me they were being sent to drug you tomorrow if you make the final. He knows that under the drugs you cannot win against the other warriors."

I glanced to Luka, Zaal, and Valentin. "Galina, the *chiri* he commanded to drug you, told me of the order. News is traveling of you and Inessa. The *chiri* don't want either of you to die. You are the champion, they respect you." Maya blushed and said, "And I have told them all of how Miss Inessa has treated me from day one. They want her to survive. We all want you both to survive."

Valentin walked off to one of the cells as Maya spoke, and Maya flinched when the sounds of his pained bellow traveled to where we stood. I gripped the bars and asked, "Is she in pain? Is she being strong?"

Maya nodded her head. "She is being very strong, but . . ." She glanced away, chased her tears. "But she is in great pain. Her back . . ." Maya shook her head like she was ridding the image from her mind. "Her back is heavily wounded. Her arms are not much better." She sucked in a breath and said, "I'm worried she won't last as long as Master wants."

I gritted my teeth and walked back to the mattress on the floor. I lifted it and hauled it against the wall. "I fucking hate him!" I screamed. My neck bunched as I shook with rage.

"Ilya!" someone called, but I couldn't calm down. "Ilya!" the male repeated. But I was lost to my anger, the red haze descending again over my eyes. The cell door opened. When I looked to see who had entered, Luka approached. "Calm," he said slowly. "Breathe."

I did as he said and took a deep breath. I saw Valentin appearing at the doorway looking equally pissed off. He stood with his hands balled at his sides, but he was holding back his anger and pain.

I had to do the same.

I forced myself to calm. When I did, Luka addressed Maya. "Can she hold on? Can you help her keep strong until tomorrow?"

Maya looked among us all, and nodded her head. "Master will be busy with the tournament. I'll try to feed her and keep her as strong as possible." Maya then looked to me and timidly walked forward. I stared down at the small *chiri* and watched her lift her head to me. My stomach tightened on seeing her scarred face. I remembered

Inessa had told me it was an acid attack because she had refused to fuck a guard.

I felt nothing but respect for the young female in this moment.

I waited for her to speak. When she did, my heart shattered. "Miss Inessa sent me here to tell you that you are in her heart forever." She swallowed, her gaze racked with pain. When Maya managed to regain her composure, she said, "Miss Inessa said she has your name readied on her lips and will find you in the next life."

I heard Valentin curse under his breath. I stared at her brother falling apart. Then I looked to Luka and Zaal. Luka nodded. "Maya," I said, and she blinked back her tears, "tell *moy prekrasnyy* to hold on. Tell her that her brother is here. Tell her that he, along with me and a few others, are going to win us our freedom." Maya gasped and swept her eyes around all the males in the group.

"So it is true?" she exclaimed. "I have heard rumors of a revolt, but the older *chiri* that have discussed it in private will not speak of it when questioned."

"Yes," I replied. "It is tomorrow, during the final." I reached out and touched Maya's arm. She flinched. I immediately withdrew my hand.

"I'm sorry," she mumbled. The skin on her good cheek reddened. "I . . . I find it hard to be touched by males since . . ." She pointed to her scar, and I nodded in understanding.

"It's okay," I soothed. Maya's shoulders sagged in relief. "Just tell my Inessa that we are coming for her. Tell her that her wish will soon come true. We will leave this place together. We will choose our lives. We will be together every day aboveground."

"You will?"

"We *all* will," I responded, and saw the flame of hope flicker in her gaze.

"I'll return to her now," Maya stated, and turned to leave the cell. Just before she did, Maya added, "You are the champion of the Blood Pit. You must win today. Win it for her."

Maya left, but her words struck my heart. I would win it for Inessa. I wouldn't put on a show. I would take the kill, then rest for tomorrow.

Luka placed his hand on my shoulder. "We have to go to our cells while the tournament is on. We must keep up appearances. But you win this next fight, then tonight, we will go over the plan for tomorrow."

I nodded, then sat on the floor. Luka and Zaal left the cell. I felt someone hovering in the doorway and looked up. Valentin was watching me with suspicious eyes. His arms were folded over his chest. I waited for him to speak. When he did, he said, "My sister has had nothing but pain and heartache in her life." He pointed to his chest, then said, "I failed to save her. I couldn't secure her freedom." His strict and forceful voice softened, then cracked with emotion. I saw his blue eyes glisten with tears, as he said in a husky voice, "She deserves someone to love her. Really love her. Treat her right. Treat her like the *printsessa* she is. Inessa deserves a warrior. A champion that will protect her and keep her safe."

I paused, then replied, "I know."

Valentin's eyes narrowed, then he darted to his cell. My mind raced with a mixture of excitement and fear. Because although many obstacles stood in our way, freedom was close. Inessa had to hold on so we could be together.

An hour or two passed, then a guard walked in to take me to the tunnel. My muscles were weakened and my body was tired. But I was energized more than ever before.

I wouldn't lose this fight.

I jumped to my feet, and the guard handed over my Kindjals. They had been removed from my cell when Master took Inessa away. I held them in my hands as the guard held the gun to my head. When the cell door opened, I looked across to the other cells. Luka, Zaal, and Valentin watched me go.

This time I didn't jog to the tunnel; I sprinted. I sprinted all the way, pushing my legs to their absolute limit until I burst from the mouth and launched myself, Kindjals high, into the pit. My opponent charged, swinging his scythe, but I didn't play his game. Ducking the curved blade, I sent not one, but both of my long Russian Cossack daggers, one after the other, flying through his stomach until their sharp blades sliced through his spine. My opponent separated, torso and legs now sliced apart. As they thudded into the sand, I turned and ran back to the cells.

Luka, Zaal, and Valentin nodded their heads in approval as I reentered my cell, coated in my opponent's blood. I threw my Kindjals to the ground and righted my bed. I slumped down to the mattress and forced myself to close my eyes. When the tournament was done tonight, I would convene with the remaining champions and plot out tomorrow's riot.

Tomorrow, when I walked out of this place.

With *moy prekrasnyy* by my side.

Sleep hadn't come easy. My mind was clogged with what today would bring. But most of all I had pictured Inessa with Master. I had pictured her in pain, tied with rope between two posts. I felt sick when I thought of her being lashed.

I pushed myself off the floor, up and down, as I finished my push-ups. I needed my body warm and prepped. My muscles protested, pushed too far over the past few weeks. But I knew they had in them one more day.

The most important day I would ever live.

This day would bring only one of two possible outcomes: liberty or death. I faced both with a smile on my face.

The sound of Luka, Zaal, and Valentin warming up echoed outside my cell. Luka with his bladed knuckle-dusters, Zaal with his black sais, and Valentin with his unpowered steel picanas.

I replayed last night in my head. The plan. The rules and the show we must perform until it was time to strike. Until Luka gave the signal. Viktor and the rebel Wraiths would ensure everyone moved into position as we fought. I shook my head at that news. At the knowledge that not all of the guards were true Wraiths. That, like me and many others, they had been forced into servitude by Master. The rebels, as we fought, would take out as many Wraiths as they could. Master and all his guests would be in the crowd, watching the four-man fight. Unbeknownst to them, the doors would be sealed. There would be no escape.

Not for a single one of them.

The sound of footsteps approached the champions' quarters. I detected three, two heavier than the third. I jumped to my feet, stretching my muscles, when there was movement at my cell door.

I didn't need to look to see which fucker stood there. I closed my eyes and forced myself to keep from charging the bars and killing him on the spot. I held in my thirst to kill.

Just barely.

"901," Master's voice said, the sound of it slitting down my spine like shards of broken glass.

I turned and glared at the soon to be fallen king of the pit. I was on a countdown to slay.

He smiled at me. It was proud. It was victorious. He stood close to the bars, a guard and a *chiri* flanking him. The *chiri* held an injection pack in her hands. Her head was bowed, and I knew this was the female that Maya had told me about last night. The one that was sent to drug me.

"So," Master said coldly, "you made it to the final?" I didn't answer. My jaw ached at how hard it was clenched. He laughed, then pointed at the other cells behind him. "I never really doubted you could. After all, you're the greatest fighter the Blood Pit has ever produced." Master dropped his hand and said, "But you won't be after today."

Master clicked his fingers, and the guard cautiously opened the cell door. He kept his gun aimed at my head as Master pushed the *chiri* inside. The older woman stumbled in and quickly righted herself. She silently opened her bag and made quick work of retrieving the needle filled with the drugs that would make me weak.

As she held it, Master raised his hand, signaling for her to pause. The *chiri* did as commanded. I glared at Master, and he shrugged nonchalantly. "You didn't think I would allow you to win, did you? Not after you pathetically fell in love with my High Mona and decided to covet what was mine."

I lifted my chin, refusing to show any remorse for falling in love with Inessa. Master's face lit with challenge at my defiance. He shook his head, tutting loudly like he was reprimanding a child. "You see, 901, this has always been your problem. Even as a child, you never quite conformed. You never took a *mona*. You never built friendships with the other fighters. You lived alone."

Master slipped his hands into the pockets of his slacks. Shrugging, he added, "And now you will die alone." Master's taunting face fell. Then a cruel, sadistic smile appeared on his face. "As will she." My blood ran cold when he added, "Alone. Racked with pain. Slowly, in the most cruel manner possible."

I heard a livid roar coming from Valentin's cell. Master raised an eyebrow as he looked that way. When he faced me again, he said, "You fucked up, 901. If you had obeyed me from the beginning, you could have been great. You could have gained your freedom if you had simply played by the rules."

"I wouldn't have," I replied in a low hoarse voice.

Master tipped his head to the side. "No?"

Balling my fists, I said, "No. Because there is no such thing with you." I pointed out of the cell. "You tell these champions that the winner will gain his freedom, but we know it isn't true." Master's face froze. "Freedom doesn't exist in your world. You exploit. You use and you bring pain. You strip people of their choice and punish them if any morsel of happiness is found. You force the males to kill. You force the *monebi* to fuck, and you force the *chiri* to exist in the shadows." I inhaled deeply, and continued, "You delude your-self into thinking you are our Master. No soul in this place respects you. You have no honor. No female that you force to take your cock welcomes it unless forced or on drugs." I took a step closer, then another. Mere inches from his face, I said, "Inessa was repulsed by you. Every time you took her, she hated it. She would tell me how her skin crawled when you touched her. She would tell me how she avoided your eyes as you stroked her hair and rutted above her like a desperate fool." I watched as Master's face filled with red. He was holding his breath, his anger rising to boiling point.

Allowing myself to smile, I leaned forward and emphasized, "But with me, she wanted it all." I lifted my hand and showed my palm. "She wanted me to touch her." I held out my arms. "She wanted me to hold her." Reaching down, I gripped my cock and locked onto his stare. "And she loved me freely. Without the drugs, she gave herself to me . . . simply because I *was* me. No demands, no coercion."

A part of me felt sick talking of Inessa this way. But what I said was true. We never fucked. With us it was something else entirely. And I could see my words striking Master as effectively as if I were slicing into his bare flesh.

Delivering the final blow, I announced proudly, "And every time you took her after me, she told me she would picture my face hovering above her. She would imagine it was me that was filling her."

Master couldn't take it anymore. Slamming his hand on the metal bars, he snarled, "I will watch you die today, 901. I will watch you die slowly and painfully in the sand, where you've killed so many others. I will laugh as you draw your last breath, then spit on your corpse when your blood has drained away." Stepping back as if he hadn't just exploded with rage, he promised, "Then I will end 152. I will strip her flesh in your honor. Her slow death will be down to you. She will die hating you. She will die knowing that wanting you was the stupidest thing she could have ever done."

Master flicked his wrist at the *chiri*. I stood resolute, furious eyes fixed on the male that had imprisoned me from a child as the needle broke my skin. I watched as he smiled triumphantly.

He had no idea what was coming his way.

Sticking to the plan, I closed my eyes when the *chiri* stepped away. I swayed on my feet, reaching out to grip the wall as the liquid traveled through my veins. When I opened my eyes, I saw Master smile.

Turning on his heel, he said, "I'll be in my seat, watching you take your last breath. Unlike every other match, I'm going to enjoy you dying quickly, 901. No games this time. Just death. I should have done it years ago."

With that, Master walked away, his guard following behind. When he was out of sight, I straightened, feeling the drug infuse my muscles. But this wasn't the drug that Master had demanded I receive. It was adrenaline to keep my body strong and able while we slaughtered them all.

The *chiri* female looked up at me. She met my eyes and a smile pulled on her lips. Closing in, she said, "We are all ready."

I nodded in acknowledgment. Just as she was about to leave, she said, "Master has taken every one of the *chiri* females against our will. We are not so different from your Inessa. When you fight today, you fight for us all. When you stop his heart, you *free* our hearts. We are with you, Champion. We are all behind you. The fighters. The *chiri*. Anyone who is enslaved. We will follow your lead and we will die if we must. Today the Blood Pit falls."

"Thank you," I rasped. The turncoat guard that had been watching us since yesterday let her out. The *chiri* rushed away, I assumed to take her position. My cell door had been left open and I entered the hallway. In seconds, Luka, Zaal, and Valentin walked out, too. We were all dressed the same: bare chested in the obligatory black pants. I could see the adrenaline pumping in their veins. Our muscles were tense and our veins protruded from the need to kill.

I met each of their eyes, but locked a few seconds longer on Valentin's. He inhaled through his nostrils, then declared, "For Inessa."

"For Inessa," I repeated.

Viktor approached us, and Luka placed a hand on his shoulder. "Are we ready?"

Viktor nodded. "Everyone is in place. You have about seven minutes to fill before the doors will be sealed and the fighters will be in place."

Luka patted Viktor on the back. "You give me the signal"—Luka looked to us all—"then we attack."

I rocked on my feet and gripped my Kindjals tighter.

"Are we all clear on the plan?" Luka asked.

"Yes," we each replied.

Luka bowed his head and his eyes closed. I watched as he mouthed something to himself. When he lifted his head, eyes open, he said, "This, everything that we have been through, endured, and survived, ends tonight. Each of us has his own story. We have our own versions of hell. But they all stem from this place. They all exist because of one male." Luka didn't name Master; we all knew who he meant. Luka met each of our gazes and said, "We have fought for freedom, but true freedom doesn't exist until Arziani is dead and this place is razed."

Grunts and heavy breathing came from us all as we envisioned what that would be like. Luka pounded his chest with balled fists. "Freedom comes at a cost. If any of us falls, the others continue. And we don't fucking stop until every last bastard in the place is dead." He curled his lips and raised his voice. "Our bodies will ache, we will tire, but we don't stop!"

I jumped from foot to foot, hearing the crowd's volume beginning to rise in the arena. Luka glanced toward the tunnel. Facing us again, he said, "We all have females we must return to. Keep them in your heart, keep their faces in the forefront of your mind. We kill for them. We kill for the future children we will have. Children that will know nothing of this hell. Children who won't face danger because of the deeds of their fathers."

Images of Inessa, full with child, played in my mind, pushing my determination to the highest possible level. By the look on Valentin and Zaal's faces, I knew they were imagining the same.

The sound of a whistle cut through to our group, and Luka turned on his heel. He brought his hands down to his sides and looked back to say, "I'll see you in the pit." Luka ran forward toward the tunnel, his back muscles bunching as he entered the arena, spoiling for the fight. A second whistle blew, and Zaal followed suit, his long dark hair resting on his back. Valentin moved beside me and said, "When he's dead, you get my sister. Don't wait for the rest of us, just get her out." I nodded just as the third whistle blew and the scarred male sprinted to the pit. I heard the crowd roar louder when he entered.

The living monster of their nightmares.

I walked to the mouth of the tunnel and stared at the light coming from the pit beyond. I had traveled this tunnel many times before, thousands of males had fallen at my feet in this sand. But as I heard the crowd screaming for blood . . . when I caught sight of the three champions circling the ring . . . I knew this was different.

This would be the last time my feet pounded on the sand-covered stone. It would be the last time my blood spilled on this sand.

This was the end, but . . .

. . . It could also be a beginning.

As the fourth whistle blew, my feet led me forth. And with every crunch of sand under my feet, I recited two names: "Inessa, Ilya. Inessa, Ilya. Inessa, Ilya." As I trudged toward the open mouth of the tunnel, playing the part of a heavily drugged male, my voice built in volume. As I broke through into the light, focused on the pit, I screamed out, "INESSA!" as Zaal ran my way, slicing across my stomach with his sai. Slowly lifting my blade, I swung back. The crowd roared when I missed. I purposely missed. My gaze drifted to Luka and Valentin, who were going through the motions of a fight.

A fist smacked across my lip. When I spun, Zaal had struck. Using the blunt handle of my blade, I struck him, too. Minutes and minutes passed; we hit and fought. Blood spilled from mouths and noses, surface wounds. But no one had fallen.

We were giving the crowd a fight, whipping them into a frenzy.

Luka ducked under my arm, and as he did, he shouted, "Ready!"

My heart slammed into a new beat, one that was about to get its kill. I faced Valentin, slicing a cut on his arm with my blade. Then just as Valentin moved to strike back, Luka threw back his head and roared out a deafening bellow.

In one practiced move, the four of us closed in, shifting to face the bloodthirsty crowd. The people watching glanced to one another, questioning what was happening. As I raised my blades, Luka,

Zaal, and Valentin raised their weapons, too. I then searched for one male only.

Master.

Catching his confused gaze, I smiled, blood from my lips rolling down my chin. Master saw my smile, but before he could signal for his precious guards to come to his aid, the exit doors all opened. The footsteps of the fighters sounded like a stampede as they rushed through the doors, war cries screamed from their throats.

The crowd began to move, scurrying like the scared rats they were. But the fighters were fueled with rage, minds clear after God knows how long.

They clearly felt the need to kill.

Master's guards charged at the fighters, but the rebel Wraiths turned on them first. The sound of machine guns joined the cacophony of terrified screams and victorious shouts. Luka raised his fist into the air as guards charged our way. When he ordered the attack, the four of us charged forward, weapons held high, rage in our hearts. My vision clouded with red as I swung. My blades cut through flesh and bone. One by one, I cut through the guards. The screams and the tinny scent of blood grew strong with every passing second. When I glanced up at the stands, some of the crowd had tried to fight back. The warriors cut them down. Monsters preying on the weak.

Finishing off the final guard in my path, I then looked up to Master's seat. Two guards, including the head guard, shielded him from view.

My blood scalded my veins, flooding every muscle. My legs began to move with greater strength. I pushed my muscles to the very edge as I leapt into the stands. I jumped up the seats, slaying anyone in my path. The high guard didn't see me coming until it was too late. He fired his gun, but the bullet only grazed my arm. His face paled as my blade pierced his heart. I kicked his dying body to the ground, his lifeless limbs rolling down the stairs by my side. The other guard ran, his loyalty to Master forgotten at the sight of my unleashed wrath. But before he could escape, I sliced the tip of my blades across his hamstrings. He fell to the floor. Making sure Master watched, I slit his guard's throat, kicking his back until he smashed his face on the floor.

Then I turned. I turned, my torso blanketed with the blood of the many I had already killed. When I locked gazes with Master, I smiled. His face paled and he tried to search for a way out. I shook my head, telling him silently that there was nowhere to go.

Reaching forward, I gripped the collar of his jacket and wrenched him close. A terrified cry left his throat as I did, then I spat in his face. I dragged him down the stairs, pulling him down until we reached the pit. My heart thudded with excitement when I heard his perfectly polished shoes crunch on the bloodstained sand of the pit. Around me, the volume of the riot quieted.

Reaching the center of the pit, I threw Master to the ground. I took hold of his hair and wrenched him up until he was on his knees. I looked up, and my breath caught when I saw that every other fighter in the pit was looking my way. The crowd that had not yet met their death watched with wide eyes as I circled Master.

Luka, Valentin, and Zaal moved closer to me. Their eyes were bright with their recent kills. Blood covered us all. We looked wild and insane.

We looked like Blood Pit warriors.

The fighters around us closed in, until a large circle kept Master trapped. I watched as he raised his head and met the eyes of every fighter. Then I saw his face drain of blood even more when he clicked his fingers. That click would once have ordered his males to obey.

As they stared at their former master with circled lips and clenched hands, I could see the realization sink in.

"They are no longer your slaves," I informed him, my voice rough from the fight.

Master blinked and I stepped back, holding out my hand to Luka, Zaal, and Valentin. Master watched every move I made.

"Master," I said dryly, "it seems your tournament has been taken over. You cannot command loyalty. Loyalty is earned."

The Wraiths that had helped in the revolt pushed to the front of the circle, led by an older man in a suit. "Abel," Master hissed. Abel nodded slowly.

"The champions you so love, *Master*," I said sarcastically, "are the Volkov Bratva and the Kostava Clan of Georgia." Master stared at Luka, Zaal, and Valentin. I pointed to Luka. "Luka is the *knayz*, once a prisoner of the Alaskan gulag. Zaal, one of the Kostava twins you experimented on for years right here in the pit." I then pointed to Valentin, who was rocking rabidly on his feet. His knuckles were white as he clutched his picanas. "And this," I said, "was your sister's—"

"Bitch sister's," Valentin corrected and bared his teeth.

"*Bitch* sister's *Ubiytsa*." Valentin stepped closer to Master, and I added, "His name is Valentin Belrov . . . he is Inessa's brother. Inessa, you know. But to you she is 152. Your High Mona. The one you left tied up and hanging on for life in the basement."

I didn't think it was possible for Master's skin to blanch even more. But as he stared at Valentin, Valentin who had tipped his head back and roared out his pain, I was wrong. Valentin ran forward, and sent the tips of his picanas through the back of Master's calves. Master roared out as the picanas pegged him to the ground.

Luka reached out and dragged Valentin back. For a second I thought he would fight Luka to kill Master. But Zaal stepped up to his side, helping keep him in place. Valentin glared at me instead.

"Finish him," he ordered with a deep harshness. "End him!"

Casting a glance around the room, I saw every fighter that Master had enslaved watch me, pure hope in their eyes. Hope this was it. This was the liberation every one of us craved but never believed we would get.

As I stepped closer to him, Master looked up at me. Narrowing my eyes, I said, "This ends today. From this point on, this pit will not exist. The gulags that Luka has told me of will be destroyed one by one. Your associates will be murdered. Your name will be forgotten." I pointed my Kindjal to every one of the fighters thirsting for his blood. "We will all leave this place." Bending down, I said, "We will all get our names back. We will live . . . in freedom!"

"I made you!" Master hissed, and stuttered through the pain Valentin's picanas where causing. "I made all of you! In this arena you were gods!"

"No," I said, slowly shaking my head for emphasis, "we were slaves. But out there, we will be whatever we want. As I have been told it should be."

"Ilya," Luka said, and I met his eyes. He nodded, telling me to get it done.

So I did.

Walking to stand behind Master, I surveyed all of the fighters and the mesmerized crowd, Master's investors who had profited from our imprisonment. Taking one of my beloved Kindjals, I slowly raised it high. With a thunderous roar, I plunged it straight through the top of his skull. I kept screaming as I did. The remainder of my hatred and fury released and drifted to the ceiling.

The males were quiet in the aftermath. They all stared at Master, dead, bent on his knees.

This time *he* was below us.

He had submitted to our collective strength.

Valentin broke the silence by facing the fighters in the stands and calmly ordering, "Kill them all." He pointed to the rest of Master's people. The fighters didn't move. Then they all looked to me. My chest filled with pride when they waited for my command.

Luka stepped forward. "You are their champion. They will only take orders from you."

Taking hold of my blade's handle, I ripped it from Master and kicked his corpse to the floor. Turning in a circle, I then raised my blade into the air and ordered, "Fucking kill them all!"

The room seemed to shake violently with revenge and the sheer need to cull. The fighters attacked as one. They charged the crowd, weapons held high.

Valentin gripped my arm as he retrieved his picanas from Master's legs. "Go," he pushed. "Get Inessa." He looked to the crowd. "We'll get these dicks."

I nodded and ran. Racing out of the tunnel, I pushed my legs as fast as they would go and followed the directions Maya had told Valentin last night. Valentin remembered everything, including the way to *moy prekrasnyy*.

Descending the steps that led to the lower basement, I then rounded the corner, sprinting down the narrow hallway. I arrived at a metal door and without pause kicked it wide open.

My stomach dropped at the sight that greeted me. Inessa was tied up by ropes, her pale skin dripping with blood. Maya was holding her up, the young female easing Inessa's pain.

Hearing me at the door, Maya looked up. Her eyes immediately filled with tears and she said, "She is losing consciousness." Maya sniffed. "I have tried to keep her awake, but the blood . . ."

I took my Kindjals and, moving to the tight ropes, sliced through them both. Inessa immediately collapsed on Maya. Before Maya herself fell, I grabbed Inessa. When I saw her lashed bare back, her blood pooled on the floor, I instantly saw red.

I breathed through the anger until I composed myself enough

to push Inessa's hair from her face. She moaned as I held her in my arms. I tried my best to avoid touching her open wounds. Inessa's eyes rolled open and her sleepy gaze met mine. She tried to smile through bruised lips. "*Moy voin,*" she whispered. "My Ilya. You have come for me."

Her eyes closed. Pressing a kiss to her forehead, I called, "Inessa?"

Maya moved beside us. "She keeps slipping in and out of consciousness. She needs help."

I turned to sprint back upstairs, when Maya asked, "Is it over?"

I heard hope lace her words. Turning, I replied, "Yes."

Her hand lifted to her mouth and tears fell down her cheeks. When I moved to the door, I realized Maya didn't follow. When I looked back, she rocked on her feet and said, "I . . . I don't know what to do now. This is all I've known. My family doesn't want me." She lifted her hand to her scarred face. I saw the fear of the unknown in her expression.

My chest cracked at the little-girl-lost look on her face. I stared down at Inessa and recalled how much affection she had for the young female. Looking up, I said, "You come with us. Inessa loves you like a sister. You belong with us."

Maya stared for several frozen seconds, then she choked out a sob. My heart squeezed for the youngster. "Come," I ordered, and fled into the hallway. I smiled when I heard the sound of Maya's light feet following behind us.

I raced up the stairs and through the tunnel. I suddenly stopped when I looked at the pit. It was done. There were fighters milling round the pit. When I looked to the stands, I saw Luka climbing to speak to the fighters, Zaal by his side. The Bratva *knayz* and the Georgian *Lideri*. Valentin hung back and waited at the bottom. The fighters all stared up, waiting for what needed to be said.

Luka cleared his throat. His knuckle-dusters were still on his hands. "Warriors," he began. The males all listened intently in absolute silence. "My name is Luka Tolstoi. This will not mean much to you yet, but I am a product of the gulags that Arziani—your slain master—owned." He next pointed to Zaal. "This is Zaal Kostava. He was raised in this pit. He is one of you." He pointed to Valentin. "As is he. Valentin Belrov."

The males looked to one another in confusion. "I'll keep this short. I belong to a powerful family in New York City. It is in another country, America. We have recovered the files of most of you. In those files are your names and where you are from. Many of you have family. Some, like Valentin and Ilya, your champions, were kidnapped from an orphanage. You have no family." He paused, then said, "Today, you are free. You get to choose what to do with your life. For those who discover they have family, the guards that helped plan this riot will help you find your way home. Those of you who have none, you are welcome to join me in New York." Luka placed his hand over his chest. "If you want, there is a place for you in my organization."

Zaal stepped forward. "I am Georgian, the leader of my people in Brooklyn, New York. If you are Georgian and have nowhere to go, I will give you a place among our people." Zaal looked at Luka. "Our two families are joined. It is your choice."

Luka looked to Viktor, who was waiting at the rear of the pit. He nodded and Viktor disappeared. "Right now, we must leave." Luka's face frosted with coldness. "We are going to destroy this pit and all the dead will remain in it. You have thirty minutes to leave."

Then the males turned and headed for the exit doors. A sound from behind caught my attention. When I listened harder, Maya said, "It is the *monebi*. They are being released, too." Maya sighed. "There are children here, too. The *chiri* are getting them out. There has been housing made available for them by these males." Maya pointed to Luka and Zaal. "For the *monebi,* too."

My head swam with a thick fog. It was all too much to take in.

Inessa moaned again, her eyes fluttering open. Spurred forward by her glazed gaze, I ran into the pit. Valentin saw me first. In no time at all, he rushed to me.

"Inessa," he called. I stopped when he reached us. I saw Valentin's expression darkening at the state she was in.

"We need to get her help," I said. Luka nodded.

"We have a plane that can get us to New York. We have a doctor waiting for us on board."

I stared at Luka in confusion. Luka placed his hand on my shoulder and said, "You have a home with us. Inessa is Valentin's blood, you are her male." He smiled over my shoulder at Maya and said, "And you are her new family. You all come with us. The males and females that need our help will follow later."

Inessa moaned again and I held her tighter. A sudden rush of emotion settled within me as I stared at her. "Thank you," I rasped to Luka, my chest tightening.

We were free.

This was real.

When Inessa moaned louder and shifted in my arms, Valentin leaned over her, pushing her matted hair from her face. "Inessa," he said softly. It was strange to see such a brutal cold male so soft and caring with my Inessa.

As his voice carried to her ears, Inessa's eyes flickered open. I could still see the weakness, the confusion in their depths. But my heart raced when she smiled and held up her little finger.

A pained sound left Valentin's mouth, and he linked his little finger with hers. Inessa smiled, then whispered brokenly, "You . . . came for me . . ." She sucked in a breath, then sighed. "Big Brother Promise . . . my Valentin . . ."

Inessa's eyes closed. When I looked to Valentin, he had tears tracking down his cheeks. In a soft voice, he said, "Let's go home. I want to go home to my Zoya."

I could tell by Luka and Zaal's shocked faces that Valentin was never this way. This calm and . . . at peace?

"Let's go," Luka agreed, and we all followed behind. When we left the stairs to enter the night, I gasped when fresh air filled my lungs. Maya had found a blanket and placed it over Inessa. As the cool breeze caressed Inessa's cheeks, I held her closer, needing her warm touch.

I scanned the outside of the pit, all metal fences and towers. A shiver ran down my spine. For a moment, I remembered being brought down these steps as a child. In a flash, the memory had gone. And I was glad. I never wanted to think of this place ever again.

Males dressed in black ran from a machine waiting in the grass. "A plane," Zaal informed me as I stared at it blankly. "It will take us home."

The machine brought me trepidation, but I climbed the stairs and entered the small space, driven by a single promise: *It will take us home* . . .

We would have a home.

I snarled when a male in a white coat tried to take Inessa from my arms. Valentin placed his hand on my arm. "He is a doctor," he told me. "He will help her."

Staring at the fearful male, I told him, "I will lay her down. Just show me where." The doctor eagerly nodded his agreement. He led the way, and I laid Inessa down on a bed, chest against the mattress so her back could be treated. I sat down on the end of the bed, taking hold of her hand. The doctor looked at me with a raised brow. "I'm not going anywhere," I told him plainly.

Maya moved beside me and patiently watched what the doctor was doing. I smirked when the doctor raised a brow at her, too. She lifted her chin to show she wasn't leaving, either.

As the machine began to move and propel us into the sky, I

kept my gaze on the doctor as he patched up *moy prekrasnyy*. As we sailed into the clouds, I glanced down at the pit. Flames were bringing down the towers. I could only imagine what it looked like inside.

Appropriate, I thought, as I watched the orange and red flames climb ever higher. The Blood Pit was my hell. Engulfed in flames with all its evil burning inside. Now it had been transformed into the hell I'd always believed it to be.

I watched it burn until it disappeared out of sight.

Then I watched my Inessa.

I watched her breathing.

I watched her sleep in peace.

The two of us now completely free.

15

LUKA

I breathed in deeply as I saw the bright lights of New York glitter in the distance. Zaal sighed beside me. "Thank God," he muttered, and I nodded my head. I felt exactly the same.

I glanced to the back of the plane. The doctor had attended to Inessa for many hours. She had been cleaned, courtesy of Maya, and was now sound asleep. The doctor had given her drugs to help her sleep peacefully. He said she needed sleep to heal. Ilya had had to be restrained when he'd seen the doctor about to inject her with the needle. Valentin had been able to calm him, promising it was nothing like those Master administered.

The doctor had removed her bracelet, too. The drugs and medication he had given her, and would administer over the coming days, were designed to clear the Type B drug from her system. When she woke, she would be cleansed of the drugs she had been forced to endure for years.

I next looked to Ilya. For most of the long flight he had kept vigil by Inessa's side. Eventually, he had washed and changed into spare track pants and a T-shirt. His hand still lay in Inessa's, his head resting on her narrow mattress. Maya slept in a chair at the end of the bed. Valentin sat in the closest seat to his sister. The scarred male hadn't said much on the flight home. Like Zaal and me, he had washed and changed. But then he had moved to be near his sister and hadn't moved since.

I'd caught him watching Ilya from time to time. But it wasn't in aggression. Valentin had always been an enigma. I had never, since the day I had met him, gotten a handle on what he was thinking at any given moment in time.

His eyes were always cold and assessing. The only time I had ever seen him soften was when he was with Zoya. Only that female seemed to be a balm to the torture he endured inside. Yet since Inessa had been found, since she had called his name in her delirious state, since she had wrapped her finger around his, something within him had changed.

Zaal and I had braced ourselves to hold him back from Ilya. But as Ilya never left Inessa's side and he now slept beside her, his hand tightly hanging onto hers, Valentin had watched him with a new expression—acceptance . . . maybe happiness?

The male appeared happy. His sister had found love. Like he had with Zoya, Inessa had with Ilya. We had all learned that life was easier to adjust to when you had someone beside you, helping you along the way.

"We will be landing in ten minutes," the pilot called over the speaker. I let my head rest against the seat.

My knee bounced up and down in excitement. In ten minutes I would see my Kisa. We would all be reunited. I allowed myself to sigh in relief that we had all come home alive. The chances that one of us would not had been high. I couldn't have faced that person's female lover if that had been the case. I knew that neither Zaal nor Valentin could have faced Kisa if it had been me.

I thanked God that we were all home safe.

Minutes later, the plane's wheels touched tarmac. When we

rolled to a stop, Viktor helped the *byki* open the plane. I looked out the window, and my heart flipped and swelled in my chest when I saw Kisa get out of a car. Her brown hair blew in the evening breeze. I could see her eyes searching for me through the windows. Several more cars arrived. I smiled when Zoya and Talia got out and stood beside my wife.

I felt Zaal tense beside me. He immediately heaved a sigh of relief when he saw his fiancée. The door opened and the stairs were brought to the plane by one of our males that worked at the airfield.

Valentin got to his feet, pressing his hand to Ilya's shoulder. Ilya jumped to his feet, his fists braced to fight. Valentin didn't flinch. Ilya blinked the sleep from his eyes and then relaxed his shoulders. His blue eyes immediately looked down to Inessa.

"She is okay," Valentin told him in his gruff voice. He guided his thumb toward the window and announced, "We are home."

"Home," Ilya repeated and bent down to Inessa. "Did you hear that, *moy prekrasnyy*? We are home."

Inessa didn't move, still asleep under the medication. The doctor came from the back of the plane and began preparing Inessa to disembark. Valentin bent down to look out the window. His eyes closed momentarily, and he whispered, "Zoya."

"Go," Ilya said, seeing Valentin's conflict. "She's my female. I have her," Ilya assured him. Valentin paused, then nodded.

Turning, Valentin headed toward Zaal and me. Not stopping, he brushed past us and turned to leave through the door. Zaal and I followed behind. Valentin rushed down the steps. When Zoya saw her male heading straight for her, she smiled the widest of smiles and ran to him. Valentin wrapped Zoya in his arms and held her close.

I couldn't hear what was being said. Before I could listen in, I heard my sister's excited shriek. Zaal flew down the steps two at a time. Talia jumped into his arms. When Zaal drew back, she began kissing him all over his face.

I glanced down the plane to see Ilya and the *byki* lifting Inessa onto a stretcher. Maya hovered at Inessa's side. I could see by her face that she was terrified.

Leaving them to it, I stepped out of the plane onto the top of the stairs. As soon as I did, I saw Kisa smile in relief. Her hands were on her swollen stomach as I walked down the stairs. Zoya was hugging Zaal, checking her big brother was okay.

As I reached the bottom step, Kisa's tear-filled eyes met mine and my heart almost split in two. *"Solnyshko,"* I whispered, and held out my hand. Kisa didn't hesitate. She came straight to me and folded into my chest. I breathed in her sweet scent and simply held her close.

"You came home," she said, sighing.

"Always," I whispered. Placing my hands on the side of Kisa's head, I drew her back and studied her beautiful face. "I have missed you," I confessed, and wiped away a happy tear from her soft cheek.

"I have missed you too, *lyubov moya*." She placed my hand on her stomach and laughed as our baby kicked. "We both have."

My pulse thudded, and I pressed another kiss to her lips. When I drew back, I heard, "Am I gonna get a hug, big brother?"

I smiled as Talia pushed her arms around my waist. She squeezed me tightly and I laughed. When she pulled back, she looked up at me and asked, "Are you done now?" Although her voice was playful, I could hear the sincerity of the question in her tone. I could see it in her worried expression. Kisa's hand took hold of mine and she squeezed. She wanted to know, too.

Inhaling deeply, I embraced the sense of peace that now resided in my stomach. "We're done," I said, and felt every last one of my residual chains break away from my corrupted soul. Valentin and

Zaal moved behind me, and I met each of my brothers' eyes. "We are done," I repeated.

They nodded in response, and I saw the heaviness rise from their spirits.

"Good! About damn time!" Talia joked, and Zaal pulled her back into his arms. She laughed as he kept her trapped against his chest.

"Valentin," Zoya gasped, just as I wrapped Kisa in my arms.

When I followed Zoya's wide gaze, I saw Ilya standing on the top of the stairs. Kisa looked at me and asked, "Who is that?"

Ilya looked huge against the executive plane's entrance. His assessing eyes were locked on all of us below. "That is Ilya Konev," I announced loud enough for them all to hear. "He was the reigning Blood Pit Champion."

"He's huge," Talia remarked.

"He is Inessa's," Valentin added when the group had gone silent.

Zoya looked at her male. "Inessa? She is okay? Safe?"

Almost on cue, Ilya began walking down the stairs. He turned his back to us as he helped the *byki* carry Inessa's stretcher. Kisa's worried eyes looked up at me. Without taking my eyes from the stretcher, I said, "Her master punished her. She had fallen in love with Ilya, and he had found out. He lashed her."

"No!" Zoya cried.

Ilya stepped onto the tarmac, holding Inessa's stretcher. He glanced over to us with wary eyes. Releasing Kisa, I walked to meet him. I placed my hand on his shoulder.

"You're okay. We're going to get Inessa into one of our vans and take her home."

Ilya nodded. Valentin was suddenly at my side. "My home," he insisted. Zoya came to stand beside him and looked down to Inessa. "Valentin," she whispered. I could hear the thick sorrow in her voice. Valentin's teeth clenched as he stared at his sister, then he looked up. Reaching for Zoya's hand, he lifted it up and kissed her palm. "*Kotyonok,* this is Ilya. Ilya, this is my female, Zoya."

"Nice to meet you, Ilya," Zoya said.

Ilya nodded. "You, too," he replied, then cast his gaze over all of us. I waved them over. Kisa's arms came around my waist and Ilya stared at her, before looking to her stomach. His eyes flared.

"You are to be a father?" he questioned.

"Yes," I replied. Ilya looked again to Inessa. I saw the hope in his expression.

"Freedom allows you to do whatever you want," I explained. Ilya looked overwhelmed. "You will understand in time," I told him. He slowly nodded his head. "Ilya, this is Kisa, my wife."

"Hello," Ilya said quietly.

"Nice to meet you, Ilya," Kisa replied.

Zaal held Talia tightly. "This is my fiancée, Talia," he announced proudly.

Ilya repeated his hello, then movement came from the stairs. Maya timidly began descending the steps, clutching the rail as her wide eyes surveyed the crowd.

"Who is that?" Kisa whispered. I heard Kisa's maternal side rise to the surface as she watched Maya awkwardly reach the tarmac.

"Maya," I replied. "She was one of the *chiri* in the pit."

"A plague?" Zoya questioned, interpreting the Georgian term. Maya turned her head away at that point, and I felt Kisa stiffen. "Her face," Zoya whispered, so low that Maya couldn't have heard.

"The *chiri* were the lowest caste in the pit. They were the servant slaves. She was Inessa's. They are best friends. Maya wouldn't leave her side the entire way here. She helped keep my sister alive," Valentin said to his female.

"She refused a guard taking her at a young age so Master

ordered that acid be poured over her face. Then she was demoted from a *mona* to a *chiri*," Ilya said. Kisa, Talia, and Zoya flinched at the information the champion supplied. "She is only sixteen," Ilya added sadly. "But she defended my Inessa's life like a warrior."

Zoya immediately broke from Valentin's side and approached Maya. Maya froze in fear. Zoya smiled and held out her hand. "Maya, is it?"

Maya lifted her head and timidly nodded. "Yes, miss," she replied in Georgian. Zoya smiled again. "It's a beautiful name." Zoya spoke to her in Georgian, too.

Maya looked to the stretcher and asked, "Is Miss Inessa okay?"

Zoya held out her hand and nodded. "I am Zoya, Valentin's female. Inessa and Ilya will be coming to our house." She paused, then added, "You are welcome, too. You are Inessa's closest friend, after all."

Maya stared at Zoya, and her dark eyes filled with tears. "Really?" she questioned, as though she were being tricked.

Zoya edged closer and kept holding out her hand. "Truly," she responded. "I am recently freed myself. I understand what it's like to have this new world thrust upon you."

"You do?" Maya asked warily.

"I do," she replied.

Maya stared at Zoya's hand like it was a forbidden fruit. But when Zoya persisted, nodding her head in encouragement, Maya gently placed her shaking hand in Zoya's.

"Come," Zoya coaxed gently. "Let us go home."

Maya sighed and whispered, "Home." I heard Kisa sniff and her hands held me that much tighter.

"Bless her heart," Talia said, but broke away from Zaal when Zoya led Maya to us. I watched as my sister introduced herself. Then I watched, with pride in my heart, as Kisa took Maya's other hand.

Maya, along with Ilya, appeared overwhelmed with emotion. But then, when you have never seen kindness before, it is difficult to accept its power.

Signaling to the cars, I announced, "Let's go home." We all made our way to the cars and Ilya took Inessa to the van. As Kisa slipped beside me in the backseat, I threaded my arm around her shoulder and pulled her close. When I closed my eyes, I felt Kisa's hand drawing lazy circles on my stomach. As the cars pulled away to take us all home, I left the pit and the kills I had made on the tarmac.

It was done.

It was an impossible feeling to accept, but as I held my Kisa in my arms, I knew it would hit home eventually. I was finally in New York to stay. The threats from my past now put to bed.

At long last.

"They are all settled?" I asked Valentin and Zoya as they came down the stairs in their house.

Valentin rubbed his hand over his closely shaved hair and nodded. "Yes. They're all sleeping. It took awhile to show them everything, but they're all exhausted."

Zoya sat back on the couch and ran her hand over her face. Valentin sat beside her, laying his hand on her knee. Zoya shook her head at something in her mind. "That pit is truly a place of hell," she uttered, and Valentin nodded his in agreement.

Zoya looked to Kisa and me standing in the room and said, "What that Master did is beyond anything I could have imagined in my nightmares. What he created through greed and hate." She shook her head. "What he did to my brothers." She placed her hand on Valentin's face. The male turned to his female, and I could see his adoration for her shine through. "What he put my Valentin through . . . Inessa, Ilya, and poor little Maya." She shook her head again. "I wish I could have killed him myself. The gulags, everything because one man saw people as disposable and subhuman. It makes me so mad."

"He's dead," Valentin said with finality. "They all are. That's all that matters." Zoya exhaled through her nose and nodded. She then smiled. "And you have your sister back."

"I just want her to wake," he said, and Zoya kissed his scarred cheek.

"She will. And when she does, she will know that you kept your Big Brother Promise. You never gave up." Valentin lay down with his head in Zoya's lap. Her hands ran over his shorn hair.

This was Valentin in love.

"Lyubov moya?" Kisa said quietly. "Let's go."

I nodded my agreement and waved to Zoya and Valentin. Valentin's eyes were being pulled by sleep. Zoya moved to get up. I held out my hand and shook my head. She gave me a grateful smile. *"Thank you,"* she mouthed. I knew she was thanking me for more than sparing her the need to see us out. She was thanking me for Inessa.

It wasn't just me who was responsible.

As we climbed into the back of the car, Mikhail asked, "Home, *knayz*?"

I opened my mouth to say yes, but at the last minute I changed my mind. "To our cove, please, Mikhail."

Kisa lifted her head from my shoulder, her eyebrows pulled down in confusion. She must have seen something in my eyes as she sighed and contentedly lay back down.

When we arrived at our cove, Mikhail opened our door. As we stepped onto the sand, I said, "We won't be long."

Mikhail signaled that he understood. He got back in the driver's seat as Kisa linked her arm through mine. The warm breeze drifted over our skin as we walked along the soft sand. I inhaled the salty air and filled my lungs.

When we reached our spot, I helped Kisa navigate the stone wall and we sat down where we always did. I leaned my back against the wall and Kisa lay on her back, supporting her head on my lap.

She was staring up at me, smiling. "What?" I questioned, my hand traveling down Kisa's pretty face and neck.

"You are still the most handsome man I've ever seen." She smiled her smile just for me, then added, "Those eyes, those eyes that tell me to whom they belong."

Leaning down, I pressed a kiss to her lips. When I lifted my head, I stared out over the dark sea, listening to the waves crashing against the shore. "You've never seen anything like the Blood Pit, *solnyshko*," I confided. I shook my head. "I thought the gulag was bad. Then with Zaal and Valentin, I wondered how it could possibly get worse." I huffed an incredulous laugh. "But it did, it was worse. A nightmare."

"Do you want to talk about it?" Kisa asked. When I stared down at her looking up at me in concern, I knew she meant it. Every word. Kisa had always been there for me. She had never shied away from the hard times and the gruesome details that were never easy to hear.

Moving my hand to her stomach, I opened my mouth to confide in her, to tell her all that I did . . . but then I just . . . didn't.

I slowly shook my head and genuinely surprised myself by saying, "No."

"No?" Kisa questioned, now confused.

I shook my head again, and with a newfound peace, I repeated, "No." I lifted Kisa's hand to lie over my steadily beating heart and whispered, "It's over." As those words left my lips, the reality really sank in. Kisa had stilled. With the heady sense of completion settling within me, I confidently voiced my thoughts, "It's really over."

Kisa moved until she was on her knees beside me. She pressed both her palms to my cheeks. "Luka," she hushed out and wiped away a tear I didn't know I had shed. "Baby . . ." she murmured, kissing my dampening cheeks.

"It's over, *solnyshko*," I rasped, "all of it. Everything that chained me. *Us*."

Kisa swallowed back her emotion and softly asked, "And how does it feel?"

I searched for the right word. I smiled, when the only thing I could think of was, "Free." I inhaled, my lungs no longer heavy and my heart no longer pained. "I am free."

"Luka," Kisa cried, and wrapped her arms around my neck. I held my wife. I held my wife and unborn baby in my arms.

When Kisa leaned back to meet my eyes, I said, "It was this cove where we made memories as children. It was this cove where you brought me back to you. You made Raze remember he was Luka, the male made just for you." Kisa blinked as she listened to me, and I added, "And it is in this cove where I realized all that we have been fighting, everything that had kept me imprisoned, has disappeared. It is gone . . ."

"Luka," Kisa whispered, an uncontained happiness shining through her bright smile, "I love you, *lyubov moya*. Forever."

"I love you, too," I rasped, and took her lips with my own. When Kisa drew back from the kiss, she lay back down on my lap. I stared out over the ocean, with a new calmness in my heart. Feeling Kisa's stare, I glanced down. She was looking at me and raised her hand to ghost around my eye—the brown eye that was smudged with a little of Kisa's blue.

"Luka Tolstoi," she said nostalgically. "God put a piece of my blue eye in yours so we matched. So we would always know that we were meant to be together, and that our souls were fused. So no matter where you went, you would always find your way home."

As Kisa's words washed over me, I knew they were true.

"And it worked," I said, smiling back at my *solnyshko* so wide.

"It was you who brought me home. Your soul called to mine when I was lost. And it's still here now, when I am found."

Kisa smiled through her tears and reached out to thread her fingers through mine. There was nothing left to say. Right now, as I sat in this cove with the other half of my soul, I knew that life had played out as it should.

Through tragedy, we were both stronger.

And through distance, our love was stronger.

She was mine.

I was hers.

Her, the girl, whose soul matched mine.

And I, the boy, who was made perfectly for her.

Finally home.

Happy.

At peace.

16

INESSA

Four days later . . .

"Inessa."

The low voice pulled me from sleep. I was panting, my body slick with sweat. My muscles ached, and it felt like my legs couldn't move.

"What's wrong with me?" I questioned, confused.

I looked up into Valentin's scarred face, my heart splitting with sorrow seeing his metal collar tightly around his neck.

"Shh," he soothed, "it's okay."

"She's hurting you," I said, and cried out when I tried move.

"Calm," Valentin whispered, checking around us to make sure we were alone. "I'm fine. It's you I worry about."

"How long do we have?" I asked, my stomach cramping in the aftermath of the drugs. I clenched my eyes, not able to look down at the evidence of whoever's release had soothed the drug's hold on me.

"Not long," Valentin told me sadly.

He reached for my hand and squeezed it tightly. "Just hold on, Nessa. I will get you out of here one day, I promise." Valentin released my hand, and I held out my little finger. Valentin's blue eyes filled with sorrow as he stared at my finger. But lifting his little finger too, he wrapped it around mine.

"Big Brother Promise," I said, *and smiled at his beautifully ruined face.*

"Big Brother Promise," he rasped just as the drug began to take me under again.

Feeling a kiss on my head, I heard, "I'll save you one day, Nessa. I promise. I'll free you."

As I gave in to the drugs, I saw Valentin in my mind. I saw his blue eyes, his shaved head . . . I saw the number on his chest. 194. Valentin was 194 . . . he was 194 . . .

The murmur of low voices drifted to my ears. Unfamiliar voices and scents drifted to where I lay. Forcing my heavy lids to open, I blinked away the sleep from my eyes. A white room came into view. I frowned. I had only ever seen dark walls. I frowned deeper, at least I thought I did. I tried to move my arm, but pain shot through me. My back. Something was wrong with my back.

I racked my mind, trying to remember what had happened, where I was. As I did, I suddenly became aware of a bulging arm lying over my waist. I stared down at the hand. It was rough and scarred. I didn't know whose it was.

Fighting the fear threatening to take hold, I made myself face the pain and turn to see who I lay with. I heard deep, steady breathing coming from beside me. But no more fear came. Instead I felt safe.

Discreetly turning my head, I focused on the male in the bed. My memory returned like a train, slamming image after image into my mind.

Ilya, Ilya . . . Ilya . . .

My bottom lip trembled as I realized Ilya, *my* Ilya, lay beside me. His face was peaceful in sleep. I watched him, my heart pounding so fast. Bruises and cuts were everywhere on his skin. But they were fading.

I tried to think about where he had gotten them. Then I remembered . . . Master, catching us, me being tied up, Ilya having to fight . . .

As if feeling my stare, Ilya's eyes opened. It took him a second to realize that I was awake. When he did, he sat up, covering my body with his own. "Inessa?" he asked, and searched my eyes.

Tears fell at the sound of my name on his lips. Then I remembered that we had discovered our names. We had known each other's names. We would be able to find ourselves in whatever life came next.

Happiness burst inside of me. "You found me," I whispered, and lifted my hand to Ilya's stubbled face.

Ilya's blond eyebrows pulled down. "Found you, *krasivaya*?"

"By my name," I explained. "You called my name and found me."

It took a moment for Ilya to understand my words. His face then paled and his eyes widened. His head shook. "No, *moy prekrasnyy*," he murmured. "We are alive. We made it."

I studied Ilya's eyes, looking for deception. I couldn't find any. Then I opened my mouth to ask how, when, and why, when a far-off scene played in my head.

Valentin . . . 194 . . . *You kept your promise.*

"Valentin," I whispered aloud. Ilya smiled, such a handsome smile, and nodded. "194?" I questioned. Ilya nodded again.

"194 was Valentin," Ilya explained, and a silent sob left my lips. I cried. I cried as more images from my life raced through my brain. They came so fast that I could barely focus.

Ilya leaned over and stroked his hand down my face. "What's wrong, Inessa?"

"My head," I explained. "I can remember. How can I remember?"

"You have been asleep for four days." I gasped at this information.

Ilya took my hand in his, instantly calming me down. "You have been cleared of the drugs." Ilya held up my wrist. It was free of the bracelet. There was an angry red scar, evidence the drugs had been taken away.

My eyes searched the room. "Where are we?"

Ilya sat on the side of the bed, his torso twisted to face me. I noticed he had cuts and bruises everywhere. "Inessa, we are in Valentin's house in Brooklyn, New York. He brought us back here. He and his new family helped free us all from the Blood Pit."

I froze. "Master?"

"Dead," he said flatly, but his tone was ice-cold.

"You?"

Ilya paused, then nodded. Leaning forward, I lay my forehead on his shoulder. Ilya's hand threaded through my hair. It smelled sweet and clean.

At that thought, I quickly sat up, wincing when the pain surged from my back. "Maya?" I questioned in panic.

Ilya's eyes softened. "She is here. She is safe."

Relief took my fear away. I stared at Ilya. He was watching me strangely. His chest was bare, but he wore pants. My heart thudded as I stared at his handsome face. I was so attuned to him that my heart raced whenever he was near. He made me feel alive.

But right now I couldn't read the look on his face. Reaching up my hand to run through his clean blond hair, I asked, "*Moy voin*, what is it?" Ilya's eyes momentarily closed at that endearment.

He didn't speak, so I pushed, "What?"

When his blue gaze fixed on mine, he inhaled and asked cautiously, "You still want me?"

I was so taken aback by his question that I shook my head. "I don't understand."

Ilya swallowed and shifted until he fully faced me. When I glanced down, I was wearing a black nightdress. When I looked up, Ilya was staring at me desperately. It made my heart crack. "The drugs," he finally said. "Now that you are completely free of the drugs, I didn't know if you would want me."

Sorrow took me in its hold, and I replied, "You thought I wanted you in the pit because of the drugs?"

Ilya dropped his head. "I didn't know. For four days I have never left your side. I have barely slept, fearing that you would wake and not want me. That your heart would no longer beat for me."

It was startling to see such a strong and brutal male being so crushed by fear at the thought of losing my heart. Gritting my teeth from the pain, I moved forward until I could sit in his lap and loop my arms around his neck. Ilya went to protest, but I silenced him by pressing my lips over his. Ilya groaned low as I kissed him softly, showing him with actions rather than words just how much I wanted him.

He was a part of who I was.

When I broke from the kiss, flushed and pulse racing, I said, "You are in my heart. You are in my scarred soul. You are my male. My Ilya . . . I am not free if I don't have you." Ducking my head, I added, "Do you still want me?"

Ilya's head snapped up, and a fiercely possessive expression set on his stunning face. He cradled me in his strong arms, making me feel so safe. "Inessa," he said in husky voice, "without you here with me, I'd rather be dead. With you in my heart, and me in yours, I am alive."

I smiled. I smiled so wide and true that my cheeks ached. Ilya mirrored my expression, and I laughed. I laughed, feeling true liberation in my soul. Fascinated, Ilya watched me laugh. He pressed his lips to mine when my laughter died down. I moaned against his lips.

When I pulled back, I asked, "Is Valentin . . . ?"

Ilya kissed my cheeks, then said, "He is downstairs. They all are."

"All?"

"Our new family," he explained.

My stomach flipped at his words. "New family?"

Ilya nodded, and a small smile pulled on his lips. "Yes. Valentin has found love with Zoya. He is part of a wider family now. They were the ones who helped to free us."

"I want to see him," I said, heart racing. I saw his scarred face and collared neck in my mind and shook my head. "I cannot believe he is 194. He was before me this whole time and I didn't believe it was him."

"It's okay," Ilya said, and moved me gently to the bed. "I'll go and get him."

As he reached the door, I said, "No. I'll walk to see him."

Ilya's face hardened. "But your back—"

"I won't be confined anymore. My back is painful, but I can take it."

Ilya's head tipped to the side, and a loving expression set on his face. "I know you can, *moy prekrasnyy*. You are strong and fierce."

Reaching out my hand, I said, "Please help me up." Ilya came to me and gently pulled me to my feet. I held in my hiss of pain. Ilya took hold of my arms and guided me to the door.

As we walked out into a hallway, a beautiful light hallway, I felt nerves accost me. With every step we took, I felt my body shaking.

As we turned a corner to some steps, I heard the low voices from before become clearer.

"Are you okay?" Ilya asked.

Taking a deep breath, I nodded my head. "Yes."

Ilya smiled at me in pride. The journey down the stairs was slow, but I made it to the bottom. I was breathless and in considerable pain, but I kept my head high. I wanted to see my brother. I wanted to meet the males who had helped him gain our freedom.

There was a short hallway between us and the voices. Ilya leaned in and kissed my forehead. "You ready?" he asked. I nodded in silent reply.

Ilya began helping me to walk to the room. When we reached the end, I held my breath as we turned the corner. A large room came into view . . . a room filled with many people.

The voices that had been loud grew quiet. Ilya partially blocked them from my view as he faced me and searched my expression. He raised his eyebrow at me. I knew this was him asking me if he should move. If I was ready.

I was more than ready.

Keeping hold of my arms to help me stand, Ilya moved to my side and allowed the people in the room to come into view. My eyes tracked over seven people. Three couples and . . . "Maya," I whispered when I saw the young female sitting on the couch. She looked so different. Her long black hair was down her back and she was dressed in such different clothes than in the pit. I liked them.

"Miss Inessa!" she cried out, and leapt to her feet. Maya ran toward me. She stopped at my feet and I held out a hand. Maya took it in hers. Her hand was shaking. Mine was, too.

"You look beautiful," I said proudly.

Maya dipped her head. "They said they can get me help for my face." She shook her head. "This world, miss. It is so different."

"You are no longer a slave," I said, and Maya nodded her head. "Then no more 'Miss.' " Maya laughed even through her tears.

Someone stood behind Maya across the room.

Maya saw me looking and stepped aside. I hadn't thought about how this reunion would go. I hadn't had the luxury, or the curse, to think of my brother every day. The male who held me close as a little girl, the boy who fought so hard to save my life. The male who endured years of slavery to ensure I kept my life. I knew that he had never ever given up.

As Valentin stood before me, I could see the fear in his blue eyes. I stared at his ruined face and huge body. He was no longer the young boy from my memories but the male from my shattered adulthood.

Yet I loved him now as much as I had then. Time hadn't changed anything. I had my big brother back. My vision blurred as I whispered, "Valentin."

Ilya guided me slowly forward, but Valentin rushed to me in an instant and wrapped me in his thick arms. He was careful not to touch my back. But I didn't care if he did. I had my brother back. I had my savior back. He was my family.

"Inessa," he hushed out as he held me to his broad chest. I closed my eyes. An image of him cradling me in his arms as I lay in a cell sprang to mind. Leaning back, I met his blue eyes—replicas of my own—and said, "I remember this." Valentin watched me carefully. Smiling, I lifted my hand to touch his face. Valentin flinched. I frowned, wondering why.

Answering my unspoken question, he said, "My face . . . the scars . . ." He ducked his head and I heard someone sniffing lightly from the side.

Studying my brother, broken by his appearance, I reached behind me for Ilya's hand. It slipped into mine in seconds. Using his strength to hold me up, I turned and displayed my bare back. I heard Valentin hiss.

When Ilya guided me back to face Valentin, I felt him press a soft kiss to the uppermost scar. It warmed my heart. He wanted me regardless.

Valentin's face was red with rage when I met his gaze again. "Do my scars repulse you?" I asked.

Valentin lost his anger, only to protest, "No. Not at all."

I nodded slowly, then placing my hand on his cheek once more, said, "Well, then. Understand that you are my brother, scars or not."

Valentin's eyes closed for a long second. When they reopened, I said, "Our eyes and hair match. Now so do our scars."

Valentin stared at me, then his lips twitched. I wondered what was happening. Suddenly, a wide, joyful smile spread on his always serious face. He nodded again, then repeated, "We match."

I laughed aloud. "The proof of our survival." Ilya's hand was still in mine and he squeezed it tightly. Pulling on his hand, Ilya stepped beside me. His arm kept me strong. Looking up to the male that had stolen my heart, I then looked to my brother. "Valentin, this is Ilya." I felt my cheeks blush. "He is in my heart and I am in his."

Ilya kissed me on the cheek. Valentin watched but didn't react. "I know," he replied, and nodded at Ilya. "He is a great warrior. He fought hard to set you free."

My pulse beat faster in response. Valentin then turned to look at someone behind him. A dark-haired, dark-eyed female came forward. She was beautiful. She was dressed in similar clothes to Maya.

I found myself liking them, too.

I watched in fascination as Valentin hooked his arm around her shoulders. She was smiling at me. A kind honest smile. "Inessa," Valentin announced, "this is my Zoya." He looked back to his love and said, "This is my little sister, Inessa."

Zoya held out her hand, and I placed mine in hers. "Nice to meet you, Inessa," she said, a hint of relief to her voice.

"Nice to meet you, too," I replied. Zoya patted Valentin on his chest and said, "You have made your brother the happiest male on the planet. All he wanted was your safe return."

As I watched Valentin look to his Zoya with nothing but love and faith, I replied, "I doubt that is true. I think that honor belongs to you."

Zoya blushed, then turned to a large male behind her. "Inessa, this is my brother Zaal."

And that's how it went. I met all of the family. My new family. Ilya stayed by my side as I shook hands with each male and female. When all of the introductions had been made, I caught sight of a large set of doors at the rear of the room. The night was dark outside, but . . . it showed outside.

Turning to Ilya, I asked, "Have you been outside, *moy voin*?"

Ilya shook his head and held me closer. "I was waiting for you. We once dreamed we would walk outside together. Along with many other things. So I have waited." I stared up at my male and smiled brightly. He laughed and shook his head. "Would you like to go out now?"

I nodded in excitement. When I looked around the room, I saw the other people watching us. I caught Maya smile. "You will love it . . . Inessa," she said timidly. "It is like nothing else. The fresh air . . ."

I inhaled, steeling my nerves. Ilya led me forward. Valentin moved aside as I approached a door. Ilya opened the handle and pulled it open. Fresh air immediately dusted the hair from my face. I closed my eyes as the cool breeze washed over me, chasing my nerves away.

I felt Ilya tense beside me and knew he was feeling it also. He stepped forward, leading me off a step and down onto a patch of grass. As my bare feet sank into the soft ground, I closed my eyes. It was only for a moment as I told myself it wasn't a dream. I opened them quickly. I didn't want to miss a thing.

Ilya looked around us. Trees and fences surrounded us. But best was the coolness of the air in my lungs. The pit was dank. This evening air was a balm to all the pain I had endured. It helped me to forget.

Ilya gasped. When I turned to face him, he was looking at the sky. I followed his mesmerized gaze, and as I did, I lost my breath.

"Stars," Ilya whispered as we stared at the tiny glittering lights.

Tears filled my eyes and I squeezed his hand tightly. "Ilya," I murmured, in awe of this new life aboveground.

"I know," he replied, and lifted his arm to thread over my shoulders. "I know," he whispered again.

Inhaling deeply, my body infused with this heady feeling. Releasing this breath, I asked, "Ilya, can you feel it?"

"What?" he questioned, the warmth of peace radiating from his worn body.

"Freedom," I hushed out. "Our freedom . . . our freedom . . . at long last."

Epilogue

ILYA

Three years later . . .

"Rodian!" Kisa called to her son as he ran over to his little cousin and pushed her to the ground.

Larisa, Talia and Zaal's daughter, began to scream. Zaal, who was talking to Luka near the barbeque, turned his head and rushed to his daughter's aid. He scooped her up and brought her to his chest. His little girl wrapped her arms around his neck and cried into his long hair.

"Shh," Zaal soothed, rubbing the little girl's back. "It's okay."

Talia approached her husband and daughter, and rolled her eyes. "She's fine, Zaal!" She shook her head. "I swear, that daughter of ours has you wrapped around her little finger."

Ivan and Vera Tolstoi, Talia and Luka's parents, walked to Zaal. Ivan folded his arms across his chest. "I remember someone else wrapping her papa around her finger, too." Talia glared at her papa. Then, bursting into a smile, she threw her arms around his waist and squeezed tight.

"I still do," she quipped. Ivan and Vera both nodded their heads. Luka walked toward Zaal, his son in his arms. Rodian was scowling at Larisa. Larisa scowled back. As Luka stopped beside Zaal, he looked down to his son. "Rodian, what do you say?"

Rodian glared at his papa and crossed his arms. But Luka's stare was stronger. Kisa joined her husband, hand on her swollen belly. She too waited for their son to apologize to his cousin.

Kirill, the Pakhan, walked over and asked, "What happened?"

Luka pointed at his son. "He pushed Larisa to the floor. He's refusing to apologize." Kirill's hard eyes turned to Rodian, and with the same level of success his glare pulled out of everyone, Rodian turned to his cousin and muttered, "I'm sorry, Larisa."

Larisa hiccupped pathetically and said in the sweetest voice, "It's okay, Rodian. I forgive you." I saw Zaal almost melt on the spot when his daughter kissed his cheek, then she politely asked to be put down. Rodian immediately took her hand and they ran off to play.

A hand lay over mine, and when I looked to the side, Inessa was smiling at me watching them. "Are you envious, *moy voin*?"

Seeing Zoya and Valentin across the yard, rocking their new-born son, Alexei, in their arms, I felt a pang of jealousy. "No," I said, but Inessa leaned forward and raised an eyebrow at my lie. "Okay, yes," I admitted. I shrugged. "But I can wait. I have you. That's all I need for now."

I had married Inessa only four months after we arrived from the pit. We were both it for each other, we knew it. We had both struggled to adjust to this new life. Had no idea how to assimilate into the world aboveground. But we stumbled through, and all the time held each other up.

Inessa came in for a kiss. I placed my hand on the side of her neck. The kiss was deep and long. When she broke away, she said, "Remember in the cell, when I came to see you before Master found us, we wished for many things?"

I nodded my head. I hated being reminded of those times.

"Do you remember we wished to walk together outside the pit? To finally choose to be together?"

"Yes," I said, and brought her hand to my mouth to kiss.

"Do you remember what else we said?"

I shook my head, but then said, "That we would have a family. That we would one day have a family, by choice."

Inessa nodded slowly, then watched me as she grew silent. I searched her eyes, wondering what she wanted me to know, when my heart stuttered in excitement. I glanced down to Inessa's stomach under her pink summer dress, then looked back into her eyes.

I opened my mouth and quietly whispered, "Inessa?"

Inessa's eyes filled with tears and she laughed as my mouth gaped farther still. "Yes," she replied, answering my unspoken question. She pressed her hand on her stomach. "You're going to be a papa."

Pure joy sailed through me. Reaching forward, I pulled Inessa into my arms, then leaned back. "I'm going to be a papa?" I half exclaimed, half asked. The wish we had wanted for ourselves was surprisingly hard to digest.

Inessa threw back her head and laughed. She was at her most beautiful when she laughed. "Yes!" she said louder, seizing the attention of everyone in the yard.

Valentin walked over first, leaving Zoya cradling a sleeping Alexei in her arms. "What?" he asked.

I looked to Inessa, and she nodded, giving me permission. Looking to my brother-in-law and best friend, I said, "I'm going to be a papa."

Valentin's eyes widened and a smile broke out on his face. "Nessa," he said happily. Inessa jumped to her feet and wrapped her arms around her brother's waist.

Zoya gave me a one-armed hug. "Get ready to join the no-sleep club," she teased.

"I'm ready," I replied. "I've been ready for a while."

Luka and Kisa came next, followed by Zaal and Talia. Kirill, Ivan, and Vera came, too. Pushing through the crowd last was Maya. She targeted her best friend and ran into her arms. Maxim, her male, one of the young fighters who chose to move to New York, stood back and watched on with pride.

"Inessa," Maya said quietly, "I am so happy for you." Inessa leaned forward and kissed Maya's previously scarred skin. Over the past few years, the Volkovs had paid for Maya to have reconstructive surgery. Although all the damage couldn't be reversed, it was almost as it had been before. It had given her the confidence to live again. And fall in love. Maxim was one of forty-three males who chose to join our ranks. Due to our high numbers of highly trained warriors, our Bratva and Kostava Clan were unstoppable.

Maxim was young too, still only twenty himself. But he was a worthy male. And he adored Maya. He knew that Maya was a sister to my Inessa. And he also knew the consequences from all of us if he ever hurt her. He wouldn't, though. I could see they were forever by the look in his eyes.

When the congratulations had died down, I saw Kirill tap Luka on the back. Luka took a deep breath and nodded. I was about to question what was happening, when Kirill tapped the side of his champagne glass with a fork.

We all turned to watch the Pakhan as he stood before us, Luka by his side. Ivan joined him. I frowned. I looked to Kisa and saw her subtly wipe a stray tear from the corner of her eye.

She was tearful in happiness. In pride.

"Seeing that we are already celebrating, I think it's about time that we add another reason to be merry." Zaal and Valentin walked beside me and we shrugged at one another, all three with no idea what was going on.

Kirill placed his hand on Luka's shoulder. "I am getting old. And I have held the Pakhan position in our great brotherhood for too many years." Kirill became somber. "I always thought this day would involve my son, Rodian. But, well, that dream never transpired as it should have." Kirill nodded to his daughter. "I should have had my wife by my side too, but life didn't work out that way for me, either." Turning to Luka, he said, "When you were taken as a child, I gave up believing that we would have a strong leader."

Ivan nodded in agreement. Kirill edged closer to Luka and placed a hand upon his cheek. "But then you came back. You came back changed, but stronger. You had so much to overcome when you returned that I worried you would never be the boy we all once knew. But you proved us all wrong. Instead, you developed. You became better. You rose with pride and honor. You became the best *knayz* there ever was."

Kirill took in a breath, then addressed all of us. "You brought three males back from their personal hells. You did the impossible and united rival families who, in the past, wouldn't have hesitated to kill each other in cold blood." I saw Talia rest her head on Zaal's shoulder in response.

Kirill met each of our eyes. "One week ago I decided to officially step down as Pakhan." He put his arm around Luka's broad shoulders and announced, "And I have appointed Luka as my replacement." Kirill turned to Luka and said, "In the past few years, you have listened and grown as a Bratva brother. But more than that, you have become a better leader than I ever was. You have built this family to be an impenetrable force. You have doubled our income and you have made us great once again."

Kirill took the Volkov Bratva ring from his finger and placed it in Luka's palm. Luka swallowed as he lifted the ring and slid it on the third finger of his right hand.

He stared down at the ring for several seconds before raising his head. "Thank you," he said to Kirill, his voice chock-full of emotion. He next turned to his father, who brought him into his chest.

I couldn't keep the smile from my face as I watched him accept the honor he so richly deserved. As one, we all readied to congratulate him. Suddenly, Kirill held out his hand. Looking back to Luka, he said, "For decades the Pakhan has ruled with others. It makes his decision making easier. It makes him strong." Kirill paused and issued an invitation, "Luka, if you will, please choose your Red Kings."

My heart kicked into a sprint as Luka's eyes fell on Zaal, Valentin, and myself. The four of us over the three few years had done everything together. We helped guide Luka and enforce rules. Valentin and I were Russians loyal to the Bratva. Zaal was *Lideri,* partnered with us Russians.

Stepping forward, Luka took a deep breath and said, "I won't delay my choice. There is *no* choice. I have three brothers, males I would trust with my life . . . and my family's life." He pointed to Zaal. "Zaal, I know you lead your own people, but my circle would not be complete without you by my side."

Zaal walked forward and shook Luka's hand. "I am honored, brother," he replied.

Luka then looked to Valentin. "Valentin, you are the fiercest solider I have ever known. But equally fierce as your strength and skill is your loyalty. It would be my honor to have you as a fellow Red King."

Valentin didn't hesitate. He walked straight to Luka and wrapped him in his arms. He silently stood beside Luka. I looked to Talia and Zoya. They were beaming with pride.

"Finally," Luka said, focusing on me, "Ilya. Over the past three years you have proved yourself to be one of the strongest and most resilient males I have ever encountered. You have led the males from the pit in their new lives. You are respected and loved by everyone you meet. I would be honored if you would take the final position by my side."

I blinked, unable to cope with all the events of today. Inessa laid her hand on my back to lift me from my shock. She smiled at me with such pride that I felt ten feet tall. I forced my feet to join Luka, Zaal, and Valentin. Luka hugged me and then looked at us all. He didn't need words. We all knew why we were here.

The four of us had survived circumstances where most males would have fallen. We had forged new lives with our females by our sides.

We had survived,

We had risen.

And we would never fall again.

LUKA

As evening fell, I stood from our place by the fireplace and signaled to my kings to follow. As I moved to walk into my office, Kisa's hand threaded through mine. I leaned down to kiss her on her head, then our sleeping son in her arms.

She was proud of me. I could see it in her eyes.

I walked passed Kirill and my father; both nodded at me, signaling their approval. I crossed the hallway to my office and opened the door. I heard my brothers falling into step behind me. I hovered at the door, staring at the seat behind the mahogany desk.

"Go," Zaal urged. "You have earned it."

Taking a deep breath, I walked slowly to the leather chair, then pulled it out and sat down. I savored every second of this feeling. Zaal, Valentin, and Ilya sat before me, all beaming with pride.

"How does it feel?" Zaal asked.

I sighed. "Right. It feels . . . right."

Pulling my chair farther under the desk, I laid my arms on the desktop and asked, "So, brothers . . . any new business?"

As Ilya began to brief me about a dispute with the Italians, I let my birthright find peace in my heart. This was the role I was born to fulfill. This moment is what I was destined to grasp. I had the strongest crime organization in the world. I had my brothers by my side and my perfect wife in my arms.

For now, we were safe, secure in our roles. We had all moved on from our pasts. But I knew, if the time ever came, that we four would call upon the savages we were raised and trained to be, the monsters we held at bay deep inside.

If anyone ever decided to fuck with us again, then as one:

We would maim.

We would slaughter.

We would kill.

Together, we would fucking *raze* hell.